THE BELL OF THE BAR

THE BELL OF THE BAR

LIZ GORDON

This is a work of fiction. Unless otherwise indicated, all the names, characters, businesses, places, events and incidents in this book are either the product of the author's imagination or used in a fictitious manner. Any resemblance to actual persons, living or dead, or actual events is purely coincidental.

Cover Design by Charcole LLC @charcoledesigns

This book may be purchased for educational, business, or sales promotional use. For more information, please email Charcole LLC at charcoledesigns@gmail.com.

SECOND EDITION

Published in the United States through Kindle Direct Publishing and Ingram Spark Publishing.
www.ingramspark.com
www.kdp.amazon.com

Ingram Spark ISBN: 978-1-7377749-2-1
KDP ISBN: 978-1-7377749-0-7
eBook ISBN: 978-1-7377749-1-4

Printed in the United States of America

To Adam, Cole, and Charlotte
Thank you for always being there for me

To Kristin and Kirstyn
Thank you for reading multiple iterations of this book

To my family
Please disregard the bad words and sex scenes

ONE

GREAT FALLS, MONTANA, a small town nestled just west of the Little Belt Mountains and a three-hour, no cell service drive to East Glacier National Park. The main street that ran from North to South was lined with about every retail store you could possibly need. Typical chain restaurants were all over the place but could never compete with the welcoming small mom and pop diners whose parking lots were always packed.

Great Falls quickly became home when I separated from the military after serving as a Heating, Ventilation, and Air Condition technician for over eight years and landed a job as a civilian employee in the same squadron. I gained some weight that still fit my almost six-foot-tall frame, grew a beard that I kept trimmed short, somewhat sacrificed my dark American Indian tan, and settled into my comfortable life as a civilian. I even adopted a lab mix puppy Tim who tagged along on fishing weekends and rode home in the bed of the truck, his legs coated in dark creek muck.

The season was nearing the tail end of autumn, leaving me and everyone else in the bleak town with our fingers crossed the weather would soon break and make way for a mild entry into the harsh winter months.

The previous winter had been a tough one where the daily temperatures teetered back and forth on either side of zero, and the outside air made its way down as far as negative thirty with a sharp breeze that made the tiny hairs in your nose freeze.

After going a little stir crazy inside, I ventured out to visit a local brewery with some friends in the small downtown. Earlier in the day, an unexpected cloud passed and dropped two inches of snow that lightly dusted the sidewalks. I followed the footsteps that were gently pressed into the snow from those that had also braved the weather earlier, not minding the below-freezing temperatures.

Although I enjoyed all the Montana seasons, the climate was ever-changing and unpredictable. One week people walked around town in shorts and a tank top with the AC in their vehicles on full blast, and the next, the sidewalks were lined with entire families up to their knees in snow, shoveling their driveways into tall piles in their lawn.

Trying not to slip on the ice-crusted sidewalk in my work boots, I stepped out to cross the street, and a sharp gust found its way between my zipper. I pulled my Carhartt jacket closed tightly, expediting my walk over to the illuminated brewery.

A loud, unfamiliar jingle rang from the top of the door when I pushed it open, finally escaping the blowing cold. I politely knocked the snow accumulation off my boots at the threshold and hung my coat up on the rack.

I strolled through the short hallway and entered the central area of the spacious taproom. I scanned the room and saw people scattered around at various wooden high-top tables, enjoying themselves.

My eyes glanced over to the taps, and the bartender instantly caught my gaze. She looked me over for a moment; then, she swiftly returned her attention to the man currently staring her way at the counter.

It had been two, maybe three months since I had visited, and I found I unknowingly missed the smell of fresh pizza dough and hot wings that hit you when you entered the front door. The brewery always felt warm and inviting and even had arcade games lining the wall, giving it a family-friendly vibe. Although I hadn't been in recently, I felt confident I had never seen that bartender working at the small-town brewery before.

I noticed her hair that hung loosely and halted near the middle of her back. It boasted a deep auburn color with scattered natural highlights that didn't appear to come from a box of salon dye. She bent over to select a glass for her customer, and when she stood tall, I watched her push it back over her shoulders with an annoyed brush.

As I made my way to the line to get a pint, I eyed the wall-mounted chalkboard menu, trying to see if there were any new brews on the handwritten list. One side had all the classics, and the other had their rotating beers currently housed in the taps.

"Had had, didn't like, had," I quietly said to myself, realizing I had already tried all their new brews.

The bartender's bright grin showed as she helped the guy in front of me decide which beer to order. He seemed indecisive and asked multiple questions as he leaned forward on his tippy-toes across the wooden bar. Even over the music falling from the speakers, I could hear her rambling on and learned how educated and attractive she sounded as she described the different varieties of beer he could pick.

She put her left hand on the counter, and my eyes moved towards it, intentionally taking note of the fact that there was no ring encircling any finger on her left hand.

With two shot glass sized samples on the counter, she took the time to point and explain their differences before allowing the man to try them both.

"It's not that hard, dude, just pick one," I thought to myself.

After he finally decided, she carefully poured him a Belgian dark ale from the rotating list into a snifter glass. Her manner was both careful and poised as she worked, ensuring the foam made the perfect crest at the top of the glass.

"Hi, how are you today?" she asked, smile unfaltering when it was my turn at the bar.

"I'm great, just trying to stay warm out there. You?" I asked, feeling my lips turn upwards on the left side of my mouth.

After tapping on the screen, she looked up, and her eyes met mine, leaving me struck by her deep emerald-colored iris'. Her smile widened, and she showed me her well-polished, straight teeth that she didn't hide behind her lips. Then, before I could admire her features more, her head shot to the door as that newly placed bell chimed at the entryway.

With her attention directed to her left, I took note of the outline of a scar under her right eye that reminded me of the aftermath of a road rash injury on my knee.

"Good, good, just another day in paradise," she replied as she shook her head and widened her eyes, bringing her attention back to me. "Can I get something started for you?" she asked as she leaned forward, letting her elbows rest on the wooden counter.

"Sure, the Lip Ripper any good?" I asked, already knowing it was my favorite.

"Well, that is one of my favorites. Do you wanna try it?" the bartender asked.

"Yes, please," I responded. "I don't think I've seen you here before, and I would say I come here somewhat often. Did you just start working here?" I asked.

Again the bell sang from the door, causing her to glance at the new guest. She stared for a second, then redirected her attention back to me.

"Sorry," she responded, shaking her head as if erasing an etch-a-sketch. "I am, well…kinda. I've been working here since I was old enough to help measure out hops. My mom and dad own the place, so I've worked here on and of my whole life. I just recently moved back to town. So, for now, it's a job."

"That's awesome," I overeagerly responded, trying to dim my expanding smile. "Well, it's nice to meet you…," I paused, continuing our eye contact, hoping she would fill in the gap.

"Kate," she quickly responded with a smile.

"Kate," I echoed. "Nice to meet you, Kate. I'm Brandon," I added as I stuck my hand out across the bar to shake hers.

"It's nice to meet you too, Brandon," she said as my hand continued floating in the space between us.

She turned and grabbed my beer from the tap with a smile and placed it near my outstretched hand, completely disregarding my gesture.

"Would you like me to start a tab?" she asked.

My ignored hand slowly moved to the side and wrapped itself around my chilled pint glass.

"Yes, please," I responded, also placing an order for a large margarita pizza.

Her finger tapped a couple of times on the touchscreen in front of her. Watching her work the computer, I noticed her nails were cut short, and the skin around them looked picked at.

"So, where are you from?" she asked politely.

"Florida, it's a little different living here now," I replied.

My mom and I moved down south after losing my dad when I was two. I didn't love Florida, and with how much I loved Montana, it wasn't often I made an effort to book a three-stop flight across the country to go back.

"Okay then, I'll bring out your pizza when it's ready," she chirped, handing me a number on a stick to display on my table.

Silently toasting the air in Kate's direction, I grabbed my order sign and walked over to a high-top table. I fished out my phone that had buzzed four times while I was wrapped up in conversation with the beautiful new bartender.

"On the way," Clay said.

"Sorry guys, I can't make it tonight. Elena's not feeling so hot. Dad duty. Next time!" Randall's message read.

"I'll be there in thirty," Stephen said.

"Sorry, I'm not coming," Justin stated with no further explanation.

Our group had a very loosely coordinated plan to get together every couple of weeks when it worked out, but it had been months since we had gotten together. We each took turns, picking different places in town for a low-key guy's night. Being single with no kids and not much else to do enabled me to make it just about every time. I would go every week if someone set it up, but it seemed like we were meeting less and less as more people's lives became busier.

While I sat at the table and waited for my friends, I played around on my phone, scrolling through social media stories and checking my email as if I was waiting for something important. Every so often, I glanced across the room at Kate working behind the bar, cautious to remain discreet.

I watched her hands and noticed how precisely she handled the tap and the glass simultaneously as if her style was mathematical and rehearsed. As she watched the liquid cascade into the tumbler, there was an apparent craft to her pour, and her pride in the ability to create the perfect fill was obvious.

The consistency of how she darted her head to the door every time the bell sang was also blatantly noticeable. Without fail, she gave the new entrant a good look over and then returned to her customer, only skipping a mere beat.

My pizza finally finished, and Kate hand-delivered it to me just as Clay entered the taproom. His bell ringing entrance caused her to pivot one hundred and eighty degrees to get a quick view of him.

She turned back around and cheerfully slid the warm tray onto the table and grabbed the tall metal number sign, hiding it behind her back. Clay joined me at the high-top with a loud sigh, and Kate took two steps back and fixated her attention on him.

"Welcome," she delightfully greeted, tipping her head slightly, "What can I get started for you today?"

"Well, hello there. Baby girl, just bring me anything you have that's dark, please," Clay responded with a sideways smile as he shot me a wink.

His eyes then looked back at her, and I watched him openly gazing at her chest as the politeness in her eyes dampened from his violating stare.

She took a deep breath in and out then put on a muted grin. "Okay, sounds good," she said as she turned to walk away.

"Oh, and sweetheart, come back over here please," he beckoned.

She stopped in her tracks for briefly as I watched her shoulders gently shrug before turning around and reluctantly returning to the table. "I also want some of those wings and an order of cheese bread, please and thank you," Clay said with a wink.

"Okay, you got it," she said, flashing him a slightly irritated smile.

As she walked away, Clay cocked his head down and to the left to ensure he also took the time to examine her lower half as well.

"Hmm," Clay said after turning his head back to me with a curious look. "Who was that?"

"I don't know. That's the first time I've seen her here," I answered. "Her mom and dad own the place, and I guess she just moved back to town."

"Well, not bad, not bad," Clay said with a soft chuckle.

We talked about work and the weather for a few minutes, trying to pass some time while we didn't have food to use as an excuse for silence. Being alone with Clay wasn't typical for me, so I was at a loss for words when it came to small talk. Over a couple of outings, I learned he wasn't the kind of guy I would be friends with if it hadn't been for the small group of buddies we shared.

Clay worked as an accountant in town and found special grants and loopholes to keep small businesses open when they saw rough times. His ability to help these mom-and-pop places afloat led to him being a well-respected and known man in the community, even though he often had a bad habit of getting too drunk and overly flirty with waitresses.

Across the room, I saw Kate talk to the manager Luke behind the bar. I couldn't make out her words, but the irritated look spread across her face became apparent when the duo quickly glanced in sync in the general direction of our table.

Luke said a few words back, but Kate gently shook her head no as she looked over towards us and our eyes met across the room. I quickly directed my attention back at Clay, trying to hide that I had been staring at her, hoping she wasn't overly offended.

Kate returned with Clay's beer a few minutes later, the dark bock cresting the stemmed glass' rim just right. Her smile returned to her face as though she let his gawking and annoying pet names wash over her. Then, with the beer out of her hand and safely on the table, she quickly backed up three paces.

"Ah, perfect love, thanks a ton," Clay responded as he toasted the air towards her.

Cute little nicknames seemed to be his go-to when it came to conversing with women. He always left the male bartenders alone, but Clay had a certain confidence in the effect he believed he had on women.

Thankfully, Kate didn't seem offended by his pet names and responded, "My pleasure," as she walked away.

Clay and I continued our forced conversation as we sat around waiting for our pizza to cool off.

Stephen finally arrived and added to the list of those that took notice of the new girl. He too, expressed that she seemed unfamiliar and made a subtle comment about her being attractive.

Luke had begun doing most of the interactions at the counter while Kate ran food from the kitchen and did other tasks behind the bar. He had always seemed like a nice guy, and a few times, I had sat on a barstool and chatted with him about fly fishing.

When Stephen walked up to place an order, Luke waved Kate off and made his way to the counter to serve him while she returned to washing glasses in a small prep sink.

The two talked for a minute before Stephen returned to the table with a glass topped off with a good amount of foam, proving that Kate was better at pouring beer.

When I looked Kate's direction, I watched her effortlessly perform her job, maintaining her smile and apparent happiness as she worked. Every person that came up to the bar received the same welcoming smile and genuinely nice treatment from her.

Without fail, I saw her quickly glance every time the bell at the door jingled. When it went off, I found myself not looking towards the door but watching her, waiting to see if someone that came in would change her reaction, but her expression remained consistently blank at the toll of every bell.

After three beers, I decided I probably shouldn't take my chances on being able to drive home by indulging in a fourth. Stephen had already gone home while Clay and I remained, but soon he too decided he should get going.

The night hadn't been a complete failure, but it solidified my belief that Clay and I didn't have much in common. He came across as loud and arrogant, which contrasted significantly with my quiet and reserved personality.

Clay made his way to the bar to close out his tab, purposely walking over to the side where Kate was standing. She stood propped up behind the bar against the wall lining half of its back, looking downwards at her phone.

He leaned down with one elbow as he put his fist to his temple and started talking to her, displaying his deeply rooted belief that he was an irrefutable ladies' man. Although I couldn't hear what he was saying to her, Kate seemed short with him, and her happy smile had faded yet again. She slid her phone into her pocket, and her eyes darted sharply down the bar until they finally locked onto Luke's.

He caught onto her signal and walked down towards them, and greeted Clay, exchanging a handshake. I knew the two had gone to high school together, and Luke was likely able to interject and distract Clay's attention from Kate.

Kate stood on her tippy toes and put her hand up to her mouth, oddly remaining an arm's length away from Luke as she appeared to try to say something discreetly. He looked up at the ceiling and nodded his head while she spoke.

She gave Clay one last half-smile and waved at him with a lack of sincerity before making her way down the hallway towards the back of the brewery. Clay signed his check, then left with a two-finger wave to me. Again, I heard the new jingle at the door while I sat alone.

Being alone had kind of become my thing in both my personal and love life. I was quiet, somewhat shy, and reserved, so I wasn't often forward when it came to talking to a woman I didn't know.

My beer sat empty, leaving the glass in front of me with only some dry foam glued to its sides while I sat at my table alone before paying my tab and wandering back out alone into the cold and windy Montana night.

TWO

AFTER SEEING HER at the brewery, Kate's face actively remained in the forefront of my mind. I craved the chance to see her friendly smile again, but I wanted to find a way to be tactful in my approach, so I didn't come off like some creepy guy.

Scouring the brewery's website, Facebook, and Instagram didn't help me find a reason to drop in casually. As hard as I dug, I saw no posts of any upcoming trivia nights or live bands playing for at least three weeks, but I didn't want to wait that long to get the chance to see her again.

Stepping out of my comfort zone, I went for it and went back in on Friday.

The bell's familiar toll yet again announced my entrance as I crossed the threshold and felt the warmth of the room.

After casually scanning the place, I saw no sign of the auburn-haired beauty who successfully made a brewing company t-shirt look incredible. I made my way over and ordered my usual from the guy managing the taps. The short brown-haired male bartender seemed to work here often, but I typically saw him sitting behind a desk more than he tended bar.

He poured me a beer and passed it across the bar without a smile as the foam gently billowed over the sides of the tumbler and left a ring on the countertop.

"Thanks," I said with a muted smile.

As I finished off my first draft, the bell chimed, and I glanced over to see Kate storming through the hallway with her hands full and a frazzled look spread across her face.

On top of her head, her hair sat loosely twisted in a messy bun that toed the line between lazy and stylish. She had on a pair of tortoiseshell rimmed glasses that I guessed were just for looks, and a large purse tossed over her shoulder that she hung. The olive drab jacket draped over her arm was also placed on the wall-mounted peg, and she finally walked back behind the bar to wash her hands.

She shook her wet hands in the air a couple of times before finding a stack of paper towels to finish the job, then rubbed it down her face, washing away whatever worries away she had come in wearing.

I discreetly watched across the room as she talked inaudibly to the male bartender that had poured my beer without much skill in her absence. While she spoke, her hands and head moved in sync with her words, allowing her whole body to join in on the conversation and aid her in conveying her emotion.

The male bartender spoke back to her, and she gently nodded, listening to what he had to say. Something he said brought a smile to his face, and her smile finally emerged as she covered her eyes with one hand and chuckled. I saw her release an overdramatized deep breath as he rested his hand on her shoulder as she turned and headed to the computer.

Again, the bell adorning the door chimed, and I saw Kate's eyes look up from the touchscreen and instantly stare at the door, glancing to see who had entered. But, again, the woman that strolled in did nothing for Kate, who quickly redirected her attention to the screen at waist level.

I looked down and saw my glass had run dry, so I scooped it up and made my way to the bar for a refill, purposely going to the kiosk where Kate stood.

"Hi, can I get something started for you?" Kate asked as she remained fixated on the screen in front of her, continuing her tapping.

"Sure," I began, "I'll have another Lip Ripper."

Finally finishing what she was doing, Kate looked up and made eye contact with me, flashing her warm smile my way.

"Hi!" she cheered, "Brendan, right?"

"Brandon," I responded, joyous that she had at least remembered some semblance of my name, "How are you today?"

"I've been better, but overall, not too bad, just the craze of running a little behind today. How about yourself?" Kate returned.

"I'm good, glad it's the weekend. Hey, I wanted to apologize for my friend the other night. He sometimes starts talking, and for some reason, at thirty-five years old, still doesn't understand what he should and shouldn't say to a woman he doesn't know." I offered.

"Ah, it's no worry," she responded, casually shrugging.

I watched as she yet again meticulously handled both the tap and the pint glass simultaneously, pouring at just the right angle and creating the perfect crest of foam that brimmed the brewery branded glass.

"Well, he shouldn't do that, so I'm sorry on his behalf," I said, pausing briefly. "You seem to be pretty good at pouring a pint of beer," I said, hoping to change the subject.

"Well," she started on, "when your parents own a bar, you get some practice early on. When I was little, we had root beer on tap as well. Of course, it wasn't the same to fill, but I would say that's probably where I learned the basics from."

"Well, good job," I returned, "I guess growing up around booze paid off for you in the end."

"I guess it did," she responded, clasping her hands in front of her as she leaned against the wall behind the bar, crossing her legs at the ankles. "Is there anything else I can get you right now?"

"Uh, this is it for now," I responded.

The bell echoed through the hall, and Kate turned her gaze to the door again. She met eyes with the woman who entered with a smile and quick feet that hurried to the bar.

"OMG, Kate, hi!" the girl squealed as she arrived at the countertop.

She rested her chest on the countertop, and one foot came off the floor as she leaned over the bar with her arms out wide as though she was inviting Kate in for a hug. But, instead, Kate remained fortified in her position and stayed where she was, using the wall as her support.

"Hey!" she cheerfully returned.

A forced look of excitement spread across Kate's face as she smiled without showing any teeth as the girl sank into her seat after having her hug rejected.

"I have a tab open," I interjected, sticking my hand out towards her.

"Sorry, sorry, sorry," she blurted as she flashed her palms in my direction, then placed them over her eyes.

Her hands lowered, and she tapped the screen in front of her. When her fingers stopped, she flashed her jade eyes my way and replied, "You're all set. Let me know if you need anything else."

My smile showed her way as I thanked her.

As I ate my pizza, I partially watched whatever rerun football game played on the TV while subtly stealing glances in Kate's direction.

She entranced me, and I still had no clue why.

Their conversation seemed to roll on without a break, and even the other guy working joined in for brief moments. Then, on occasion, the door's bell would echo from the front, and Kate would take a glance to her left, doing her usual routine.

As I casually watched her, I learned that she frequently used her hands as tools of emphasis. When she spoke, her hands moved in rhythm with her words and didn't stop until her lips did. Her small feminine hands were constantly engaged in the conversation, trying to show the depth of her words and feelings.

Kate finally removed herself from where she had taken up residence on the wall and positioned herself more directly in front of her friend. Her hands rested on the backside of the bar, supporting some of her weight as she leaned forward.

Realizing I had been looking at the bartender far too long, I shifted my attention back to the game playing in front of me.

The football and my beer finished about the same time. Checking my inhibitions, I concluded I could have one more drink before I called it a night. Slowly, I made my way again to the bar, hoping not to interrupt the group mid-conversation.

Kate's eyes slowly shifted from her friends when she realized I was back. The way she edged towards me hinted she attempted to wrap up their conversation but didn't want to come off as rude. So instead, she flashed me a subtle smile and stuck one finger in my direction, and made eye contact with me while mouthing, "one second."

I gave her a slight nod.

The glass in front of her friend had run dry, and when she realized Kate's gaze had moved momentarily, the girl's eyes shifted towards me. She looked me over once, then quickly glanced away with a smile I could see expressed on her profile. Her hand raised to the left side of her mouth as she whispered something in Kate's direction.

Kate's eyes widened as she smiled and kept her teeth hidden. I watched as she batted her hand at the girl twice before glancing at me.

I heard Kate say goodbye and watched as her friend reached across the bar in an attempt to place her hand on Kate's. Kate quickly retracted her hand and moved it to the backside of her neck, rubbing it with an awkward smile on her face.

"Right, sorry. I forgot," the girl sitting at the bar said.

Kate slowly twisted her body in my direction and inched towards me as she continued to smile and say goodbye, clearly eager to rush the girl out of the brewery.

The girl climbed down from her barstool and finally quit talking. She donned her jacket and threw her overstuffed purse that looked like she was living out of it over her shoulder.

Her eyes glanced my way as she looked me over, starting her gaze at my feet and finally ending at my hat. Then, lifting her eyebrows, she flashed a playful smile towards me but said nothing before making her way to the door, the bell signaling her departure.

Kate sighed loudly, "I am so sorry about that," she apologized. "I hadn't seen that girl in close to ten years. To be honest, I wasn't even sure who she was till I saw her name when she started a tab," she said, slightly cringing.

I chucked at Kate, and she saw my empty glass.

"Anyways, another?" she asked.

"Yes, please," I responded, pushing my empty tumbler her way.

"Same as before?" she questioned.

I silently nodded, but she had turned around to wash her hands in the low sink seated near the middle of her thighs. As she bent over, her tightly fit t-shirt crept up, and her exposed mid-drift revealed the edge lines of a tattoo that brandished her lower left back and wrapped around her hip.

I wanted to see more of that tattoo.

Before she caught me staring, I returned my gaze to eye level, "Yes, please," I answered.

Once the foam on my IPA was just right, she carried my beer back over, wiping the side of it with a freshly bleached white towel.

"Whitefish, huh?" she questioned.

I realized she was looking at my chest, not my eyes, and I looked down to see the left breast of my shirt branded with the Whitefish Mountain Ski Resort logo.

"Yeah, I love it there. Have you ever been?" I asked.

"Yeah, I went in the summer a couple of years ago, but I haven't been up during winter in a while," she answered.

Whitefish had quickly become one of my favorite towns in Montana, and someplace I saw myself retiring in the future. On top of the resort's summit, you could see the small town below, and looking out to the east, the snowcapped peaks of Glacier National Park felt like they were almost close enough to touch.

We talked about skiing for a couple of minutes, sharing our mutual love of fresh powder falling on the mountains. She smiled and listened as I detailed out my disastrous tale of learning how to snowboard for the first time.

In sync, her smile dropped, and her head turned as the chime of the bell sang from the door, the unchanging look on her face clueing me in that it wasn't anyone special. However, her smile quickly returned as her attention refocused on me.

"I should probably help him," Kate said, after we talked for a few more minutes, "Keep it open or close it out?"

"Uhh, I'll keep it open for now, thank you," I answered, using it as one more chance to come up and talk to her.

"Sorry," I said, stepping out of the way.

Finishing my beer quickly, I stood up, ready to pay and call it a night. Kate was alone at the bar with no one bothering her, so I purposely walked over to her to close out my tab.

"Another?" she asked.

"No, I think that's it for tonight," I returned. "Just the bill, please."

With her attention fixated on the screen in front of her, I again noticed the small road rash scar marked under her right eye, which appeared more noticeable.

She printed my receipt and pushed it across the bar with a pink gel pin laying on top.

"Pink?" I questioned, subtly laughing as we locked eyes.

"I know, right. I have no idea what happened to all our pens. I'm sorry, pink is the only color I can find right now," she answered with a smile.

"Pink is my favorite color anyway," I replied, trying to get her to laugh.

She shot me a skeptical smile and let out a soft chuckle.

I scribbled something that resembled my name with the flowing florescent pink pen and left her a handsome tip. I turned the receipt over, hiding my total momentarily before pushing it back across the bar.

"Thank you for coming in," she said with a smile.

"I do love it here," I replied as I grabbed my card off the counter and tucked it away back in my wallet.

I bid the beautiful woman goodnight and ventured back towards the door, knowing the chime of my exit would trigger her attention once more.

Two days later some friends called, inviting me to go out to watch a basketball game. My first inclination was to say no, but realizing it was at the brewery, my answer quickly flipped to yes, hoping that I would get to see Kate again.

While I was there, I spoke to Kate whenever I went to the bar, but the restaurant was unusually crowded. So even though we didn't talk much, our eyes met across the crowded room on more than one occasion, and I saw Kate brush the glance off and go back to what she was doing, trying to hide her subtle smile from me.

The following week, I came back after work three more times.

She wasn't working early in the week, and I sat alone and enjoyed one draft before calling it a night.

Mid-week when I visited, I was glad to see her working again. Sticking to my usual routine, I got my beer and made my way to sit in the taproom. On the two occasions I strolled over to the bar, I made sure to speak to Kate. We had short and light exchanges, and I learned a little more about her each time.

As the night went on, the clientele slowly died down until only three other people and I were left. Kate came out from behind the bar, and out of nowhere, slid into a chair at my table. She only stayed for about five minutes on three occasions, but we took turns talking, dropping little bits of information about ourselves.

On my last visit of the week, on cue, Kate glanced at the chime, and I saw her smile as she identified me. Then, she moved to the end of the bar closest to the door, and her hand gently tapped the wood surface. Interpreting this as an invitation, I pulled out a barstool and joined her.

Sadly, she was leaving soon to meet her mom, but she had a couple of minutes to chat if I was alone. So for the fifteen minutes she could give me, we spent it bantering back and forth.

When she spoke, her tone felt confident and natural. No long pauses or awkward body language accompanied her dialog, and it seemed like Kate could keep talking about anything and everything for hours if she had the time.

"Oh, my mom is out front; I have to go. I hope you come back soon," she stated, ending our conversation.

"I will," I replied, smiling in her direction.

THREE

WITH THE WEEKEND complete, I began planning for the busy upcoming week.

At work, most of my time would be spent in the field, driving out and back to the various missile sites littered across Montana to do annual checks and maintenance on the remotely located systems.

I loved getting paid to be in a warm truck, driving through the gorgeous countryside all alone during the cold winter season. Once out of town, I found myself on the long straight roads with only some cows and a couple of farmhouses littered across the horizon. The snow-covered mountains that jutted up from the farmlands in the distance felt as though you could reach out and touch them even though they were hundreds of miles away.

The slick roads didn't have many drivers willing to risk the conditions, leaving them relatively empty for miles. I would turn the knob as far as it went and listen to my music as loud as the government vehicle speakers would allow, simply enjoying the Montana landscape.

Thinking through my week as I drove, I was deliberate to ensure I penciled in time to go to the brewery and hopefully see Kate. But, unfortunately, she hadn't given me her schedule, so I figured I'd try midweek with the hopes that I would get to see her.

My gamble was spot on.

Our eyes met as I strolled in, and without an invitation, I pulled out a barstool and sat down at the end of the bar.

"Let me guess, Lip Ripper?" she asked confidently with a grin.

"But of course," I answered, smiling back.

I looked up and down the bar and around the taproom, realizing Kate was the only bartender on duty.

"So, tell me about your week," I prompted, eager to hear about what she had been up to.

Kate explained how she had been chopping away on a long-term backyard renovation with her mom, and the week's task had been stringing lights on large posts in the backyard when the weather allowed.

I loved watching the excitement spread across her face as her head bobbing around as she detailed out their remodeling plans. Their projects included new patio furniture, a custom-made outdoor grill, and a fire pit built from concrete paving stones to have a beautiful backyard ready for entertaining guests.

She sat down on a barstool and talked on and on about her parent's house. A sense of ownership hidden in her voice gave me the impression she still lived at home.

"So, what about your week?" she asked.

Work seemed to be all I muster up to talk about from my week so far, and I found myself telling Kate about the hundreds of miles I had driven, rambling on and on about my love of the beautiful Montana countryside.

"I remember driving those long, empty roads when I moved back, and I couldn't believe how much I had missed them," she explained.

"How long ago was that?" I asked.

"Uh, like a year and a half ago," she answered, shrugging her shoulders.

"So, what did you do the year after you moved back? I feel like I would have remembered you working here that long ago." I asked.

"Um, just stuff around the house, kind of just took some downtime. I wasn't working here then," she answered, shoving her hands between the inside of her thighs.

Kate's eyes navigated to the ground, and a moment of awkward silence hung between the two of us.

"Another beer?" she asked, pepping up and rising from her stool.

Although my beer had warmed up some, there was still just over a third of it left in the tumbler. So I chugged the rest of my draft and pushed the empty glass back across the bar to her.

"Sure," I responded, feeling like I had brought up a topic she would rather circumnavigate.

She slid my refilled glass across the bar while I dug for something to talk about while dancing around the taboo topic of her past.

"So, tell me about when you were in the military. Did you love it? Did you get to do anything cool?" she asked, leading me with conversation starters.

I spoke of my decision to join and detailed some highlights from my uneventful deployment to Afghanistan while she sat on her stool and listened intently. With her ears open, her eyes remained locked on my face as she gently nodded her head with a faint smile present on her lips.

"I loved the military and what it gave me, but I am not sad I got out," I explained honestly.

"That's because now you get to have those nice things," she commented as she lifted her hand and twirled it around as she pointed at my hair that messily stuck out from under the edges of my baseball hat, flipping upwards all around the rim. Her attention then moved to my face as she motioned to my beard I had neatly trimmed and shaped that morning.

"You're not wrong. These babies have been one of my best parts," I agreed, stroking my facial hair lovingly.

The night continued as our conversation rolled on with ease.

Kate told me about her parents and explained their dedication to the brewery. I sat patiently and waited for her to ask me about my family history.

"What about your parents?" she asked, almost on cue.

"My mom is in Florida, and she's great, but my dad died when I was two, so I don't remember much about him," I explained.

One warm April night, a twenty-year-old college kid was driving drunk and hit my dad's truck broadside at a four-way stop on his way home from work. The driver died upon impact, and after the door was ripped off, my dad was pulled from his destroyed car that ended up on its side just past the intersection. They rushed him to the hospital, where the doctors determined he had suffered significant brain damage and a broken back and pelvis. My mom had to bring herself to make the difficult decision to pull the plug, causing my dad's whole family to alienate us, but she knew it was what he would have wanted.

"I'm so sorry to hear that. It must have been awful," she said with a sincere look of sadness.

"My mom worked a lot to make ends meet, but even if it meant she was exhausted from working double shifts, she always made time for me. I didn't have a dad, but my mom was essentially two parents," I replied.

"Wow, she sounds amazing," Kate said.

"She is," I said with a grin and a nod.

To steer the conversation away from dead parents, Kate told me about the time their family had taken a trip to visit Disney Land in California. I watched her eyes light up and her hands move around as she relived the magic of her childhood memories.

"Can I get one more?' I asked when my glass was almost empty.

"Of course," she responded with a smile.

"Okay, I'll be right back," I said, sliding off my barstool and heading towards the back to use the restroom.

As I made my way to the back end of the brewery, I realized Kate wasn't alone in the building like I had initially thought. As I walked past the hall door, the guy that had been working the bar with Kate lately emerged from the office and stood in the doorway, leaning smugly against the wood framing.

He remained silent in his stance at the door with his hands crossed in front of him but intentionally locked his eyes on mine as he gave me an odd glare while I walked by. I gave him a good look over and realized I had about six inches and twenty pounds on him while I tried not to read into his stare.

In the restroom, I thought into it.

I assumed his subtle grill was due to the amount of time I had spent talking to Kate lately, and maybe he believed I was stepping on his toes.

"Oh well, I haven't done anything wrong," I quietly said to myself.

I made my way back to the bar and found the doorway he had been standing in to now be empty, and Kate was still behind the bar alone. I sat back down at the bar and disregarded the off-putting look.

Without hesitation, Kate started our conversation back up as soon as I was entirely in my seat. She liked to talk, and we could easily feed on one another's words, ensuring the conversation was a mutual discussion. The topics we discussed came easy and smoothly shifted to something new as we rambled on.

After finishing off my third drink, I realized it was getting late, and I had been sitting at the bar for a couple of hours, hogging all of Kate's time.

She printed a check that only charged me for one drink and laid it face down on the bar in front of me with a soft smile. I smiled back and again tipped her well, but with a black ballpoint pen.

She walked away for a minute to help another customer close out his tab at the other end of the bar as I waited with my signed slip. I sat alone in silence and contemplated the idea of asking her out to dinner with me.

"Stop being so shy," I said to myself, trying to ease my nerves.

She walked back towards me and brushed her braid back over her shoulder with the back of her thumb.

"So, are you sure that's going to be it for tonight?" she asked, tilting her head slightly to the side.

"I was wondering, and I don't normally do this, but I was wondering… hoping that you would uh want to go out sometime. Nothing crazy, just a drink or something," I asked shakily.

She moved towards the counter beside her and leaned into it as she placed her palm on its top. She rhythmically drummed her fingers back and forth on the surface and gently bit her bottom lip.

"You seem way nicer than most of the guys that come in here. I want to say yes, but I kind of just got out of a relationship recently, and I don't think I am ready to start dating anyone else yet," she sadly answered.

Instantly, I assumed the recent relationship she referenced had been with the guy in the office that had shot me the dirty look.

"Okay yeah, I get that," I responded, feeling awkward.

"Well, I'm sure I'll see you around here next time then," I added, putting a smile on my face, so she didn't feel uncomfortable.

"Yeah, for sure, I'd like that," she said, smiling again.

I stood from my seat with a slight feeling of disappointment. It had been a long time since I had taken the leap and found the courage to ask a girl out, and I was hoping it would have ended better.

She came closer to me, placing herself halfway between the rear counter she had been leaning on and the bar where I was, and seemed comfortable again.

I smiled and responded, "Well, good, I'd like that. I hope you have a good night, Kate. Until next time."

"Until next time," she copied.

Next time was going to be a while. I didn't want to come to the brewery multiple nights a week, and risk number one, looking like an alcoholic and number two, appear to be stalking her after she told me no.

"Oh well," I thought to myself as I left.

With a wholehearted smile, I walked out and made my way to my truck, trying hard to avoid the slush piles that had accumulated on the sidewalk from the recently melted snow. Hopefully, the cold night air didn't cause the wet roads to freeze before my final long drive the following day.

As I neared my truck, I pushed the automatic start on my key fob and heard the roar of its' engine starting. Knowing how cold the leather seats would be, I cussed under my breath for not coming out to start the heat sooner.

The cold was bitter, and the wind blew at a slow but constant speed, causing me to wrap my jacket around myself tighter as I attempted to preserve the warmth of my body from the brewery. When the wind caught me, the hair tucked behind my ears gently tickled the sides of my neck and sent a shiver down my back.

Just before I stepped off the curb, I heard the gentle tapping of tenderly approaching footsteps behind me, not even trying to avoid the slush piles.

Kate had walked out of the brewery and was about twenty paces behind me when I heard her voice ring out. She quickly moved across the treacherous sidewalk, not being careful, causing me to cringe at the thought of her hitting a patch of ice in her rush.

"Hey Brandon," she annunciated at a volume I could barely hear over the obnoxious sound of my aftermarket exhaust.

I patted down my jacket and pants pockets thinking I had left something behind but felt both my phone and wallet tucked warmly inside.

"Hey, what's up," I bellowed as I walked towards her.

Looking over her shoulder, I noticed that about forty yards behind her, the male bartender from the office had also exited the brewery and stood just outside the entrance on the sidewalk, watching Kate from afar.

I couldn't make out his facial expression due to the distance, but I could see that he stood there looking our way, leaving me unsure of where his attention was directed.

"Hey," she said as she slowed down when she neared me, shivering against the brutal cold.

She started to talk before I could return her greeting.

"I'm not ready to go out on a date or anything, but if you want to, I'll be working the bar on Friday. It isn't usually swamped the day after Thanksgiving. So if you want to stop by and sit at the bar, I thought maybe we could chat like we have been?" she said as she tilted her head sideways, putting on a half-smile.

The thought crossed my mind to say no, but I enjoyed being around her and wanted to do it again. Maybe she wasn't ready for a relationship, but we were just getting to know each other.

In the rush of walking outside and finding me, she had forgotten to put on her coat, gloves, hat, or anything to help keep her warm, and she stood there in front of me, visibly shivering.

The office guy was still peering at us from a distance and was also visibly cold as he stood on the sidewalk. His feet were hardened in place as he slightly swayed back and forth with his hands shoved into his pants pockets, trying to combat the weather. It was apparent he was cold, but not once did he remove his eyes from us.

"Yeah, I'd like that," I finally responded, awkwardly shoving my hands into my jacket pockets as I began to sway side to side in place, trying to generate some heat.

"Okay, sounds great," she beamed, converting her half-smile into a full smile as she continued shivering.

"I should probably go," she said.

"Okay, have a good night," I replied.

"Yeah, you too," she said as she flashed me a wide smile.

Her head turned towards me one last time when she started her walk back to the warm brewery; her high-top weatherproofed Vans staying dry through the slush.

When she was back in front of the entrance, the male bartender stuck out his hand, guiding her inside first. Then, still in my place, he flashed his attention back in my direction briefly before turning and disappearing with her into the building.

FOUR

MY WEEKEND WAS spent doing some much-needed trekking through the nearby mountains. My guide, and good friend Kendall was a skilled and knowledgeable hunter, proven by the fact that he had tagged just about one of everything in the continental United States and Alaska.

That morning we hiked into the snow dusted mountains at my request. The hunting season expiration date was approaching quickly, and I was hoping to tag a bull elk worthy of mounting by the seasons end so I could be like ever other Montanan that had their best game mounted on the walls of their home.

Kendall had already filled his tags for the season and was kind enough to join me on my trip to share all the fancy gadgets and equipment that a beginner hunter like me hadn't invested in yet and help if I was successful.

Thankfully, the wind throughout the morning had remained calm, with only the occasional gust blowing through the trees, but even with the stillness, the day had turned out to be blistering cold. Looking up hoping to see the sun peeking through the clouds, snow blew off the trees, dusting my face. A chill ran throughout my entire body as I glanced at my watch to check the temperature.

"Damn, it's six degrees up here," I said quietly to Kendall.

"Nah, you don't say?" he said, shooting me a sarcastic look.

We had almost canceled our trip, but remained committed to our plans, pushing through the cold on our search. As I felt myself getting colder, I silently admitted to myself that we should have held off for a warmer day.

We walked about two miles into the wilderness, quietly searching for my prize-winning elk, but had yet to catch sight of anything tag worthy and had only had a couple small leads.

Sadly, the scattered tracks we did happen upon led us nowhere.

Starting to feel the cold reaching into my bones, I shoved some shake-activated heating packets into my gloves, hoping they would help ease the pain of the icy chill. My toes were starting to freeze, and I wiggled them around in my boots that were allegedly rated to withstand the low temperature. As cold as I was getting, I didn't want to be the one to speak up and end the expedition that I had planned and insisted we commit to.

After about another half mile, Kendall finally spoke up.

"Alright, I quit. How the hell are you not cold?" he asked.

"Man, I wanted to quit an hour ago. I'm freezing," I admitted.

Chuckling at our stubbornness, we turned around and began our trek back to our starting point, both no longer hiding how cold we were. Sadly, on this trip, we were leaving both freezing and empty-handed.

On the bright side, there were still a couple of good weekends left in the season to hopefully nail something worthy of hanging on my barren walls.

I knew if it didn't work out, my search would continue for the seasons to come until I got what I was looking for even though I would have to find a new guide once Kendall moved to his next assignment in Korea.

"Anything new with you?" Kendall asked, slightly winded as we walked up a rather steep and snowy hill.

"Nah, not really," I replied.

My personal life was something I didn't usually talk about much. I had always been kind of private in that aspect.

"Nothing at all? Sounds fun," Kendall said, shrugging off my silence.

He then took over the conversation by telling me about how things had been difficult for his wife, who was due to have their daughter any day. With him also now married and having a child soon, I felt like I was slowly losing all my friends to marital or parental duties.

"No new women in your life?" he asked and saw me shake my head no. "What about Tim the dog? How's he?"

"He's good, just hanging in there being lazy as usual," I explained.

After a few silent moments, I detailed out some of the projects I had gotten into around the house to have something to talk about. When I finally fell quiet again Kendall looked at me and stopped in his tracks with his eyes squinted towards me.

"Any new girls since that Taylor chick ran off and broke your heart?" he asked.

Taking a moment to consider my short list of what I would call relationships, I reflected on his question and tried to think of someone to use as an example but came up blank. There were a few girls I had taken out a couple of times, and some had even come home with me, but none of them ever ended up being anything serious.

"Yeah, there was that one girl," I paused, struggling to remember her name, "Michelle," I finally blurted out.

The brief relationship Michelle and I had was not classified as dating, but I knew that he would remember her, so I used her as my defense to get him off my case.

"Okay," he said, putting his hand up with a smile on his face. "You have to admit you weren't actually dating Michelle. Shelly and I were there with you guys that one time. Even we could tell nothing was gonna happen."

The date he recalled was the first time I had met Michelle.

Michelle was a tall and extremely attractive Hispanic girl that worked at the Medical Group on base as a medical technician. When we matched online, I was shocked to see she was also in the military.

Trying not to make my first online date a complete disaster, we met up for a double date with Kendall and his wife at a relatively new Mexican restaurant in town that we had all agreed to try out that night.

Sitting at a round booth with a pitcher of margaritas, we all seemed to be having a good time until Michelle started acting strange suddenly. Out of the blue, she tucked herself farther into the booth beside me and started being quiet, ceasing her previous laughter and trying to hide beside me. Moments later, she started stammering, saying she wasn't feeling good and asking if we could just leave.

"Everything okay?" Kendall asked as we got up to leave.

"I guess?" I said shrugging my shoulders with a confused look as I handed him some cash for our portion.

Out in the parking lot, I searched for an answer to her sudden interest in leaving, asking for some clarity. Her face saddened some as she detailed a brief history, informing me she had just finalized her divorce the week before, and her ex-husband had just walked into the restaurant with a new woman.

She wanted our date to continue but wanted to go somewhere where she wasn't going to run into her ex-husband again. The rest of the night went well, and it was one of the more enjoyable dates that I had been on in a while.

Admitting Kendall was right about Michelle, I replied, "Well, yeah, that was a weird night, I won't lie. I told you why, though. But, I did take her home with me that night, so I wouldn't say that nothing happened."

"Heyyyy, attaboy," Kendall cheered as he patted me on the back. "And did you see her again?"

"Nah, she was too hung up on her ex," I said.

He was right, and I didn't want to admit it. Ever since my relationship with Taylor ended, I hadn't been with or made any effort to be with anyone else seriously.

"Alright, fine, I guess I really haven't," I finally admitted with a gentle shoulder shrug. "But Taylor didn't break my heart, I just haven't really been looking for anything," I defended, knowing that wasn't the truth.

"Whatever you say man," Kendall replied.

We continued our walk again while I maintained my silence, thinking about how accurate he was and realizing I hadn't bounced back from Taylor yet. It wasn't that I missed her or thought about her every day, but I hadn't found a reason to try to find someone else either.

"She was fun, and we had fun, but that was it. I was never going to be good enough for her or her successful family. I miss some of the times we had, but I'm not still hung up on her," I responded, realizing that I was lying to him and myself.

We had been friends for a couple of years, but I was shocked from the fact that Kendall had taken note of the lack of things going on in my personal life.

We continued our hike, and I shut my mouth, not wanting to reveal any more about my personal life to my hunting buddy. The silence of it all, and pretending it didn't exist was working for me.

After walking quietly for a few more minutes, I spoke up in an effort to defend myself even though the topic had been dropped.

"Well, I did meet this girl. She seems pretty nice. I'm gonna see her again on Thursday," I responded, trying not to sound too winded for the steep walk.

"Nice, good for you," he returned with a deep grunt. "I am not ready for my daughter to start dating, and she's not even born yet. Hmm, well, maybe this new chick will break the Brandon dry spell that you seem to have to go on then, eh," Kendall answered with his Wisconsin native accent.

"Hey, no one ever said I had a dry spell going on. I just haven't been on a date in a while," I replied, knowing there had been no women in my bed in months.

"Uh-huh," Kendall answered.

"And I don't know if it's really a date yet. I'd like to take her out, but she said she wasn't really ready for that right now, so I am just gonna go hang out with her at the brewery," I explained, remaining vague.

Kendall stopped in his tracks and turned to me, causing the mud beneath his foot to squish around the sole of his boot.

"I mean… A girl, at a bar, with you… granted, I haven't done this dating thing in a while, but this sounds like a good old-fashioned date to me," he said.

"Well, she works at this bar, so I'm just going to hang out and talk to her. She said she's recently single and not really sure that she's ready to date," I explained.

"Ah, okay, well, you have fun with that then. I hope it works out for you. You're a nice guy. So just let go of that Taylor gi….," Kendall said, silencing himself as he knelt to the ground.

His pointer finger moved to his mouth, and his other hand stuck out level with the ground, abruptly halting me. He pointed at a small clearing through the thin thatch of trees about one hundred yards from our current position with his halt signal hand. Squinting through the brush, I could see a mature cow elk with her head dipped to the ground, eating from the forest floor.

We silenced ourselves and ensured we were cautious of our movement as we crouched down on the crusty snow-hardened ground. Careful to not make any sudden moves or sounds, I moved my rifle from my backside to a more proper ready position in front of my eye. As I peered through my scope, I set my crosshairs on the appropriate spot on the elk's chestnut-colored fur.

In the silence, I listened for moves in the nearby tree line, but only heard the usual sounds of the quiet Montana winter forest.

I eyed her, surveying her size. Although it wasn't the bull elk we had been searching for, she was still an impressively sized animal. If I could tag her, it would put plenty of fresh meat in my deep freezer that was starting to run low.

As we stayed in our prone position on the ground, she perked up, quickly snapping her head in our direction. She didn't move, and neither did we as we watched and waited for her to run off into the surrounding snow dusted forest. The two of us remained still and silent as she held her gaze in our direction.

My finger remained steady and elongated alongside the trigger as I continued my gaze through the scope, my eye locked on her position. I rested my bare cheek lightly on the stock of the gun, and double-checked my aim, ensuring it was sighted in.

Once I was confident my crosshairs were right in the heart-lung kill zone, the pad of my index finger eased slowly onto the trigger, ready to pull. I took a deep breath in and released it quietly, and one last time checked my aim through my glass scope.

Her thick body remained frozen right in the position that I wanted her as I moved my crosshairs slightly to reposition. While I stared at her through my glass scope, she quickly snapped her head and returned it forward, aligning it with her chest. The wind momentarily picked up speed, increasing to a decent gust as I felt the cool air blow across my exposed cheek.

Without taking an additional steadying breath, the pad of my finger gripped the trigger and pulled, worried something had spooked her. The gun fired on command, and I felt the deep kick to the pocket of my shoulder as the rifle cycled.

As soon as the rifle returned to its resting place, I quickly brought my eye back to my scope, looking for her carcass on the ground. I moved the scope left and right as I searched but saw no visible evidence of her lying down in her previous location.

Removing the scope from my face, I looked around with my naked eye as I raised myself up on the heels of my hands and scanned the immediate surroundings. It was clear she wasn't dead on the ground, and as I looked around, I realized I saw no trace of her running off into the trees for cover.

Quickly I stood up, slinging my rifle back to its resting position across my back. Kendall moved beside me as we traversed the brush both swiftly and loudly. If there was anything else still around still lying low, it was likely it had been scared off by the gunshot.

When we arrived where she should have been dead at, we quickly noticed heavily marked hoof prints leading away to the south. We looked all around, but realized there was no blood trail leading off, the hope that I had hit her was abandoned.

After thoroughly viewing the mountainsides around us in a three-hundred-and-sixty-degree view, we determined she was gone, leaving her to die another day, by another hunter's bullet.

"Dammit," Kendall said, taking his rifle from the low ready back to over his shoulder.

"Oh well," I said, also slinging my rifle.

We continued our trip back to the truck with the thrill of the possible kill left behind, dampening my warm rush as I started to feel myself grow cold again.

"Guess that's why they call it hunting and not killing," I heard my grandpa saying.

"Sorry man, maybe next time," Kendall said, continuing our mostly uphill hike with about one mile still to go.

"Eh, it's whatever. That's how it goes," I returned optimistically.

Mashing the button on my key fob as soon as we were within range, I started up my truck, praying it would be warm enough to begin the process of thawing me.

"Have a good Thanksgiving, thanks for coming," I said.

"Yeah, you too. We'll do this again sometime. Good luck on your not a date date," Kendall said before forking off towards his truck.

I drove home looking forward to seeing Kate on that upcoming Friday, and tried not to think about Taylor and the things Kendall said.

When I came home, I took Tim for a short walk, ready to take a hot shower and thaw on the couch under a warm blanket.

After hanging up my jacket and slipping off my boots, I stepped into the hallway, and a rawhide dog bone that Tim had nosed to the middle of the hall sank right into the middle of the soft bottom of my foot. After loudly yelling a few obscenities, I grabbed onto the wall for support, waiting for the pain to pass.

While I stood there nursing my foot, a quick visual survey from my position allowed me to see what a train wreck my house had become.

There were multiple piles of both clean and dirty laundry on top and even more were lying in a heap next to the washer and dryer. I had spent the better part of a year just picking through the clean stuff and rewashing the stuff I wasn't sure about, never taking the time to put any of it away.

I shoveled the clothes into a basket and threw them onto the bed,

proudly smiling and nodding to myself that the clothes had finally made it off the washer and into my room.

Stepping back, I took notice of my master bedroom.

My dresser was a trash covered mess, the closet had old winter jackets falling out of the side, and there was a half inch of dust that had accumulated on my TV stand.

Hearing Kendall's words echoing about me and Taylor, I thought maybe he was right, and that I had been in somewhat of a slump. Before Taylor, the house had never been immaculate, but when she was around, we both worked to make sure it was in a presentable manner. But now that it was just me, my personal mess had slowly grown around me without me even noticing, and there was no one else around to complain about it.

I also never cleaned because I never had anyone over. The number of invites I had extended to anyone lately was particularly low. That number was a big zero when it referenced the number of women that had been invited into my home recently.

Every so often, I would invite the guys to come over for a playoff game of some sort if I craved adult interaction around people I didn't work with. But, it often led to them bringing their wives or kids in tow. Although I never really specified that they couldn't come, my invite turning into a family outing was never my intent. Having little kids running around my house usually led to someone wiping their Cheetos fingers and snotty noses on my couch or knocking over their "spill-proof" cups, leaving milk on my carpet.

I decided to get it together and clean up my house.

Even though there still wasn't any short-term plans on the horizon of bringing a girl back to my house, it still would be nice to feel it was possible if the opportunity presented itself. If it was clean, I would avoid the embarrassed feeling of suddenly rushing around trying to tuck things under the bed or shovel them into a closet, creating a false image of cleanliness.

Most of the things around the house were simple, so I started with the disposal of the large, accumulated pile of empty Amazon boxes that barricaded the front door I never used shut. Then I went through my dust covered video games, making two piles while I decided which warranted keeping, and which needed a return to GameStop for credit.

I also pulled out the couch to vacuum the insane amount of dog hair that had built up into tumbleweeds underneath. After pushing the couch back, I saw two small red stains on the carpet that were remnants of a night spent with Taylor.

We had finished off a bottle of wine each while watching Christmas Vacation on Christmas Eve. The bottles had been left mostly empty and placed right on the edge of the end table just asking to be knocked over.

Taylor's hand smacked down hard on my chest as she scolded me for quoting the whole movie, threatening she was going to leave. I knew she had too much to drink to drive herself home, so I kept on quoting, feeling her smiling at me from the other end of the couch.

Eventually she joined in on the quoting with me, saying the blessing before the meal by reciting the Pledge of Allegiance in sync with me and the movie.

Looking over at her, we exchanged a smile.

As the wine and movie came close to finishing, I felt her hand make its way onto my leg as she found her way up upwards into the opening in my athletic shorts. She scooted closer to me and was faced my direction as she bit on her bottom lip the way she often did, playfully smiling my way.

Her hands continued to lightly make their way up my leg and into my shorts as I felt a chill run throughout my body. I removed my hand from my lap that was blocking her way in order to not hinder her advance.

After allowing her hand to play around in my shorts for a couple of minutes, I took it out and grabbed her by the knees, straightening her legs out as I laid her down in front of me. She fell flat on her back, lying on the couch as I placed myself down on top of her.

Her neck was the first thing my lips touched.

I walked my lips up to her ear, then eventually worked my way over to her mouth. She moaned tiny sounds of enjoyment as I ran my hand down her torso and then over to her breast.

She arched her back and removed her arms from behind me, straightening them at the elbows and placing them above her head, signaling for me to begin taking her clothes off.

Her cotton t-shirt slipped off easily over her head and I tossed it to the floor and quickly found my way back to her mouth as I felt her body push upwards into mine. Our hips met, and I knew she could feel my excitement pressing towards her.

I love this," she said with a softly as she bent down to kiss me.

"Love what?" I asked as she sat up.

"This, us, the way we are," she replied.

Before I knew it, I pulled her down to me and whispered, "I love you," into her ear.

She pushed up on my chest, opened her eyes, and looked at me for a brief moment. Her hands went from my chest to my face, and she lowered hers to mine. The silence broke when her lips released from mine, and her mouth moved over to my ear.

"I love you too," she replied, sending a chill down my spine.

The National Anthem played, signaling the end of the movie. Our lips parted momentarily as our foreheads pressed against one another as we both smiled as the song sang out.

I pushed up from Taylor and sat between her legs. Her hands reached up and encouraged me to remove my shirt as well, throwing it to the floor to join hers.

Taylors hands rubbed up and down my torso as I saw a small drunken smile build on her face in the glow of the end credits. I chuckled slightly from the gently feeling of her hands on the side of my ribs.

"What's so funny?" she asked, slightly chuckling.

"You, you're great. I love you," I said, closing my eyes and enjoying her touch.

"I love you too Brandon, always," she said softly.

I opened my eyes as she shot her arms back upwards, allowing me to slip my fingers under the edge of the tight sports bra she had on and pull it up and over her head as well, tossing her hair in her face that she pushed away with a blow.

I laid back down on her and silenced her smile by taking her face in my hands and resumed kissing her, putting my tongue in her mouth and gently biting on her bottom lip.

She moved her arms from above her head back down in a wide snow angel motion to get her hands back onto my body, when she accidently knocked one bottle of wine over sending it to domino

into the other, the two bottles tumbling to the floor and their contents forever staining my carpet.

Taylor eventually rearranged the living room randomly on a snowy Saturday we were stuck inside, and the couch was moved to cover the red spots. The couch had remained in that place ever since, leaving the stains and the memories that came with them to be forgotten about until my cleaning spree brought them back to life.

I walked away from the wine stains and went to go clean the bathroom.

I didn't want to miss Taylor anymore. I didn't want to remember how nice she felt laying naked in bed next to me or how seeing her smile in the morning would set the course of my day straight. She had pulled me into her life for that year and a half and then pushed me out of it so abruptly and questionably.

Even though I thought I had moved on years ago, I now found myself coming to terms with the fact that maybe I was still slightly hung upon her. She had moved on, so it was time that I did the same. She had found someone new that she loved and was marrying another man. A pilot that probably sent her parents swooning.

But, our relationship was over, it had been over, and it was time I accepted that and stopped subconsciously waiting for her to come back to me.

That meant the wine stain had to go.

I busted out the carpet cleaner that had been tucked away in the garage for years and dug out the cleaning solution that was buried under the sink with the other cleaning supplies that were also somewhat neglected.

With a quick read of the suggested use, I decided to quadruple the amount to get the carpet extra clean. The detergent smell rolled up into my face as I free hand poured it into the reservoir and got to cleaning.

The machine hummed loudly as I moved it back and forth across the carpet, specifically targeting those two small spots. The carpet throughout the house needed to be replaced years ago, but this was a quick fix of the problem.

The stained section of the carpet got scrubbed raw until the spots were barely visible. But when I stepped back to admire my handiwork, it shocked me how much that freshly clean chunk stuck out distinctively from the rest of my dingy carpet.

Shampooing the rest of the neglected carpet to match the clean spot became mandatory to ensure that spot didn't stick out like a sore thumb. I replaced the water and pulled the carpet cleaner back and forth across the rest of the room, being careful to make noticeable lines of where I had already been.

After two passes of the highly concentrated solution and the violent sound of the roaring brush head deafening me, I looked back and checked my work. The cleaner had brought a whole new life to the carpet and the room, removing ten plus years of stains, especially the wine ones.

After dumping the black water from my carpets down the drain and cleaning out the machines two reservoirs, I popped the cap off a beer and strolled across my freshly shampooed carpet to my couch.

I sank into the rugged couch and curled my toes in the floor, feeling the crunchy carpet that had been cleaned with two much solution become soft under my feet.

It was late, but I flicked on the TV and enjoyed some time alone with Netflix, soaking in the feeling of my clean living room before heading off to bed.

FIVE

I SPENT THANKSGIVING with my friend Wes who was in the final stages of his divorce, and his soon-to-be ex-wife had the kids for the holiday. His voice came across as sad and depressed when he explained his plans to eat leftovers and watch a movie alone. Although I wanted to spend it by myself, the good friend in me kicked in, and I invited him over to enjoy the day at my place.

Thankfully my house was clean when I agreed last minute to host the holiday. We heated some frozen pizzas, drank some cheap beers, and I even watched a game of football as we celebrated the holiday in the traditional single man's fashion.

Friday arrived, bringing a close to what had been a slow-moving week. The base had closed for a family day, allowing people the day off to recover after the Thanksgiving holiday. So, to pass some time, I took a trip out to see the freshly snowcapped mountains covered in frosty evergreens while scoping out some new possible hunting locations.

When I got home, I took a shower to freshen up for my not date date with Kate, the bartender. Even though the mop of hair on my head would be tucked under a snapback, I blew it dry before venturing out into the cold.

Trying to dress to impress, I picked through my wardrobe, being overly selective as I searched for something to wear. A quick glance at the thermometer told me the outside air was hovering just above twenty degrees. So I doubled up on jackets, throwing on a Patagonia quarter zip and topping it off with a heavier outer layer as a backup.

After a quick double-check of my appearance in the reflection of my truck window, I picked a couple of stray dog hairs off my jacket because Tim's light coat and my love of wearing dark-colored clothing had proven to be a bad combination over the years.

The bell I had become familiar with loudly jingled as I opened the door to the brewery, signaling my entrance. Not to my surprise, Kate also heard the bells chime, and when I had made it into the taproom, I saw her head jerk to the door. Catching my eyes first, she quickly realized it was me, and a soft smile spread across her face.

"Well, hello, Brandon," she said as I made myself comfortable on the padded barstool.

"Hello, Kate," I responded with a smile.

"What can I get for ya?" she asked, grabbing a freshly washed glass and started to dry it with a white towel.

"How about you surprise me, just nothing sour," I responded.

"Hmmm," she puzzled as she directed her eyes to the ceiling and rhythmically tapping her pointer finger on her bottom lip.

Her eyes returned front and center and lit up when she had finally decided on a brew. She made her way to the tap, grabbed one of the unmarked handles, and poured the draft just right.

While she was at a distance, I took the time to appreciate how well she pulled off basic casual clothing. Everything that I had seen her wear had been plain coloring and simple, and not once did I think something looked bad on her. It was remarkable how impressive she looked in just a t-shirt and jeans.

That evening she had chosen light-washed skinny jeans cuffed at the ankles that had a small hole in one knee and a black t-shirt that was knotted in the front as though it was too big for her, but she couldn't let it go. She had weaved a low braid into her hair, and it laid dangling in front of her before she pushed it back over her shoulder. Her natural beauty showed, her bare face proving she didn't require makeup.

Kate made her way back to me at the end of the bar, moving quickly in her tan slip-on leather Keds with my surprise beer in hand. Quickly I identified the brew as a red ale that I had drunk many times before.

The glass tumbler tapped gently on the counter as she set it down in front of me and pushed it halfway towards me. Kate put her elbows on the bar and rested her chin in her hands with wide eyes, waiting for me to try a beer I already knew I would enjoy.

"Bottoms up," I said, toasting in her direction and taking a long swig.

"Good call," I said, returning my glass to the counter, realizing I was right about the beer.

"Yay, I had a feeling you would like that one," she said proudly with a smile as she straightened her stance.

The bell chimed, causing Kate to obnoxiously move her head around me to look at who entered. I observed her and took note of the fact that her face remained blank. When I walked in, I had elicited an expression on her face, proving she cared in some fashion about who came through the door.

The new customer made her way from the entrance straight to the bar to order.

Being the only bartender currently posted, Kate said "one sec," as she moved over to the taps to help her.

The male bartender that had shot me the dirty look the week previous emerged from the office, making his way to the taproom to help Kate out. As he walked towards me, the look on his face wasn't the same sour one as before. Instead, he seemed in a good mood and smiled at me when he arrived at the bar. He stood next to m and drummed his hands on its top while wearing a silent and soft grin. I stared back at him, waiting for him to say something.

"Hey man, how's it going?" he finally said as he broke the silence with a subtle chuckle.

Maybe I had just caught him at a bad moment before.

"Hey," I returned awkwardly, surprised he was talking to me, "not too bad. You?"

"Well, now that I'm done with some paperwork, I'm ready to sling some drinks. I swear I get stuck doing that stupid crap every night, and it drives me crazy. I was not meant for desk work; you know what I'm saying?" he responded as he removed his hat and slicked his hair back before replacing the cap, brim to the back.

"I feel you; I hate paperwork. I'd much rather be working with my hands," I agreed.

"Mhmm, I knew there was something I liked about you," he mumbled as he waived his pointer finger at me and shook his head.

Seeing my eyes leave him and glance at Kate across the bar, he spoke up again.

"My sister's pretty cool, but she is a little delicate, just so you know," he interjected, putting his hand up to shield his words from Kate.

"Sister?" I said out loud.

"Yeah, I know it's hard to tell with how good-looking I am while still being… eh almost two years older than her," he clarified.

Unsure of what he meant by delicate, and being an only child, I determined that was sibling talk for dramatic, though she didn't seem like either to me.

Raising both eyebrows, I looked at him, "I had no idea she was your sister," I admitted.

"Yeah, I don't work here because I want to. But, mom and dad needed the help. So, a couple of years back, I worked a couple of shifts, and I guess I just never left. I'm Seth," he said as he stuck his hand out towards me but quickly retracted it. "Sorry, I was eating some chips," he added as he wiped his hand on his pants and stuck it back out towards me.

"Brandon," I returned, shaking his hand.

"Nice to meet you, man. Kate's said some things about you," he said, accepting my handshake.

"Hopefully, good things," I replied.

"Well, I don't think she mentioned anything about you being a deranged murderer. So, I guess so far so good," he said with a soft chuckle.

"Yeah, I guess so," I answered.

"Well," he said, tapping his hands on the bar top again. "I'm gonna go run some food. Nice to mee you man."

"Yeah, you too," I returned.

With one last drum on the counter, he returned to the kitchen and left me sitting at the bar, waiting for Kate to finish up with the other customer.

When the customer walked away, Kate came back and pulled up a soft-topped barstool that had been tucked up under the bar top and made herself comfortable. She crossed her legs at her ankles and wedged her hands between her butt and the stool as she bent slightly forward at the waist.

"So, how was your week?" she asked.

I told her the depressing story of the skunked hunting trip and tactfully left out all the Taylor feelings that had emerged.

"Since you've lived here forever, have you ever been into hunting?" I asked.

"I went with my dad a couple of times when I was little, but it's been a long time since I did," she responded.

Wanting to share my love of guns and trying to think of a fun and more casual date, I volunteered to take her to the shooting range sometime. She adjusted herself in her seat, tucking her hands farther underneath her as she raised her shoulders upwards towards her ears.

"Thank you. It's not that I haven't because I don't want to. I just don't particularly care for guns and don't have much interest in shooting," she sputtered out, breaking her eye contact and directing her attention to the floor.

"Yeah, I get that," I lied, shrugging it off, even though I found it incredibly sexy when a woman had confidence with any gun in her hands.

The bell rang, and as expected, Kate looked past me to see who came in. Through the door walked a loud group of nine men who looked to be in their early twenties.

Kate watched, taking longer than usual as she took the time to study each one. Then, once they had all cleared whatever inspection she was putting them through, she snapped back to the reality of our conversation.

When she finished looking at the frat party, my eyes were still staring her way as she brought her attention back to me. She smiled and began to restart our conversation as if I hadn't just lost her for ten seconds when I cut her off.

"Do you look every time the bell jingles?" I quizzed.

She returned one hand underneath her, and the other one moved to the back of her neck and rubbed it gently as her eyes looked in my direction, but never at me. There was an unmistakable sense of discomfort as she searched for an answer to my question.

"Yeah, I guess I do, just a habit," she answered with an uncomfortable smile as her eyes met mine again.

The group of guys made their way to the bar to place an order, remaining in their herd. They seemed to be bar hopping and ended up here after catching a buzz somewhere else downtown. They eyeballed the menu and prepared to place their order as some of them swayed and loudly laughed as they put their arms around one another.

A few of the patrons looked over at Kate, then whispered something to a friend, and they both looked over her way. Seth took note of this and waved her off when she stood up to help with their drinks.

"Hey, how are you doing?" one of the guys slurred as he leaned over the bar towards her.

Still talking to me, Kate wasn't paying attention when he spoke, and upon the realization that he was talking to her, she flinched and leaned closer to the counter behind her.

"She's good," I interjected, causing the guy to look at me.

"I mean, I wasn't really asking you. I was asking the pretty lady right there," he responded as his finger wobbly pointed at Kate.

As I started to stand up to ask him to leave, Seth came over to the end of the bar where we were and placed his hands on the countertop.

"Hey man, your friends went over there," Seth said, nodding his head towards the back corner of the taproom.

"Yeah, cool, thanks," the guy replied, putting his glass up towards Seth as he walked to join his friends.

"You good?" Seth asked Kate.

"Yeah, I'm fine," she responded, smiling at her brother.

"Alright," he responded as he walked back to the other side of the bar and left us alone again.

"So, you were telling me about your week," she stated, restarting our conversation.

She had removed her hands and folded them lightly in her lap. Her face had softened, and she sat more upright, appearing comfortable again.

"Right," I registered and continued to tell her about my boring week, this time skipping any more discussion about hunting or firearms.

I told her about my intense cleaning session, partially because I didn't have much discussion-worthy and because I was proud of myself for finally accomplishing it. As I described the deep clean, I found it inevitable not to sound like I had been an utter slob before.

"The bachelor life, I guess," Kate said, softly chuckling.

If she was judging me for the mess I described, it didn't show on her face as she looked at me with a soft smile that hid her teeth.

"Yeah, I'm getting better slowly. Still trying to learn how to be an adult," I admitted and laughed as well.

"I think that's a never-ending learning curve. We just take what life throws at us and try to make it work, I suppose," she replied.

We talked casually about the weather, and she sat there stationed in her seat and intently listened as I spoke without stopping.

"Sorry, I don't usually talk this much, like at all. I would consider myself to be a quiet guy generally," I admitted with a slight cringe, realizing I had been rambling. "Please, tell me about your week."

"I like hearing you talk. Your week was a lot more interesting than mine, anyway. So, I hope I don't bore you with the details of mine," she explained.

Sitting across from her and watching her talk was pleasant. She spoke clearly and concisely and had an air of confidence that emanated from her as she filled me in on her week. Her hands retreated from her lap and began to flutter around with her words as she spoke.

She told me about the two online classes she had just started taking at the local college for the graphic design degree she was working to earn. I could see the visible passion in her eyes as she described the current projects she had on her plate.

Leaning forward on her seat, she reached to grab something that had been tucked away under the bar, the stool almost losing its footing. She stood up and slapped a long piece of laminated paper on the counter in front of me.

"Take a look, tell me what you think," she said as she stood back and crossed her arms.

Upon examining the paper in my hands, I quickly realized it was a revamped version of the bar's menu. It was sturdy and detailed, which was quite an update from the clipart trifold laserjet printer ones they currently had in circulation. The page also had detailed drawings and creative fonts that accentuated the menu options.

"I made that for one of my assignments," she said with a satisfied smile.

"Wow, this is great, really great," I complimented genuinely, "Why aren't you guys using this full time?"

"We will be next month. My dad is currently getting them printed. He was actually really picky and made me revise it like fifty times," she said with a gentle eye roll.

"That's awesome, way better than what they have now," I said with a nod and chuckle.

She sat back down and put her hands back in her lap before she leaned forward with a broad smile, happy with my review.

"Thanks! I'm glad you like it," she beamed, and her hands were back out to talk alongside her, "Those had to go. I moved back and came in and couldn't believe they were still using those crappy paper ones."

The bell rang, and she adjusted herself to watch a young couple holding hands enter, wholly wrapped up in each other. She tried to make her glance subtle and quick to avoid my detection, but it was blatantly obvious.

Once she finished with their order, she looked back at me and softly smiled as if pretending she hadn't just done what I recently called her out on.

It was odd that she had come back to Montana so recently but didn't seem to talk at all about life before she came back. Of course, she made mention of her childhood, teenage years, and present life, but there was a large gap missing from Kate's story she kept locked away and left me curious to hear more.

"So, where did you live before you moved back?" I asked, hoping I wasn't prying too much.

"Ohio," she said and looked down at the ground, sliding her hands back underneath her.

"What made you decide to move back? Did you like Ohio?" I asked as her eyes remained fixated on the ground in front of her.

Kate grabbed a sweater off the bar and put her arms inside the sleeves, and pulled it around herself tightly.

"Eh, it just wasn't working out there," she said as she looked back at me with a blank look.

"Ah, okay, gotcha, I've never been there," I replied.

"You're not missing much," she explained.

The more I asked about her past, the more she broke eye contact and gave me short answers that hinted it was a topic she'd rather not discuss. Trying to take her hint, I dropped the talk about Ohio and steered the conversation elsewhere while making every effort to avoid conversations about her past.

As we talked about more current topics, I saw Kate become more comfortable and watched her loosen up again. The chatting came easy and comfortable when we weren't discussing her obvious disdain of Ohio.

Everything she said gave me the impression that she was an intelligent and driven girl. But the way she hesitated on some things made me sense something in her life was holding her back from reaching her true potential.

Her hands reemerged from underneath her and rejoined our conversation. When she spoke, she sounded passionate and educated, and her speaking pace sped up noticeably about things that invigorated her. Excitement poured out of her as she started to tell me about her many hobbies, ranging from disc golf to watercolor painting.

I enjoyed watching the way she continued to talk with her hands, using them as tools to express her emotions. The things she was passionate about caused her hands to move all over the place, and when something was less interesting to her, they would rest in her lap and only occasionally flutter about.

When it was my turn to add to the banter, she fixated on me with her jade eyes, and I could feel her want to listen and not just hear what I was saying. She intently listened to me talk and slouched forward slightly on the stool while occasionally rolling her bottom lip under her teeth and releasing it.

We were just rolling from one topic to the next, talking about whatever came up organically. A couple of times, she briefly placed our conversation on hold to help a customer while Seth remained occupied in the kitchen. But when he was free, he had, for the most part, voluntarily taken on the task of handling the bar and helping out with the food while Kate and I sat there and talked.

Kate had expertly poured me two more beers of her choice. One turned out to be Lip Ripper, which I knew she must have picked up on as my favorite, and the third beer she served me was the result of a trip back to the brewing room.

She placed two pints on the bar and scooted the one on my left across the counter closer to me. After a taste, I studied the wall-mounted chalkboard menu, trying to guess which one it was. While eyeballing the list, I took another sip and found myself unable to pinpoint it.

"I like it, and I can tell it's some kind of IPA, but what exactly is it?" I questioned.

"My dad just finished it up. It's a blood orange IPA. It'll be available in the late spring. You're welcome," she said as she closed her eyes and gave me a grin.

"And what's this one?" I asked as I pointed to the beer adjacent to mine that looked the same.

Kate grabbed the extra glass and sipped the beer while looking at me over its rim with a silent smile.

"It's the same one. I just thought I'd join you," she teased as she set the glass on the counter.

"Drinking on the job, huh? Well, aren't you a daredevil," I replied jokingly.

"It's alright. I know the owners. Hopefully, I won't get in too much trouble," she playfully returned.

While we drank our beers together, we continued talking about Montana and the things we did for fun. Talking to her was enjoyable, and I was delighted at how easily I had opened up and found anything and everything to keep her talking to me.

I was typically a quiet and more reserved guy, I didn't always find it easy just to sit around and chat with strangers, but for some reason, it was simple with Kate.

As she tried to hide a yawn, I took a quick survey of the room, realizing there were only a few guys left from the party of nine that had loudly entered the bar. They had remained in the back corner of the bar and hadn't bothered us when they came back up for refills.

Glancing down at my watch, I noticed that it was nearing ten o'clock. Seeing me do so, Kate glanced down at the time on her phone and also realized how late it had gotten.

"Dang, tonight has gone by fast," I stated.

"Yeah, it has, and I hate to kick you out, but we have to get some stuff done so we can close in just a little. I don't want Seth to do it all cause I'll never hear the end of it," she apologetically said as she rolled her eyes.

"Yeah, for sure, I liked this. I'd like to see you again sometime if that's okay with you," I admitted, not making it sound like a date.

Silently, she stood and made her way to a coat rack on my side of the bar. After a few seconds of rummaging around in her jacket pocket, she pulled out a small card and handed it over.

"Here's my number," she said shyly.

"Marketing director," I said out loud as I inspected the standard-sized black and white business card in my hand.

"My parents tried to church up my title working here, and since they're paying for my college, they keep making me design new stuff for them," she said.

"Well, that makes sense Miss Marketing Director," I replied

"Also, I just got that number not too long ago, and I haven't taken the time to learn it, nor do I ever give out my number. I know it's weird for someone to give you their number on a business card in today's world," she explained.

"Ahhh, gotcha. Well, thank you for your number Miss," I paused and examined the name printed in a slightly raised ink on the card, "Kate Dillon," I responded,

"You're very welcome," she cheerfully responded. "Tonight was nice, thank you, and I'm sorry to kick you out."

"Nah, I need to get home and let the dog out anyway," I lied.

Tim had a bladder of steel and refused to go in the house even if I had left him home alone all evening.

"Yeah, for sure," she exclaimed, "I'll walk you to the door."

"I agree. Tonight was nice, thank you again," I stated, then stopped. "I didn't pay," I exclaimed as I fished into my pocket for my wallet.

"Nah, don't worry about it," she said with a flip of the wrist and a smug smile.

Seth emerged from the kitchen that was near the front door as we passed by. He leaned on the frame as he wiped his hands on a white rag he had tucked into the side of his waistband.

"Have a good night, nice guy Brandon," he said with a smile.

"Seriously?" I heard Kate mutter to him behind my back as we kept walking.

"Well, drive safe. It's a little slick out there right now," she warned while we stood at the entryway.

"I'll try. I hope you have a good night. I'll send you a text soon, and thanks again," I stated.

Trying to be a gentleman and not try to push my luck, I opted to extend a hand to her shoulder as I walked away.

Facing each other but out of arms reach, I stepped forward and began to raise my hand to place on her shoulder. At that moment, Kate flinched, retreating two more steps back from me as she looked down at the floor. I lowered my hand, unsure of what I had done.

She moved her hands from behind her back and began scratching the skin near her thumbnail with her pointer finger.

After a moment, her eyes returned to mine, and she softly smiled and said, "Goodnight, Brandon."

Out of the corner of my eye, I saw Seth come closer to us from the kitchen. I gazed at her, feeling awkward for unintentionally making her uncomfortable.

"Sorry, I didn't mean anything," I blurted, trying to apologize.

"I hope you have a good night," she repeated, ignoring me.

"Yeah, you too," I responded, realizing our conversation was over.

I gave her one last softened smile and exited the bar, hearing the bell chime in my wake.

SIX

THE NEXT MORNING, I awoke to a painfully bright room after failing to pull the curtains closed before I fell into bed. I yanked the comforter over my eyes while I laid there for a moment and listened to the internal rhythmic sound of my head throbbing.

When I got home from my outing with Kate, I had downed the half six-pack of IPA's I still had in the fridge while I watched The Office before making my way to bed. Lying on my back with a sold buzz, I looked at the blank ceiling and dissected our evening, trying but failing to conclude what I had done wrong.

Kate had become somewhat of a mystery to me that I couldn't seem to understand. Every encounter we had, she exhibited brief moments of oddity and obvious discomfort that left me wondering their root cause.

The first time I met her, she completely disregarded my friendly outstretched hand that was just looking for a handshake, and there was no question if she had seen it. Now, she had recoiled from me at a simple, innocent hand merely intended to land on her shoulder as I said goodnight.

Then there was the whole heightened awareness every time the bell jingled at the brewery's door that seemed to have magically appeared when she started working there. She claimed she wasn't aware of her quirk, but I could see the look plastered on her face as she ran a mental checklist every time she looked at the new person that came in. There was a slight possibility that it was subconscious, but it was odd how the chime sounded, and the person that entered never went disregarded.

So many little things quickly added up in my head and left me wanting to know more about her.

After holding it as long as I could, I finally climbed out of bed and stumbled to the bathroom, not looking forward to a day of being hungover. I popped three Ibuprofen in my mouth and stuck my head under the faucet, and drank till I was full to combat my dehydration.

Desperately needing one, I climbed into the shower and tried to shake the feeling that I had done something wrong. I scrubbed well, trying to eliminate the beer stench that was probably seeping through my pores at that point.

Freshly washed, I sank into my couch in just my boxers and enjoyed my morning coffee as I flipped on the TV and started watching the local news. I rested my feet on the coffee table and looked down. I saw Kate's card lying on the table in front of me from the night before.

After checking out the card, I saw that the area code was a local one, and I toyed with the idea of sending her a text message.

I typed out a simple "Hi" message and paused when I realized the small numbers at the top of my screen read 0745. Considering most people don't wake up before eight for no reason, I decided it was probably wise to wait a while before texting her.

Also, after the awkward goodbye, I wasn't sure if she was even interested in hearing from me again.

I spent the rest of my day doing some simple tidying up around the house and running errands. I completed my least favorite chore of grocery shopping, restocking on some essentials with my mild hangover lingering. The whole day, my mind wondered if I should text Kate or just let it go and see what happens.

When I got back home from grocery shopping, I returned to my worn-in spot on the couch and pulled out my phone to gather some tidbits of light information and maybe learn something about Kate to help unlock some of her mysteries.

My Instagram search turned up a few women named Kate Dillon, but after a scroll, none of the publicly viewable profiles was the girl that had captivated me the prior evening. The private accounts took some more examination, but none of them appeared to be her either.

My Facebook search came up about the same, yielding some of the same women and pictures, but none of them were the Kate Dillon I was trying to find.

Knowing social media isn't for everyone, and I concluded maybe she just didn't use it. So, as one last-ditch effort to learn more about her, I Googled Kate Dillon and still found nothing: LinkedIn, Pinterest, Twitter, nothing. She had zero online presence from what I could easily find with my limited web searching skills.

Eventually, I found something about her.

A Google search revealed a picture from the Great Falls Gazette when she was in high school from when she ran a Clean the Park event. Unfortunately, the image quality wasn't excellent, but she looked about the same, minus the braces tracked across her teeth.

"Hey, it's Brandon," I typed out and finally hit send.

A few minutes went by as I awkwardly stared at the screen, hoping a bubble with three dots would appear, signaling her typing a response. Finally, after a minute of nothing, I locked my phone and went back to watching The Office reruns.

Although it was freezing out, I found Tim's head on my lap, his sad eyes looking at me and begging for a walk. I pushed him away a few times, but he was persistent, so I donned a couple of layers and went outside into the cold air for some exercise.

A couple of minutes into our walk, I felt my phone finally vibrate in my back pocket. I removed my glove and took a quick look at the screen.

"Hey, it's Kate," she responded, changing one word from my text.

Adding her as a contact in my phone, I toiled over my response. Should I ask her about her day? Should I ask her out again?

"How was your day?" I decided to ask her.

"Honestly, it was pretty boring. I didn't do too much," she quickly responded. Then my phone tapped in my hand again. "Yours?" she inquired.

"I guess mine was probably about the same as yours," I answered.

"Do you have any weekend plans?" she texted, stealing my line.

"No, I don't have much planned, typical errands and stuff. But, I was hoping that you were free so I could take you to lunch or dinner tomorrow," I boldly stated.

When she didn't respond right away, I typed out an additional text, "If you want, no pressure."

Her response to my invitation didn't cause my phone to buzz for close to twenty minutes.

"I can't because I already promised Seth we would go skiing tomorrow. You said you snowboard, so would you like to join us? He said it was cool with him," she replied.

"That sounds fun. I'd like that," I responded, realizing that meant it was time to go through the hassle of digging out all my snow gear that probably got put away wet and hadn't been touched since last winter.

The following day, I gathered all the stuff needed for a day in the snow and met them at the brewery's front, purposely showing up ten minutes late, so I wasn't there alone. We tossed the abundance of gear into the back, and all climbed into Kate's 4Runner.

Seth stretched his legs out in the back and covered himself up with a blanket as he sat sideways on the second-row bench seat while I rode shotgun. Kate was a ten-and-two driver and remained very concentrated as she drove through the windy roads.

The route we drove to the ski resort gave you a perfect insight into all aspects of Montana's beautiful landscape, showing you a little of everything the state had to offer. The flat plains that painted the Big Sky aspect before your eyes eventually formed into hills and coulees that scattered the countryside in dips and hills as far as you could see. The grassy-covered fields that surrounded Great Falls gradually grew upwards and slowly became mountains with sharp rocky edges.

Only two small towns between Great Falls and the ski area claimed no more than five hundred residents combined. With not much else in between, you needed to get gas before leaving the city or risk the chance of running dry in between. Driving through the small towns during any season of the year felt like you were visiting a ghost town. After coming through them during all four solstice's, I wasn't sure if either had any residents minus the people running the small "Inconvenience Store."

During our drive, Kate and I took turns telling the stories of how we got into winter sports. She got to hear the painful stories of me learning to snowboard and the challenge that was, causing her to cringe when I told her the gruesome ways my knees twisted when I fell.

Her story was completely different. She didn't even remember learning how to ski because her parents sent her down the bunny slope for the first time when she was only three years old. But, she had taken to it quickly like most kids do when they don't have a fear of injury holding them back.

We added onto our talk from the night before, but neither of us brought up the awkward moment at the door. Instead, we spent time discussing my hometown, our favorite foods, Kate's graphic design school, and anything else that flowed out organically.

"Nope, I never saw snow till I moved here," I admitted with a smile as her mouth fell open.

"Seriously? Like never?" she asked.

"Nope, and the movies make you think it snows and then never melts till summer in the north. So I was shocked when it melted a few days later and didn't come back until the next snowstorm," I explained.

"Well, aren't you lucky," she added, keeping her eyes on the windy road.

Kate told me more about her graphic design courses and her plans once she finished her degree. Once she was entirely comfortable in her work, she hoped to one day make restaurant menus and marketing supplies for other small businesses around Great Falls.

Trying to talk about something outside of Montana, I changed the conversation by telling her I wanted to start traveling again. The hard part of taking overseas trips was finding someone to commit to taking the time and spending the money to go with me. Although I could go alone, I liked the idea of having someone to tag along and see the sights alongside.

I told Kate about my plans to make my next trip a long, two-week venture to see the sights in Italy and Greece. I had been researching and trying to plan out all the spots that I wanted to hit to truly capture the history, extensive culture, and fantastic food both countries had to offer.

"Do you want to travel anywhere specific? Like, where would you go if money wasn't an issue?" I asked, hoping to get a response that wasn't Montana-related.

"Oh, I don't know, I've seen some places online, but I can't think of anywhere specific," she said, shrugging her shoulders.

Even though she didn't have something specific planned, I could tell it was something she wanted to do. The way she asked questions and listened intently to me didn't give me the impression of someone that wanted to spend the rest of her life stuck in a small Montana town.

Something was holding her back.

We kept on driving and continuing our small talk as Seth snored in the backseat, his face covered by his ski jacket and his body tucked in under his fleece blanket. Kate got chatty, and I could tell it was a struggle for her not to speak without her hands' full assistance. She spent most of the time driving, merely flipping around only her pointer fingers on the steering wheel.

The snow appeared evident on the road as the ski area finally came into sight.

We pulled into a spot that was still a decent hike to the hill's entrance but was reasonable. I looked towards the lifts, saw only a small herd of people, and realized the place wasn't overly packed.

"Wakey wakey," Kate said, turning around to slap Seth on the thigh when we parked.

"Okay, geez," he replied, rubbing his eyes.

This mountain wasn't big compared to some of the mega-resorts that Montana was also home to, but what it lacked in size and luster, it made up for with its superior customer service and homey feeling. Everyone I had ever met that worked in the lodge and on the slopes was always exceptionally polite and friendly.

There were only three chair lifts on the mountain that led to roughly sixty trails that ranged from green circle to single black diamond about their difficulty. The longest and most accessible run was a vast, green circle trail that quietly weaved down the mountain for a mile and a half on a towering evergreen-lined path.

The siblings donned their skinny rigid ski boots, and I stepped into my slightly more forgiving puffy snowboard ones and donned all the needed gear to survive when it was twenty-five degrees out.

As we trudged through the parking lot, Kate looked back to see me struggling about five paces behind her.

"You coming?" she asked as I heard her chuckle through her cheetah print face covering.

"Yeah yeah," I replied with a subtle laugh as I picked up the pace.

We bought our day passes and strapped our feet tightly into our boards as we made our way to the lift, ready to get on and hit the snow. The day was starting to warm up slightly, but the sharp breeze made me keep my face covered and caused some nerves as I watched the chairs rocking side to side on their suspension cable.

During our ride upwards, I sat on the left side of the three-person lift with my outside foot unclipped and my board hanging down, loosely ratcheted tightly to my right foot. Seth was sandwiched between Kate and me and oddly put his left arm around my back as he cupped his hand around my shoulder. He swung his legs back and forth slightly, causing the chair to move up and down on the thin cable.

"Could you not?" I asked sternly, looking over at Seth as I wrapped my arm around the chair's pole.

"What, are you scared?" Seth asked, continuing his bouncing.

"Seriously, I don't like it either, and you know that," Kate added as she put her hand on Seth's thigh, causing him to stop.

We exited the chair lift at the summit, and I tried my best not to fall as I slid down the ramp with one foot strapped in to get to the runs.

We slowly carved our way down my favorite gradual run to warm up our winter legs. At the bottom, we readied ourselves for the whack of the lift as we ventured up for our second run, this time checking out the fresh powder on the backside of the mountain.

Kate found herself in the middle of the sandwich on this lift as I returned to my consistent left-sided position. The chair was tight, forcing the three of us to cuddle up in our layered attire as we made our ascent.

Kate's hips and shoulders were squished between her brother and me as the lift escalated farther from the powder below. I recalled how snug I fit next to Seth previously. With Kate next to me, the space I had next to my hip felt like she was edging closer to her brother and trying to push farther away from me.

She kept the left side of her body held close to her on the lift as though she was trying not to risk being any closer to me. After our encounter at the brewery's doorway, I thought maybe she was simply weird about being touched, so I leaned more to the left to give her whatever space I could.

We ventured down a blue square run next, stepping the difficulty up just a tad. To stay ahead of Kate and Seth, I ended up picking up too much speed and tried to slow myself when I caught an edge with the front of my board, hitting the snow hard, flipping over, and falling on my right shoulder.

After sitting up and doing a quick function check, I realized I hadn't done any significant damage and stretched it out for a second. Kate was only about twenty yards behind me and witnessed my tumble and slid up behind me with a smile on her face.

"Yowch, you okay?" she asked as she pulled down her face covering and revealed a toothy smile.

"Yeah, I'm good. I don't know, though. Maybe I'm getting too old for this stuff," I responded with a chuckle, able to laugh at my misfortune.

"Oh whatever," she responded as she waved her pole at me and started to scoot herself down the mountain again slowly. "Let's go, old man," she yelled back at me, picking up speed.

After a couple of more trips down the mountain, we were ready to head into the lodge to take a break and warm up. Still nursing my shoulder, I grabbed a platter of chicken tenders with fries and a large glass of beer. We sat in the warm lodge and ate together while we talked about our run plans for the rest of the day.

"Let's do a couple of more, then well call it a day. Pizza and beer at our place?" Seth said, looking at me sideways across the table.

Looking over at Kate, I saw she was softly smiling and gently nodded at me while eating a cheese stick.

"Sure, why not," I replied.

Seth took our lunch break as a chance to get to know me some more and started asking me some simple questions. I was happy to answer as he sat across from me and nodded while he shoved a cheeseburger into his mouth.

We boarded the lift again, and I found Kate tucked in next to me on my right side. She appeared to have loosened up a little, no longer feeling like a statue stationed by my side.

She sat close to me, and I wanted to put my hand on her leg or drape my arm around her back, but I decided to take things one step at a time. Feeling her not fighting the requirement for her left side to be butted up next to mine was a good place for us to start.

The rest of the day, skiing was great and improved the way my weekends usually went. I probably should have taken my rifle out hunting for my elk instead, but the ski trip ended up being the better choice. Kate, Seth, and I laughed and had a good time together carving up the mountains. The two of them were fun to be around, and I found myself hoping the three of us would do it again sometime.

Just as the sun set below the mountainous horizon, we made it back to Great Falls and entered the family's brewery. We ate pizza together while Kate and Seth's parents operated the bar with Luke. Kate introduced me to her mom and dad, and they seemed delighted to meet me.

Even off the clock, Kate continued her bell chime glances like usual, peering over and scanning the new entrants. As she looked, I noticed the scar I had seen below her eye previously stick out to me. Whatever light dusting of makeup she typically covered it with had worn off during our day in the snow. The thought crossed my mind to ask where she had gotten it, but I withheld my question.

Eventually, Kate's dad called Seth to cover the bar while his parents helped the kitchen during a brief rush. Although I enjoyed our day with Seth tagging along, it was nice to get a few minutes to talk to Kate with no other ears listening in.

We talked, talked, and talked some more while I remained careful not to go too deep into her past, even though I wanted to know more. Kate leaned forward across the table with her hands in her lap as she listened to me and pulled her hands out when it was her turn to talk. Our private conversation flowed easily, and after a glance at my watch, I realized it was almost eight p.m.

Seeing me eyeball the time, Kate asked with concern, "Oh geez, you've been gone all day. Do you have to go let your dog out?"

"Oh no, he's fine. My neighbor and I take turns letting each other's dogs out if we know one of us will be gone all day. I told him I would be home late tonight. Plus, I'm having too much fun talking to you," I said.

"Oh, okay, good, and yeah, it is nice," she said, as a full smile cracking across her face.

Her eyes locked on mine, and we just sat there for a brief second in silence. Then, when she looked at me, I could see the kindness in her eyes, and the soft smile she bore made me decide to go out on a limb.

"I'd like to take you out sometime, just the two of us. What restaurant in town is your favorite?" I blurted at Kate.

She sat across from me quietly, her eyes moving away from mine as she pulled her cross-body purse in tighter. She looked down at her lap for a minute and remained silent as I saw the smile fade from her face. Then, finally, her head returned upright, and she looked at me with a blank expression hidden in her eyes.

"Brandon, I feel like you should know some things about me," she said, a weepy look of defeat appearing in her eyes.

"What are you talking about?" I asked, confused.

"Just hang on," she said.

Rising from her position at the table, Kate bared her palm in my direction with the understood direction stay put. She made her way across the taproom and walked behind the bar where her brother had just finished helping a customer.

Sitting there perplexed, I rolled over the hundreds of possible things it could be she felt I needed to know. It was a simple yes or no question that now seemed to be turning into something much more complicated.

Kate was already somewhat of a mystery to me with her obvious issue with physical contact, and now suddenly, it seemed like she had some big secret she needed to reveal to me.

Facing away from me, she leaned her back against the bar with Seth at her twelve o'clock, his back resting on the wall. Across the length of the taproom, there was no chance I would be able to catch a drift of what she was saying, but I watched their body language and tried to gauge the tone of their conversation.

Kate spoke to her brother, and he listened. Her hands were gently moving to join her words, and her head slightly bobbed, adding expression to whatever she was saying. Then she silenced herself, and her arms went crossed in front of her while Seth responded to her.

Although I wasn't able to make out the mood of the conversation, they seemed to both be calm and listening to one another without issue. The only thing I could make out was the word "okay" come from Seth's mouth as he shrugged one shoulder.

Soon after saying okay, Seth peered around his sister and met my eyes from across the room. He quickly looked away and redirected his attention to Kate standing there quietly leaning against the bar. He took her in his arms and pulled her into a hug while looking at me over her shoulder.

God, I felt so confused.

The bell at the door chimed, and the siblings both released from their embrace, turning their heads to see who came in. But, again, whoever it was didn't seem to matter to Kate or Seth, and they quickly returned their attention to one another.

Seth walked over to the kitchen while Kate stood at the bar for a minute alone. I watched her shoulders drop as she exited the backside and returned to the table where I was sitting, pondering what was about to happen.

She stood tall and silent behind her chair for a moment while I watched her, keeping my mouth shut. Then she pushed in her chair, and I assumed she had changed her mind about letting me in on whatever it was she was hiding.

"Will you come with me?" she asked.

"Where?" I responded.

"To the loft," she answered, motioning her hand to the staircase.

"Okay," I said hesitantly, wanting to know more.

She removed the rope at the bottom, and I followed her up the staircase to the loft and found myself alone with Kate.

The loft had a lower ceiling, but I could still clear the exposed piping without ducking my head. My eyes gazed around the room, and I saw all the chairs were turned upside down, their seats resting on the tabletops, giving me the impression it had been a while since they let anyone up here.

Kate began to pull a chair from a table intended for four near the staircase. Moving to help, I took down a chair, and then we both removed a second, clearing the table. We sat across from each other, and I softly frowned, unable to hide my confusion.

Kate sat in her seat with her hands intertwined in front of her and her head slightly tucked down in-between them. The bell chime was faint but still audible from our loft position as someone entered the taproom below. Kate remained in her buried position, and for the first time, she didn't seem to be startled by its sound.

A few seconds later, Kate finally lifted her head. I could see that her eyes looked glossy but didn't appear to have tears welled up in them. Her hands rubbed her face before pulling the bottoms of her eyelids down. Then, with an exaggerated sigh, she laid her hands down gently on the table in front of her.

"Okay," she finally spoke and then took another deep breath in and out as her eyes aimed upward then back to me. "Here we go," she added.

"Listen, you don't have to tell me whatever it is you think you need to, really it's fine," I explained.

"No, I like you, Brandon, but I think you need to know some things about me. Sadly, thanks to the internet and this small town, a decent number of people know this story, and I don't want you to hear it from someone else if you mention my name. Maybe after hearing it, you'll understand why I am the way that I am," she explained.

"Okay, tell me whatever you want, but know you don't have to," I told Kate.

She started to tell me her story.

SEVEN

Kate

GROWING UP, I was lucky enough to be blessed with a loving family where both my mom and dad were present and attentive to my brother and me. However, on the flip side of the coin, Ethan had grown up with just his dad, and the two of them often just barely made it.

Ethan lost his mother when he was only two, which started his father's downward spiral into alcoholism. He started heavily drinking and became not just a drunk but a violent drunk, often taking his rage and sadness out on his son.

Ethan's grandmother Shannon was a bitter older woman who also lived in Great Falls. Still, even after losing her daughter-in-law, she never helped or paid attention to her only grandson and what was happening to him behind closed doors.

When we were both juniors in high school, Ethan and I became close friends and often found ourselves just hanging out after school. Finally, our senior year, we decided to give it a go, and after a couple of dates, we quickly fell into that dreamy high school love that seemed picture-perfect, and you think would never end.

After graduation, Ethan enlisted in the Marine Corps as a diesel mechanic to get away from his dad and earn a degree for free. He used the military as his chance to break free from Great Falls and the life that was leading him nowhere.

At his graduation from boot camp, he proposed to me in the middle of a grassy field, and it didn't take a second for eighteen-year-old me to agree to marry him with tears flowing down my face. The following day we were sprinting to the courthouse to make it official.

The first couple of years of our marriage were great. Ethan loved his job in the Marines, and I had moved to North Carolina with him, finding work as a shopkeeper at a local boutique craft store. Ethan made romantic gestures, took me on dates, and constantly wanted to show me off to his friends.

Then I found out I was pregnant, and we would be adding a little boy to our small family. At this point, we were close to three years into our marriage and stable for the most part. I was nervous about how he would react, mainly for financial reasons, but thankfully Ethan was ecstatic when I told him the news.

Planning for a baby was fun for me. I read all the books and dove deep into product reviews, making sure I did everything just right. The baby's nursery was painted a gentle blue, the crib was screwed together tight, and the cute little clothes were hung on the mini hangers.

We both fell in love with the name Jack, and Ethan would gently talk to him at night while he rubbed my bare belly. Ethan was generally sweet, but his soon-to-be son was bringing out a whole new side to him as he nestled into the role of being a dad.

Ethan had so many dreams already planned out for Jack, all the classic father-son stuff he wanted to do with his dad but did. Jack had quickly become Ethan's whole world, and he wasn't even here yet.

When it came time, we snatched up the pre-packed hospital bag as we rushed to the hospital. I wasn't sure what at the time, but my body was sending me signals that something was wrong during the whole ride.

On the ultrasound, they couldn't find his tiny pattering heartbeat, but the nurse stuttered as she told me she found the umbilical cord had become wrapped around his neck.

Jack finally entered the world late on a Tuesday night after hours of pushing but was delivered stillborn and would never accomplish all the dreams we had built for him.

Holding Jack in my arms briefly before the nurses took him away was the most challenging time of my life. His lifeless body was just weight in my arms as I sobbed, begging him to breathe and come back to us. Ethan refused to hold him or get a photo of the three of us but stood by my side, crying alongside me.

The loss of our baby hit Ethan harder than I expected. We had a small funeral for Jack where we buried him and were presented with his hand and footprints forever cast in plaster, and I held the rock hands of my son close to my heart as they lowered his tiny casket into the ground.

Ethan and I were both positively devastated about the loss of our son that happened so suddenly. Nothing could have prevented the tragedy, but I still felt like it was something I had done, and I wrongly cast the blame on myself, sending me down a rabbit hole of postpartum depression.

In his grief, Ethan neglected my pain as he selfishly tended to his own. He started drinking, often heavily and to excess. He drank both at home and ventured out to bars, often endangering himself and others when he chose to drive after way too many.

The drinking quickly spiraled out of control and started affecting our ability to pay the bills when he racked up sky-high bar tabs on credit cards while the amount in our joint bank account kept dwindling.

Hoping it was just a phase of grief and it would get better, I kept silent about the excessive drinking, knowing he was drowning his emotions in a way that was numbing his pain while I kept mine bottled up inside.

But when my debit card declined as I tried to buy groceries, I checked our finances and decided that was enough.

After he came home from work one day, I finally confronted Ethan, making sure I caught him when he was still mostly sober. Almost instantly, he jumped on the defense. His excuses evolved into "I can stop whenever I want" and "I'm just a social drinker." He just wasn't ready to admit that he had a drinking problem.

His talking and defending quickly snowballed and became violent. Ethan yelled at me as he pushed over one of our kitchen chairs, causing the top corner of it to puncture a hole in the drywall. I slowly backed out of the room, afraid that I would be the next place he directed his anger.

Ethan became aware of what he had done and snapped out of it. He sat down at the table and put his face in his hands as he started sobbing uncontrollably. I went up to him and gently placed a hand on each shoulder to calm him down as he grabbed my hand gently.

He stood up and pulled me close to him. My body stiffened for a second but relaxed when I realized the rage he had exhibited was gone. He continued sobbing, and I found myself joining in on the crying too. Once the tears had stopped running, we sat down in the living room and held hands while we calmly talked for what felt like the first time in a long time.

Ethan finally admitted to his drinking problem and voluntarily agreed to get some professional help. In addition, he repeatedly promised to work towards his sobriety and swore to make our relationship a priority again.

Even though he fell off the wagon a few times, he eventually made it to the three-month mark without a setback. I beamed with pride for him and couldn't wait for three months to turn to four and so on.

With Ethan sober, our finances, sex life, and all-around marriage got back on track.

With everything happening with Ethan and the emotions I still had from losing Jack, I decided to get back on birth control. Ethan didn't need that kind of stress in his life while he was trying to rehabilitate himself, and I wasn't even sure I felt ready to think about having another baby.

Four months into his sobriety, Ethan came home from work late with a solemn look on his face. Thinking he had slipped up again, I was surprised when he broke the news that he would be shipping out to Iraq in a month for a six-month stint.

That last month together went by all too fast, and soon it was time for me to send him off. I drove him to the base with tears in my eyes and his three stuffed green duffle bags in the trunk.

"I love you, and I'll be fine. It will be over before you know it," he said, pulling me into his embrace.

I told him I loved him and stood in the terminal with tears running down my cheeks as I watched him and sixty plus other Marines funnel onto a grey military airplane.

Two days later, Ethan had finally made it to Iraq and sent me a hurriedly typed email telling me that he made it safely and that he loved me.

Over the first four months, I got letters and emails often. There was spotty Wi-Fi in his location, but he would call and text me when he got the chance. He didn't go into much detail about his location but told me positive stories about friends he'd made on the small camp and the local people they had helped.

Then came Ethan's accident.

He was working on top of an MRAP when a sandstorm blew in out of nowhere. His surroundings vanished in a matter of seconds, and he became engulfed in the cloud of clay-colored sand. Disoriented and blind, he fell almost twenty feet from the vehicle's roof to the hardened ground below.

He hit the ground below, his leg banging off the side of a pile of metal ammo cams next to the vehicle. His head struck the concrete as the sand continued to fly all-around before he blacked out alone on the ground.

Roughly a half-hour later, a fellow Marine saw Ethan lying on the ground as he returned to the vehicle to grab a radio he had left behind. He left Ethan motionless on the ground and ran off to get help from the medical team. A few minutes later, they were at his side, trying to figure out what injuries he had sustained.

Later that night, he was on a helicopter back to the main base, where he received an x-ray and was diagnosed with a shattered femur, fractured hip, and a severe concussion. After three hours of tests and imagery, he was airlifted to Germany, then back to the states for better care and recovery.

His commander called and gave me the rundown about what had happened while he was mid-flight on his way to Germany. The military made arrangements for me, and I soon found myself flying to Walter Reed to meet him.

When I arrived at the hospital, I found Ethan sleeping. His medical team fitted him with a hard black cast that ran across his waist and down the entirety of his leg. The rest of his body had developed scattered bruises, and his face was black and blue as though he had been through the wringer with someone twice his size.

His recovery was tough and long, but I was there to help him through it. After finding an apartment near Walter Reed, I stayed there till he could get back to everyday life and come home. We discussed his options, but eventually, he separated from the Marines and applied for disability.

Once he was fully mobile again, we loaded up everything and moved to Ohio, where I got accepted to a small nursing school. I felt the urge to do something more with my life after seeing how the nurses helped Ethan in the hospital.

When he finally felt up to it, Ethan started working as a mechanic for a local auto shop. I loved hearing him come home from work with excitement showing on his face as he expressed how happy he was to be off the couch and working with his hands again.

Ten months passed, and Ethan worked hard in his recovery efforts and progressively regained his previous strength. Along with his physical recovery, he always seemed in good spirits and enjoyed his life after leaving the Corps.

Ethan was prescribed an enormous concoction of pain pills that he had secretly developed an addiction for during his recovery. Although he hadn't gone back to alcohol, he was popping multiple pills a day just to get by, even long after the pain subsided.

Eventually, the pills weren't enough, and Ethan broke his sober streak when he started mixing the drugs and alcohol to get the buzz he craved.

During his attempts at defending himself, he sometimes got angry and started yelling at me and even threw things on several occasions. He often blamed me for always being on his case or saying I didn't understand what he was going through. Every time he lashed out, he ended up being apologetic and often cried and begged for me to forgive him.

Time after time, I found myself stupidly taking him back.

Ethan started to be late or even wholly miss work a lot. Then, when he did show up, he was never fully there, which eventually led him to getting fired for being drunk on the job. His anger had grown, and he started flying off the handle at me for no reason.

His addiction to alcohol and prescription pills ended in his arrest after a night of mixing the two, which resulted in him getting kicked out of a bar and passing out in a dark, musty alley. Seeing him at such a low point had me hoping it would be his wake-up call.

He climbed in the car after spending the night in the drunk tank with a sad smile and sorry eyes as he hugged me and repeatedly apologized. After three hours in the car discussing what to do, I drove him straight to an inpatient rehab center that he finally agreed to commit to

Tears ran down my face when I got back into the car alone after checking him in. He had begged me at the counter not to make him go, but I knew it was too late for us to turn back now; he had to do it.

Ethan worked on his recovery diligently. I visited him frequently and saw the drained look on his face and thin body as he started the process of working on his sobriety.

As he progressed in the program, it seemed as though he began to look better physically, but his anger had noticeably escalated. As the doctors tried to wean him off his anti-addiction medication, he grew very short-tempered and had started not to want to see me when I came to visit.

Halfway into his stay, I received an odd call from one of the doctors on staff. Dr. Branch introduced herself and detailed as much as she could without breaking confidentiality laws. She didn't divulge much about their sessions or tell me the secrets Ethan had told her, but she was able to provide me with a chilling diagnosis she was exploring.

She suspected Ethan had a mental illness.

The traits he displayed convinced her that he was only mildly bipolar and told me her team was working on creating the right prescription combination for him. However, they had to be methodical in their treatment plan, ensuring not to give him anything that would agitate the addiction issues he was working so hard to squash.

Dr. Branch called me a week later and told me they had found a suitable cocktail of drugs to try and even out Ethan's mood that seemed to be working for him. She expressed the need to keep him for a few more days to ensure they had the proper dosage before sending him home. She said great things about Ethan's progress and talked about how well he was coping with the card in life he had been dealt. Although relapse was always possible, she told me she saw nothing but good things for our future.

I saw Ethan the day before he was coming home, and we chatted for a while. The changes in him helped me feel like I was talking to the eighteen-year-old Ethan I fell in love with all over again. He kept talking about how excited he was to come home and start over, hoping to do things right this time around.

The next day, I picked Ethan up from rehab, and he leaned over kissed me repeatedly on the cheek when he got in the car. I smiled both inside and out, happy with how different he was from when he started the program.

We stopped at Chick-fil-A, at his request, and grabbed his favorite meal, which was anything if he also got one of every sauce. We took our lunch to a park and sat down at a picnic table by the water,

When he finished scarfing down his nuggets, Ethan suddenly started opening up to me. He began telling me things that he had told Dr. Branch but had never told me before, which included stories with new details about sexual and physical abuse that had happened to him as a child. I cried for him, feeling terrible for the events in his life that he had kept bottled up for so long. Finally, he took ahold of my hand and interlaced his fingers in mine, promising me everything would be better.

The months went by, and we fell back into the swing of things. His meds leveled his mood perfectly almost all days. We laughed, joked, and enjoyed everything about being an average married couple again.

Some days were darker, and I could see he was tired and holding back a slight bout of depression that had crept up on him. Occasionally, his temper would flare up, but I was happy with the life we were living.

Nursing school just wasn't for me. I thought I would love so many things about the career field but ended up hating it. After the first year, I quit and found myself working full-time as a nanny to a set of triplets with a wealthy father who couldn't stop hitting on me.

Three months after leaving rehab, it seemed as though Ethan's mood had drastically changed for the worse out of the blue, leaving me clueless as to why. Every morning I counted his pills, and the right amount was always missing from the bottles. His demeanor became a concerning problem, and I was beginning to question if he was taking his medication at all.

As he grew more noticeably agitated, I more than once begged him to go back to Dr. Branch and see if they could do some recalibrations to his medicine. Finally, he took offense, accusing me of calling him "crazy," and struck me hard across the face. My head whipped sideways as the back of his hand made hard contact with my face. My hand shot to my cheek and rubbed the place the warm place he hit while my eyes watered from the pain.

That was the first time he had ever hit me. There had been times he had thrown things, but I never felt they were aimed to cause harm to me, but the hit had. Standing there, I was at a complete loss for words as tears began rolling down my face.

Every bone in my body told me to run, leave him for what he had done to me and never come back to listen to an apology. My mind quickly flashed to me, saying how stupid the women were on those TV shows that stayed in an abusive relationship, a woman I vowed never to be.

Now there I was, that woman.

He quickly apologized to me, falling to his knees as his tears began to mirror mine. Still loving this man, I knew he was struggling, and I was trying to be compassionate while my mind fought a mental war on what to do. Then, taking him in my arms, he swore to me that he would call Dr. Branch the next day and see what she could do for him.

The following day, I rolled over as the sun peeked through the curtains to find our bed empty. After looking around the house, I realized Ethan wasn't anywhere inside or outside. Repeatedly I called his cell phone, begging him to pick it up. After calling six times and getting no response, it started to go straight to his voicemail. I sent him multiple text messages pleading for him to let me know he was okay.

When he didn't answer, I called his work, the couple of friends he had, and even his grandmother in a desperate attempt to find him, but not one of them had heard anything from him.

After rummaging around the house looking for a note or clue to tell me where he would have gone, I realized that he had emptied the small cedar box on the counter we kept close to two grand of cash in and saw the key holder looked empty. I rushed to the garage and found my car missing, but his still parked in the street.

I called the police to report him missing, and they told me I would have to wait forty-eight hours before being able to file a report. But the police didn't understand, and I didn't tell them, but I felt there was a chance that he could be dangerous to himself and those around him.

It became clear that he had left on his own accord, purposely leaving his meds behind.

Two days later, with no word or sign of my husband, I called the police back and made the official missing person's report. I detailed his history to them, told them about his diagnosis, and revealed how he had struck me.

As soon as I got off the phone, I sat on my living room floor as tears streamed down my face while I looked through shoeboxes to find pictures to help identify Ethan and create a profile to begin their search. I pulled out a wedding photo and compared it to a recent one on my phone. I cried even harder as I compared the men in both pictures, seeing how far he had gone downhill in only a couple of years.

Now deep bags were sunken in under his eyes, making them look sad and lonely, and the nearly fifty pounds of weight he had lost left his cheekbones visible and his face hollow. His hair was constantly in disarray and had become almost patchy in certain spots. Blinking through my tears, I could barely recognize Ethan in the photo.

After a couple of days of searching, the police finally called me up and told me they had no news of Ethan's whereabouts. He hadn't used any of our credit cards or his phone, but they continued to monitor them both.

He was good at hiding.

I called the rehab center and asked to speak with Dr. Branch to tell her what was going on and gauge her opinion. I could hear the worry she tried to hide in her voice when she asked, "not taking his medication?"

She told me things she hadn't been able to previously, expressing the severity of him being on the loose and off his medication. Ethan had expressed thoughts of killing himself while he was in rehab, thoughts she sat with him all night talking through till he broke down. She mostly said that she felt worried that he could be dangerous to others while off his medication.

I promised to let her know if I heard anything from him, and she offered her prayers for both Ethan and me.

Not knowing what else I could do to find someone that didn't want to be found, I kept working with the triplets and posting on Facebook and other sites, hoping that someone would hear from him or see him. No one reported anything, but many offered their condolences.

I checked religiously, but the credit card hadn't been used in over two weeks, sending me into a downward spiral of concern that something terrible had happened to him.

Three weeks after he left, I came home late, exhausted from being with the triplets all day during spring break. After pushing the button on my visor, the garage door slowly rose.

Inside the garage, I saw my car nicely parked in its spot again as though it had never been missing. A chill dashed from my head to my toes as the door came to a stop, and my car, I believed to be gone forever, came fully into view.

My lights shone in the garage as I sat in the car and pondered my next move. The hum of the garage was loud and must have alerted him I was home because a few moments later, I saw the door to the house open, and Ethan stood in its frame.

Confusion ran through me as I sat in my car, unsure of what to do. Do I call the police? Dr. Branch? Do I just drive away? I sat there frozen, trying to decide what the right move was.

He raised his hand from behind his back, revealing a large bouquet of multicolored tulips in it, my favorite. He held them in front of his chest and stayed in his place in the garage.

If I just left, there was a chance he would just disappear again, and deep down, I thought I would be that one that would be able to reach him before he flew off the handle. I convinced myself that he wouldn't hurt me again, and if I let him go, maybe he would hurt someone else.

Shooting Dr. Branch a quick text, I informed her that he had come back home. Before she texted back, I sent her an additional text, telling her I was going inside to talk to him. Hopefully, she would be able to come over and reason with him if I couldn't.

As I walked into the house, I felt a drone camera hovering over me, recording me as I starred in the opening of a horror movie. Inside, my body was screaming, "no, you dumbass, don't go inside to your mentally unstable husband," but my heart wanted to take care of him.

At first, I kept my distance, silently standing at the edge of the garage and giving him a quick look over. The time he spent away, while likely off his medication, had done well for him.

He neatly combed his ill-kept hair, and his skin looked like it had regained some of its previous hues. I knew the clothes he was wearing were clean ones that had been hanging in the closet while he was gone.

A smile cracked across his face, revealing a glimpse of the man he used to be again. It looked like a sincere smile, with hints of an apology and regret showing in his eyes.

"Hi Katie girl," his voice said, slightly cracking, forcing him to follow his greeting with a cough.

My lips stayed sealed, offering no response, relieved to see that he was okay.

As our issues continued to compound, exasperated by him striking me, I still really cared about him, but I could sense that I was starting to feel differently. I still loved him as a person and wanted him to get better, but when he was gone, the realization of how trapped I had become hit me hard. I was no longer his wife but his caretaker and mother. I waited up at night worrying about him like he was a high school kid that stayed out past his curfew. I had run off all my friends over time because he was jealous and always seemed to have some issue with them.

When he was gone, I was worried about his wellbeing and anyone that might rile him up and get hurt as a result. But I concluded that I didn't miss him or want him back. I just wanted to know he was okay.

Seeing him standing in the garage, I knew; our marriage was over.

"Hey, where have you been?" I asked, a little snarky.

"Around, trying to figure things out," he responded shortly, "Will you come in so we can talk? I made dinner."

He didn't seem intimidating, and I didn't want him to flee, so I followed him into our home.

Sincere apologies spilled from his mouth as we walked into the house, me trailing behind him. He kept his hands to himself, and he didn't even try to hug me. When we walked into the living room, I saw had freshly vacuumed the floors, perfect lines streaking across the carpet the way I liked. I could hear the gentle beat of the washing machine running downstairs in the basement as we made our way into the kitchen.

He asked me to join him at our kitchen table, and I strategically selected a chair directly across from his, trying to use the table as a physical barrier between us.

Once we were situated, he began talking. Still unsure of the situation, I sat politely and listened to him talk, all the while maintaining situational awareness of my surroundings.

The front door and the garage door were both behind me but were easily reachable. The glass door behind Ethan would require me to get past him, which would have to be plan B. I pulled my purse, which housed my keys and phone, closer into my lap in case I needed to run.

He realized many things during his stint in rehab, things he had never talked about with me or anyone, and he now found himself trying to get a grip on all of them. His early morning departure and weeks of being missing was allegedly him trying to cut those demons on his own, not wanting to burden me with them.

The look on his face appeared sad as he described all of this to me. The apologies for hitting me continued, while his words and body language showed me a broken man who desperately wanted to put the pieces back together.

Standing, he grabbed my favorite bottle of red wine that had been chilling in the fridge and poured me a glass. His hand reached for the glass of water placed in front of him. Taking small sips from the glass, he looked at me. Slowly I sipped the wine, ensuring not to drink too much and hinder my inhibitions.

A moment later, he stood up and fished two plates of spaghetti out from the deep pot on the stove. After covering it with a heavy basil sauce, he tossed on a couple of meatballs and placed the plate gently in front of me.

Ethan didn't eat. He just played with his fork in the mountain of noodles while he kept looking up and softly smiling at me in my silence. Even though I hadn't eaten much all day, I picked at my food, being more nervous than hungry.

The look on his face remained sad and disappointed. Since I wasn't speaking, he apologized for leaving without saying anything and the worry it brought me. However, unlike his usual apologies, no tears were streaming down his face, and throughout our conversation, he maintained his composure and kept his head calm.

Mainly just being worried, I explained I wasn't upset with him.

The most important part of our conversation was telling him I wanted him to make an appointment to see Dr. Branch and confirm his medication was dialed in ASAP. Although everything seemed okay on his end, I wanted to hear that confidently from her.

While he was gone, he explained that being off the medication felt great because he was clear of the fog the meds weighed him down with, a state he didn't want to feel again. Getting by without the medication worked for him, and he wanted to continue doing it the old-fashioned way. After a mental battle he had with my request for him to go in for a consult, he finally agreed to see her.

Reaching across the table, I offered one hand to him. His hand stretched out and laid down on mine, and I felt his warm and smooth fingers as he rolled my hand over and placed his other hand on top.

Ready to talk about my feelings, I started the discussion by expressing just how much I loved him. Promising I would always be there for him, I begged him to get everything situated with the doctors.

His recovery was going to be a living, breathing treatment and not just something that he could only pay attention to when it failed.

He agreed to get and maintain the help he needed.

Finally, I told him that I thought it was best we go our separate ways. I made sure to tell him I still wanted to be there for him in every form of his rehab, but I just couldn't continue the charade of pretending we were happily married when the last four years had been nothing but hell for both of us.

Trying to put it gently, I told him I didn't think we were happy together anymore. It wasn't about his current state or anything specific, but something that just had happened over time with our broken past always following us.

He sat across from me silently and listened, maintaining the same stoic face as I talked. Hoping he would agree, I told him I loved him, but we both needed to move on. After the loss of Jack, the drinking, drugs, and eventually the physical abuse, I had lost parts of myself throughout our marriage.

I finished my rant by telling him that I would always love him and that he deserved a clean slate with someone new. He was still a good person, and someone out there would bring the light in him that he once had, but that person was no longer me.

A soft smile spread across his face, and I hoped that he would agree and understand. I wasn't trying to be mean or break his heart. I just thought he needed to know the truth, so we could both move forward and navigate the process together.

My phone began to ring, the ringtone loudly echoing in the kitchen. I looked at Ethan and saw him still just sitting there staring at me with a blank look on his face. Then, fishing my phone from my purse, I looked down to see Dr. Branch's name scrolling across my screen.

I looked across the table to Ethan, who had pushed his chair back add stood up from his seat. My finger had just hit the answer button on my phone when he grabbed the wine bottle that was still three-quarters full and swung it, smashing it across the side of my head.

EIGHT

Kate

I AWOKE TO thin lines of sunlight filtering through the small basement window and streaked across my face, causing me to squint as they beamed in my eyes.

Once I came to and examined my surroundings, I realized I found myself shoved in the back corner of our small basement laundry room. The clothes that I heard beating around in the washer the night before remained trapped behind the glass door, wet and building up mildew.

Seated in a straight-back wooden chair from our eat-in kitchen, I tried wiggling around to assess the status of my feet and hands. Hard plastic dug into my wrists, and I moved my feet and felt the tiny hairs on my legs pull as the duct tape failed to give way.

"No, no, no, come on," I repeatedly said as I wiggled around in the chair, hoping something would break loose.

Sitting there alone in the room, I didn't feel scared. I felt terrified.

I closed my eyes and listened to the steady pulse beating inside my head as the images of the wine bottle breaking across my temple returned.

Dr. Branch, I instantly remembered.

Shortly before my world went black, I had mashed the green button on the screen, so surely she must have heard what happened. I prayed she would talk him off the ledge and free me from the prison I found myself stuck in.

Trying to grip the situation better, I shut off my thoughts and closed my eyes, listening for anything.

After thirty minutes, I had heard nothing but a heavy silence floating in the air. As much as I tried to imagine my ears caught something rustling, there were no audible sounds or hints of movement coming from the house above.

I screamed at the top of my lungs, and then I screamed again. My screaming continued until my throat ached, and I had grown hoarse. Unfortunately, our neighborhood was pretty quiet, and we didn't have many daytime streetwalkers that were likely to hear my desperate call for help.

Defeated, I slumped back down in my seat and tried to use my spit to soothe my throat I had irritated.

I sat still and upright in the hard wooden kitchen chair for an entire day, just looking around the room and gently fighting with my restraints, trying not to dig them deeper into my irritated flesh.

I was growing thirsty and hungry, and I started to worry that Ethan had tied me up and left town again, and I surprisingly prayed he would come back for me before I died from dehydration.

There was blood that I could feel had dried on my face near my eye from where he had struck me with the almost full wine bottle. In nursing school, they taught us that scalp bleeds are often dramatic, so the severity of my actual injury may have been somewhat minor.

The chair and my pants were sopping wet, and I had no other choice but to sit in my urine-soaked clothes.

Tears began streaming down my face as I cried and loudly cursed myself for being so stupid and falling for his show. It was idiotic that I had agreed to go into the house with him and then continued by spilling my guts about wanting a divorce.

Just as I stopped crying, my head hanging down, the hum of the garage door became audible overhead. My body froze, and instantly I felt both fear and relief at the fact that Ethan was home.

Footsteps lightly tapped on the laminate floor above me as I heard someone enter the house. He roughly chucked keys onto the kitchen counter, and I listened to the crack of an aluminum can hiss through the ceiling.

After a couple of minutes, his footsteps made their way across the house. The slight squeal of the basement door creaked as his feet started to make their way down the stairs. I struggled with my restrains more than before, trying to make a last-ditch effort to break my hands or feet free.

The door swung open, and I saw Ethan's silhouette positioned in the doorway. On his frame hung the same clothes from our conversation at the table, but when I took a closer look, I saw he appeared to have my blood splattered on a corner of his shirt.

The delicate appearance he had in the garage had disappeared entirely, revealing a strung-out look again. He was pale and looked disheveled as he silently stared at me in the doorway.

"Ethan, please, I'm sorry. I didn't mean any of it," I pleaded.

He said nothing but came closer as I continued to tug on my wrists and ankles. My efforts proved futile, and I merely dug the zip ties in farther, leaving me exhausted and in even more pain.

"I love you, Katie girl. You know me, and I know you. We were meant for each other, and you know that," he said, squatting down in front of me.

He stood and ran his index finger upwards from my shoulder to right behind my ear that kept progressively getting harder, sending a sickening fear racing throughout my body.

"Ethan, we will be okay, I promise. I'm really sorry, and we can find a way to figure things out," I lied, trying to reason with him.

As soon as I finished blabbering, he thrust my chair back to the wall as his hand slammed down hard on my face, covering my mouth and completely silencing me while I squirmed beneath him.

"Shut up, Kate, you're lying to me," he snarled, pulling a bandana from his pocket.

With a look of anger embedded in his eyes, he shoved the sweaty cloth into my mouth, and I gagged against it.

The door shut, and his footsteps retreated up the stairs, leaving me alone in the laundry room with tears streaming down my face. Then, above me, I heard another can crack, and Ethan flipped on the TV, and I listened to the remote get dropped on the coffee table. I closed my eyes and took in the muffled sounds of daytime television as they dripped slowly to my ears through the drop ceiling.

A couple of hours later, he returned to the laundry room. This time it was clear he was halfway intoxicated but came bearing gifts. I saw a plate with a ham and cheese sandwich in one hand, and the other hand held a plastic cup filled with water.

"I see you spit the bandana out, but I'll let you have a free hand to eat as long as you behave," he said.

I nodded my head rapidly in his direction, desperate for the food and water in his grasp.

He handed me the plate and the glass and placed his back on the doorframe, and slid himself to the floor. He looked at his toes and picked at his nails while he said there and allowed me to eat.

I chugged the entire tumbler of water first, almost throwing it up as I guzzled it down. The water deprivation had left me completely dehydrated, my body dying for a refill. Disregarding the mustard I despised, I devoured the sandwich, not wanting to risk it getting taken away.

"Can I have a refill?" I asked, showing him my empty cup.

"Sure," Ethan said, standing up unsteadily.

He left the room, going around the corner to the half bath to fill my glass. I quickly reached my free hand down to my left ankle, trying to loosen it with the hope of freeing my ankle, then laying the tape back across, giving the false appearance my extremities were still bound.

Ethan silently re-entered the room as I was fidgeting with the tape. Dropping the water glass and allowing it to spill all over the concrete floor, he looked at me with a terrifying grin.

"Stupid Katie girl," he said.

He instantly charged at me, and my leg came free, allowing me to react quickly. I landed a hard kick to his thigh with my heel and tried pushing him back with my one free hand. He backed up for a second before he grabbed me by the throat and stared at me as he slammed my head against the cinder block wall multiple times.

After about four solid blows to the head, he released me from his grip, my hands reaching to my neck. A throbbing headache instantly washed over me, leaving my whole body feeling disoriented.

Although I wanted desperately to pass out, leaving consciousness to escape the pain, I fought the urge, terrified of what would become of me if I slipped away. My brain and vision were foggy as Ethan came back over to me with shaking hands as he fumbled with my ankles and wrists, reapplying the restraints again, tighter this time.

Allowing my body and mind to give in to the fact that I was again stuck, I passed out.

At some point that day, I finally came to, awakening to the sound of Ethan opening the door to the laundry room. He was very drunk and holding a pair of scissors loosely in his hand. My whole body shook with terror as I used my tippy toes to try to scoot my chair back.

He stumbled over to me, leaving me scared he would fall and accidentally stab me with the blunt scissors in his drunken walk. He held onto the washer for support and grabbed the back of my chair. Sliding it forward, he wrapped his hands around my wrists at the binding.

He mumbled, the smell of booze wafting out of his mouth, "I swear to God Kate, you pull any shit, and I will bring you right back down here, but you need a shower. Understand?"

I nodded and felt a slight feeling of relief.

As he cut through my restraints, the thought crossed my mind to try something new once all my limbs were free. But, knowing I would still have to beat him up the stairs, I waited.

My bare feet moved forward, stepping through the puddle of pee I had created underneath me. Once out of the laundry room and in the fresher air, I could smell how much I reeked.

Ethan's hand lightly held only my shoulder as we made our way up the staircase, leading me out of the basement I had that felt like a prison. I rubbed my wrists, trying to ease some of the pain from the digging zip ties, hoping I wouldn't be put right back into them after I bathed.

I looked up and saw we had about three stairs left when I smelled something more putrid than me. The cloud of smell that hit my nose wasn't garbage or something coming wafting off of Ethan. It was coming from the main floor of the house.

In the kitchen, I looked around to see a couple of dishes piled in the sink but noticed Ethan had cleaned up the mess that slamming a bottle of wine across my head had caused. I looked on the counter and saw the knife block while thinking of a way to dart over and grab one when Ethan turned me towards the living room.

As I entered the living room, the smell quickly grew, becoming even more potent as I hit its wall.

When we walked in, I looked behind the tufted loveseat and saw a body lying face down in my living room. A pile of blood had leaked from under her abdomen and was spread out perpendicular to her body, but I saw no other signs of injury. I saw the thin frame, simple clothes, and dark hair that almost reached her butt when I looked closely.

Dr. Branch was lying on the ground, dead in my living room.

Still gently holding me by the shoulder, I threw my head downwards and vomited the little my body could muster while I heaved violently. Unfortunately, some of what I retched landed on Ethan's right foot, causing him to scoff at me as he shook the fluid off.

A thick silence hung in the air as we passed by her body, Ethan not even bothering to look or acknowledge it. I kept my mouth shut, afraid to ask what had happened. As we ascended the stairs, the stench slightly dissipated, and I felt myself breathing more freely again.

Seeing her body from above, I remembered that I had answered her call right before Ethan hit me. She likely heard the events transpiring on my side of the phone, causing her to come and check on us. I felt sick when I thought that my actions had led this poor woman to her death while she was only trying to help her patient.

Ethan pointed to the master bathroom and directed me to strip down and get into the shower. Although he had seen my nude body countless times previously, he now felt like a stranger, and I felt exposed and degraded.

I did as I was told.

Ethan moved to the tub shower combo and tuned on the water for me as he adjusted the temperature with his fingers like he would for a child. Looking into the shower, I saw that he had removed almost everything, leaving only my loofah, body wash, shampoo, and conditioner. Water splashed as it ran from the head and puddled on the floor with no curtain keeping it in.

The warm waterfall of the shower felt amazing, and I turned around to let it run down my face and opened my mouth to refill my dehydrated body. Then, worried Ethan would change his mind or limit my time; I cleaned myself quickly. But, instead, he remained seated on the floor, his back to the wall and paying no attention to me while I showered.

When I was fully clean, and the hot water had almost run out, Ethan walked over and smiled a soft grin at me as he handed me a clean towel from under the sink. While I was drying off, he scoured my dresser and finally gave me a pair of clean pajamas.

Ethan, still silent, sat on the bed while I dressed in the corner of our room, still trying to hide my naked body from him. Once clothed, I hurried back to the bathroom before he could tell me no, and found my hairbrush still lying on the vanity in the exact place I had left it before the madness began. Again, I hurriedly brushed both my hair and teeth, finally feeling clean.

With a deep look of defeat hanging on his face, Ethan looked up at me and looked me in the eyes.

"I'm sorry," he murmured, slurring his r's together. "I didn't mean to hurt you, and I don't want to hurt you. But I don't want to lose you, Kate. I love you too much."

Pretending to be still brushing my hair in case I needed to use my plastic hairbrush as a likely ineffective weapon, I stared back at him while he waited for me to say something.

"Alright, just play along," I decided silently.

He had calmed down finally, and the last thing I wanted was to go back to the basement again. Maybe I could just keep him calm enough to find the perfect time to slip out unnoticed and take my chance to sprint to the police.

Laying down my brush, I made my way to him, ready to execute my charade. Remaining an arm's length away, I joined him on the edge of the mattress, reached my hand out, and lightly placed it on his shoulder.

"I know you're sorry, but look, I'm okay. I'm still here, right? I'm not going anywhere, Ethan. I love you," I lied.

Although I knew he had some stuff going on in his head that he wasn't handling well, the truth behind my words was that I no longer felt pity for him.

"How about we go to a clinic and see if they can help you?" I asked, hoping that would get him in the hands of medical professionals who could see how dangerous he had become.

He silently turned his head towards me, but his eyes didn't land on me as he stared out the window, the sun finally beginning its descent behind the house across the street.

"Tomorrow," he responded.

"I just think tonight would be the best time to go; get it all situated now," I explained. "For us."

"Tomorrow," he responded again, his eyes leaving the window and sternly looking straight into mine.

Shutting my mouth and breaking our eye contact, I accepted tomorrow was better than nothing.

Ethan collapsed backward onto the bed, and his hand patted gently on the quilt my mom made for us, asking me to lay with him. I laid down beside him with my arms glued to my side, thankful it wasn't the chair in the basement. He reached over and grabbed my hand, pulling it towards him and causing my whole body to stiffen naturally. He rolled over and had his arm stretched across my chest, his beer-scented breath billowing in my face.

All through the night, I faded in and out of consciousness as I fought to stay awake and vigilant. He didn't seem as though he was fully asleep and often made small grunts and movements that hinted he was only lightly sleeping, scaring me more about trying to flee.

When I woke up from the airy sleep I had finally fallen into, we were still laying there in the same position, me stiff to the side of the bed, and Ethan's arm laid across me. The sun was just coming up, the gap in the curtains allowing it to shine on the wall. I could feel through his shorts that he had an erection that was pushing against my leg. Silently, I found myself praying he wouldn't take the opportunity to add sexual abuse to his list of crimes.

After lying motionless in the bed for about an hour, Ethan finally woke up and removed his arm from my chest, stretching and letting out a slight grunt.

"Good morning, Katie girl," he said with a smile, leaning over and kissing me on the cheek, causing my whole body to flinch at his touch.

Appalled at my reaction, Ethan stared at me with confused sadness stricken across his face briefly before he climbed out of bed.

"Come here," he said, directing me into the bathroom.

I took this opportunity to finally pee somewhere other than the floor as he started to get undressed and warmed up the water for his shower.

"Just stay in here while I shower, please," he instructed.

I prepared his toothbrush, handing it to him in the shower while trying to avoid looking at his naked body.

Finally, he was clean, and we both got dressed for the day.

"So, are we ready to get going?" I asked, hoping he would say yes.

"Yeah, we will later," he said unconvincingly.

"Oh, okay," I said.

We went down the stairs again, me never leaving his sight.

"We should probably do something with her, don't you think?" Ethan asked with zero remorse as he nodded towards the body in the living room.

Terrified, I stood there silently as the color drained from my face at the idea of touching a dead body.

"Yeah, let's get her out of here," he said while I was still staring at the corpse.

Trying not to rock the boat, I grabbed her arms while he grabbed her legs, and together we picked her up and heaved her onto a blanket. Her lifeless body felt much heavier than I could have imagined, and the clammy feeling of her cold skin made mine quiver. We carried/dragged her body towards the back door as tears built up in my eyes.

She had been nothing but kind to him, and I felt terrible that coming to check on him was the last action that led to her death.

He unlocked the shed, and we tossed her body inside, hearing it hit the plastic floor of the small building. Ethan nudged her slightly, and Dr. Branch's body rolled over and showed the knife from the block on the counter that was deeply lodged in her abdomen.

I fearfully followed Ethan back into the house, and we both worked to open some of the downstairs windows to air out the stench of her rotting body. He grabbed a blanket my late grandmother made me and haphazardly threw it over the spot where she had bled out.

"Let's have breakfast," he said, clapping his hands once in front of himself.

Wanting to leave but also not being able to eat after moving a corpse, I replied, "Well, should we go see the doctor first? Maybe get some breakfast on the way?"

"I said later," he snapped back at me, his teeth clenched.

Fear shot through my body as the look on his face sent my mind back to the night he had struck me.

I didn't want to end up like Dr. Branch, so I ate my bacon and eggs in silence and decided not to do anything rash.

When we finished eating and our dishes were in the sink, Ethan gently placed his hand on my back and ushered me over to the couch with him. We awkwardly sat in the living room and watched TV, binge-watching Outlander just as we had been before he left, as if nothing had happened.

Midday, we ate ham and cheese sandwiches while sitting at the table in silence. Not once did Ethan let me out of his sight unless it was for a trip to our windowless half bathroom.

At about two in the afternoon, Ethan started stirring from boredom and suggested we go for a drive to get out of the house. I agreed, hoping it would lead to us going to a clinic or me getting a chance to run away from him.

I quickly planned everything out in my head. As soon as we were at the first stoplight, I would throw off my seatbelt, jump out of the car, print as fast as my legs could go, and bang on the first door I could find, begging for help.

There were tons of gas stations and small restaurants nearby we were bound to drive by. One of them had to have someone inside willing to help me. Then, after calling the police, Ethan would leave in cuffs, Dr. Branch's body would be found, and I would be free of him.

As soon as he buckled his seatbelt, he reached in his waistband and pulled out a Glock 19 that he laid in his lap. My whole body became covered in goosebumps. Ethan hadn't owned a gun before, leaving me to wonder when he had gotten it from and knowing it ruined my escape plans.

For about two hours, we just drove around with no real destination in mind. Occasionally some semblance of small talk would come out of his mouth, and I would respond shortly, intentionally not adding much to the conversation.

When he tired of the driving venture, we went straight back home. It was clear he wasn't going to be getting help any that night, and worry built up inside of me as I wondered what his plans were for me.

We heated a frozen pizza and ate together in silence at the table. My appetite was still minimal, but if there were a chance I'd be in the basement again, I didn't want to be hungry. So I forced myself to eat.

Then it was back to the TV.

After finishing season three, we moved on to season four without pause. Inside I just wanted to run, scream, do something, but knowing the gun was somewhere on him or in the house led me to fear he would pull it out again and maybe even fire it.

As we watched TV, Ethan had gone back and forth to the fridge very frequently, fishing out beers, offering me one a couple of times. Occasionally I accepted, trying to play along but ensuring to nurse it, trying not to dull my senses.

After probably seven or eight beers, his unsteady demeanor signaled that he had reached a detectable level of intoxication. He was up and down constantly with all the liquid intake and started leaving me alone in the living room on his trips to the bathroom.

"Okay, the next time he goes, I'm going to make a run for it. He's drunk enough. It should work," I thought to myself as I scanned the room and tried to visualize myself running out the door.

Almost a half-hour later, he got up and shuffled his way to the bathroom at the end of a somewhat long hall. Quickly, I took the opportunity and quietly sprinted on my toes to the front door.

With shaky hands, I fumbled with the lock on the handle as I heard my breathing growing faster and louder until it finally gave. My hands moved to the always sticky deadbolt as I tried to slow my breathing down. My foot wedged against the bottom of the door, slightly pushing it in until I heard it gently pop as it released. With both bolts loosened, I fidgeted with the chain strung to the frame at eye level, holding me inside. When the last lock finally gave way, the sound of the metal flying down and hitting against the door felt like anyone with ears could have heard it for miles. I held my breath for a brief second, knowing I had been obnoxiously loud when I heard the booming cough from behind me that echoed throughout the whole room.

Ethan was back from the bathroom, standing ten yards behind me and drilling a hole into my back with his devilish eyes. Knowing it was too late to turn around, I threw open the door and instantly became engulfed in the darkness of the night.

Through the heavy black evening, I looked around, trying to see signs of anyone outside. After seeing no one in my brief scan, my legs continued running into the cul-de-sac we lived on, frantically making my way towards the neighbor's house.

Ethan quickly ran out the door and bolted after me. When I had made it about fifty yards from the house, he finally caught up to me. He reached out and latched his hand onto the back of my shirt. My body quickly fell, landing hard on the bumpy asphalt as my cheekbone and shoulder slid on the road beneath. Lying on the ground, he held the gun to the back of my head and laughed.

"Good try, baby," he said.

After he helped me up, he guided me back into the house with the gun firmly pressed into my ribcage and his other hand holding strongly on my shoulder.

In my home that had become my prison, Ethan quickly refastened the locks behind us while I stood beside him, gently shaking with fear. Then, removing his hand from my shoulder, Ethan turned and landed two hard blows on my body. The first hit landed right in the middle of my stomach, sending me doubling over in pain, and the second blow came when I stood back up, landing right below my right eye.

"Seriously, Katie?" he asked, shaking his head and squinting at me.

Now on the floor on my knees, Ethan went over and sat down on the couch. With blood oozing out of my road rash, he patted the spot next to him on the sofa.

"Now can we finish this episode?" he asked.

He didn't acknowledge what happened, and I did as told, joining him on the couch, doing whatever I had to do to avoid going back down to the basement.

With the episode complete, Ethan let out a loud sigh and stretched his arms high above his head, "How about we go to bed?" he asked with a smile.

I followed him up the stairs, grateful my stunt hadn't condemned me back to the basement. I brushed my teeth, and just as I went to lay down, I saw the Glock again, this time lying exposed and alone on the nightstand.

"Goodnight Katie girl," he whispered as he flopped down next to me and kissed me on the cheek.

"Goodnight Ethan," I replied through my teeth.

Unable to sleep, I laid there listening to the silence, wanting nothing more than to get away as I stared at the wobbly ceiling fan above me. It was apparent I needed to come up with a better escape plan.

Eventually, he rolled to his side, taking the arm he laid on me with him. It seemed like the almost eight beers he downed had finally done their job, knocking him out good. Both sides of my face throbbed as I laid there quietly, trying to construct a game plan on how to get away from him, the mental planning keeping me awake.

All I could craft in my head was desperate sprints to the door when I had a chance. Maybe during hours of daylight, someone would see a stunt like the one from last night and help me, or perhaps I would never make it out of the door. I had no idea where Ethan had stashed either of our cell phones, and the phone that hung on the wall had been disconnected for years because we never needed it.

Just after one a.m., I heard a convincing voice in my head telling me to get out of bed and make a silent run for the door. Instead, I waited just a few minutes and heard Ethan grunt in his sleep a couple of times before he got up and appeared dazed as he made his way to the bathroom. I rolled over to his side of the bed and quickly grabbed the gun from its home on the nightstand and placed it near my pillow on the mattress, adjusting my position so I could have my finger ready alongside the trigger.

Like a statue, I laid there, waiting for the sound of the toilet to flush. Grabbing the gun had been a spur-of-the-moment plan, and I had to decide what to do quickly in case he happened to notice it missing when he came back.

I thought it would be, but it wasn't a hard decision.

"I'm gonna have to shot him," I thought to myself as I felt an indescribable sadness wash over me.

The thought of shooting the man I promised to love till death do us part had never once seemed to be something in our future when we said I do at the courthouse. But I was lying there, face oozing, stomach bruised, hands shaking, ready to shoot to kill if I had to.

He came back a few moments later and failed to notice his missing pistol when he flopped back onto his side of the queen-sized mattress, facing away from me.

I waited, waited, and waited some more until I heard the promising sound of his snore echoing throughout the dark room.

Quietly, I slid out of our bed, gently moving the blanket and trying not to move the mattress as I stood. My direct path was aimed directly at the bedroom door, trying to move slowly and make as little noise as possible. In the heavy silence, I slowly breathed in and out of my mouth and listened, only hearing the small joints in my knees and ankles cracking.

I held the pistol in my right hand, which shook slightly, feeling its power in my grasp, but kept my finger elongated alongside the trigger, just like I remembered my dad teaching me.

I tiptoed almost three yards which felt like a mile, to the bedroom door and found it locked from the inside. Being extremely gentle, I tried to turn the small handle lock ever so quietly until it gave, sounding off with a very faint pop that reverberated like a bomb in the heavy silence. After it clicked, I paused for a moment before waiting to open the door, listening to the room.

It was quiet, and the snoring had stopped.

With the faint moonlight coming through the window, I slowly turned while keeping my hand grasped onto the door and saw Ethan sitting on the edge of the bed, staring directly at me. A bottomless pit formed in my stomach as fear built up inside me, freezing me in place.

"Oh, Katie girl, why?" he asked, clicking his tongue after.

Frozen in place, my hand gripped to knob harder as I looked at him silently, barely seeing the whites of his eyes in the dim room. He lunged at me, and my instincts instantly kicked in, and I threw open the door.

I quickly skirted out the door, slamming it hard behind me. Grabbing onto the handrail to my right, I raced down the stairs, ensuring I hit every step. The last thing I needed in my flight was to get injured on the staircase and allow him to catch up to me.

Only a couple of stairs in, I heard the eerie sound of the door reopen behind me. Following in trail, he chased me down in his boxers, stumbling a couple of times on the carpeted stairs.

Finally reaching the bottom, I ran through the living room in a desperate attempt to get to the back door. I hurriedly slid my hand across the counter on purpose as I ran by, sending a couple of the dishes and glass tumblers to shatter on the floor. The glasses bounced, then shattered, creating a minefield for Ethan to traverse in my wake.

After a few more strategic steps, I was at the back sliding door just as Ethan arrived at the threshold of the kitchen. I fumbled with the lock using my left hand while the right one continued to shake with the gun gripped tightly.

I knew he could get to me before I had the door unlocked. So I turned around and put my back against the glass door, making eye contact with my husband, who stood before me out of breath. My hand, still shaking, rose, gripping the gun as I pointed it in his direction while my other hand worked behind me, trying to undo the locks.

"Kate, I swear, I love you. Please don't leave me," he begged.

Stopping with the locks, I raised the gun higher and more directly at Ethan. At this point, I had the upper hand, and I was leaving alive one way or another.

"Don't come any closer, or I'll shoot," I cried. "You and I don't belong together Ethan, this is over, and you know it. If you just let me go and leave me alone, then this can be over, and I won't tell anyone," I lied.

He crossed his arms and chucked a little, revealing a smile that told me he wasn't too keen on that idea.

"I can't do that, and you know it," he said, flipping an internal switch and running towards me through the glass littered across the floor.

Quickly moving my finger to the trigger, I closed my eyes as I pulled it three times, hoping they flew in his general direction. Finally, the red from my vision cleared as I slipped back into the moment to survey the damage, my ears ringing from the shots.

Ethan stopped and fell to the ground clutching his stomach. With him lying on the ground, his chest still rising and falling with each labored breath; I knew I needed to get out while he was down. I kept fighting with the door, begging the locks to release until finally, both gave way.

I threw open the door with everything I had and ran out of the house as fast as my feet would move. Looking back over my shoulder twice, I saw no one chasing after me as I ran to the neighbor's house at a full sprint, feeling tiny pieces of glass embedding themselves deeper into my feet.

The house next door turned on some lights as I neared. My encounters with those neighbors had been very brief, but I found myself pounding on their door as I screamed for help until the older man that lived there opened the door, leaving the chain still intact.

"PLEASE HELP ME!" I screamed through the small opening.

Swiftly shutting the door, I heard the chain rattle, then finally, the door opened. The older man looked at me for a second, standing in the doorway, blocking me from entering.

"Please, it was my husband, not me," I said, gently placing the gun on the porch.

I raised my shaking hands at him, trying to show that I was innocent, begging him to let me in. Instead, the older man picked up the gun off his stoop and ushered me in, locking the door behind us. Quickly, I rattled off the short version of my story in my frazzled state. He helped me over to the couch while he left the room and phoned the police.

About five minutes later, the police arrived, causing other neighbors to come out and see what happened as their blue lights flooded the night and sirens echoed all around. They took an armed team in to clear our house but found no sign of Ethan. His blood trail was evident, but he cleaned out the downstairs medicine cabinet, and his car was gone.

The police got on their radios and sent out a description of Ethan and the car, hoping they would catch him nearby. They sat me down and took notes as I told them the story of what had happened, no sparing any of the gruesome details. They asked questions about the body in the shed, sending tears down my face as I told them what had happened to her.

They searched the woods around our house, questioned the neighbors, and even called local hospitals to ask if anyone with his appearance and possible injuries had shown up, but there wasn't a single trace.

The police marked the house as a crime scene and finally removed Dr. Branch's body. After draping the place in caution tape, it became off-limits until they could complete their investigation. As soon as we arrived at the station, I instantly called my parents to tell them what had happened.

They immediately flew in and got us a room in town. After that, I never left their sight and locked myself in the hotel room whenever I could. I knew my husband wasn't stable, and I didn't want to risk him finding me again. I gave them the entire story, causing my mom to cry when she heard that I had been dealing with so many issues in my marriage alone.

When the police finally wrapped up the investigation, we took the next flight back to Montana. I wore a hat and sunglasses while walking through the terminal, desperately trying to hide who I was, while I realized my life would never be the same again.

I stared out the window as we drove home from the airport and let my head bounce gently on the glass, feeling a little weary about coming back to Montana. The Big Sky state was also where Ethan had grown up and considered it home too. Thankfully he wasn't close with his family, and I didn't see him coming back to visit.

Moving back home was my only option.

My parents bought a different house in town in a gated community and made sure nothing personal about us was listed. They wanted to try and at least make it difficult if Ethan ever wanted to find me.

Eventually, I sold our house as-is, causing me to lose a large sum of money since it had been the sight of a brutal murder. There were many hoops to jump through when it came to selling the house and filing for divorce from a missing man, but eventually, I was successful on both accounts and finally felt the freedom I needed.

When we were back in Montana, Ethan's grandmother called my parents and apologized for her grandson's behavior and promised me she would call if he ever got in contact with her,

For all any of us knew, he was dead.

My first year back in Montana, I was scared to leave my house and only ventured out into the backyard for fresh air. There were no trips to the store, no casual walks around the neighborhood, and no meeting girlfriends for wine and appetizers downtown like every other girl in their mid-twenties did.

Based on what my brother told me, quite a few people had come into the brewery to ask about me. Some people that had been close to Ethan were contacted and questioned in the hopes of finding him, and others were just gossip-hungry small-towners who enjoyed hearing more about my misfortune they read about online.

Since I wouldn't leave the house, my therapist visited me, trying to help me get over my agoraphobia. The fear of being on the street and spotted by Ethan, or someone who would tell him, was overwhelming. Staying inside felt comfortable and safe.

A lot of trauma surrounded what happened to me that I had to figure out a way to get over. I didn't want anyone to touch me, and the idea of being anywhere alone was terrifying to me. I needed someone with me all the time.

One afternoon, Seth had left to run to the gas station down the street real quick once while I was napping. I woke up and found the house empty, sending me running frantically around searching for my brother. I huddled in my closet, trying to hide from my crippling fear of being alone.

When he came back home, he found me curled up in the closet. After many apologies, he promised never to leave me like that again.

He repeatedly apologized, and the look on his face read like someone who had just left a baby in a hot car. The pity and fear on his face at that moment forced me to come to grips with my issues and try to work to figure out my new normal.

I was still super spooked when I started thinking about getting my life back, sometimes even having mild panic attacks when I just thought about leaving the house. I started with baby steps, going for walks around the neighborhood with someone and riding in the car around town. Eventually, I graduated and moved on to bigger things, and finally went to the grocery store with my dad.

Eventually, life started to feel okay again. After two months of slow progress, I became comfortable being around people and out in public again as long as I knew my dad or brother was nearby. It felt good to leave the hermit phase of my life behind me.

Working the bar with my family seemed like something that I could do. Also, being in the brewery with someone there gave me a feeling of security while I got to be out around people.

Every time I left the house, I ensured that one of my family members was with me, which became a habit that I was comfortable with and scared to deviate from. In the beginning, I was super shy with every customer, trying to keep my distance, but eventually, I warmed up and enjoyed being able to talk to people again.

While tending the taps with my dad, he often caught me staring at the door. If I had a moment free, my eyes were glued to the entrance, waiting for the next person to come in. Every entrant got a rundown from me, ensuring it wasn't Ethan because I had convinced myself he was coming back for me.

I always looked, checking for his deep brown hair or his dark brown eyes. I knew his walk and other specific mannerisms that I could pick out of a lineup. I was scared of seeing him again but kept that to myself as I tried to work through my fear on my own.

The bell was my dad's idea as an attempt at supporting my need to see who came in while still allowing me to work and not feel the need to stare at the door constantly.

Even after a year and a half, the general fear of someone that wasn't my family placing a hand on me chilled me to my core, and I recoiled from every attempt at physical gestures.

At some point, I wanted to be rid of that fear.

Finally, I met someone who liked me for me, recently blind to my past and the damage that accompanied me. Brandon seemed like a great guy and someone I wanted to touch and touch me back eventually. I wanted my history to be erased and start fresh the way I had intended when I told Ethan I wanted out.

It was still new, but maybe Brandon would be that fresh start.

Being with him was going to take a lot of work for both of us. I was going to have to step out of my comfort zone, allowing him into my life, and he would have to bear with me through it all. It wasn't fair of me to ask him to wait for an undetermined amount of time to fully conquer my fears before I could live an everyday life again.

He sat there and intently listened to me relive the worst couple of days of my life. Hopefully, my story explained some things to him, and he understood why I was the way I was. I wanted him to wait for me, but I was unsure if he would or even should.

NINE

Kate

I WATCHED BRANDON'S face while I weaved the tale of my misfortune. During my story, his face displayed a vast array of emotions from beginning to end. There were a couple of smiles in the beginning, but they quickly faded when he realized it was going downhill face. Nevertheless, he had a look of basic compassion coming from his eyes the whole time I talked, and not once did he try to interrupt me.

He was sweet and kind, but I could also see an appearance of pity hiding in his eyes, a look I never wanted from anyone. What happened to me was in the past, and all I wanted to do was move forward from it. I didn't need him or anyone else displaying any pitiful reaction to my situation.

I was over, and I was finally picking up the pieces and still hoping that Ethan had finally let me go.

Brandon knowing everything would help him understand, at least I had hoped it would,

"So that's why I'm telling you everything, so you can know why I don't go anywhere without my family, why I don't like being touched, and why I probably seem so damn weird. I don't know how many people in town know what happened, but it's a small town, and I see you have friends here. I didn't want one of them to tell you before I could," I explained, finally allowing myself to take a deep breath.

I stopped talking, hoping Brandon would say something. But, instead, he just looked at me for a minute with a sad look as his lips remained shut and he gathered his thoughts.

"I don't think you're weird, and Kate, I'm so sorry that happened to you," he stated with genuine concern. "I can't imagine what it was like going through all that back then, and I can imagine what it's like still living with that fear in your life."

Just as I went to interject, telling him not to be sorry for me, he continued his speech.

"Thank you for telling me all of this. It answers a lot of questions that I had about you. I know times are weird for you right now, so I just want you to know I'm here for you in whatever way you want me to be. I like you, though, and I'd like to get to know you even more," he exclaimed.

"Thank you. I really appreciate it. I don't want you to feel bad for me, it's in the past, and I like you too," I said.

There was a lot I liked about Brandon. He seemed nice, and everything he said felt genuine. On top of his personality, I found him extremely attractive, for the first time in my life, liking a guy with a beard. I wanted this to work and get to know him better and feel like an average person again. I wanted to go on dates, have my hair brushed out of my face, feel the touch of someone that wasn't in my family. I wanted so much, and Brandon just gave me the impression he was a guy worth taking a chance and jumping in headfirst.

But if we were ever going to work, and I would get all the things I missed about having a typical life and relationship, I would have to get over the fear of being touched and act like a normal person again.

I didn't want to push him. Taking me on wasn't an easy job and probably something most guys would say no to if asked. I was going to need everything to move slow, real slow, and that wasn't something I wanted to ask someone else to do or feel as though they had to.

"So here's my deal. I'm gonna be out of town with my dad this week in Missoula doing some stuff for the brewery. How about we take the week and figure out if this is something we both want to do. I'm a burden right now and not exactly the easiest girl to take out," I explained.

"Kate, I," Brandon started, and I raised my hand, cutting him off.

"I want to get better. I don't want to recoil from a handshake or feel the need to have my family with me all the time. Honestly, I hadn't thought about how trivial it was to my life until I met you. Please, take a week to think about what being with me would mean for you. I also need some time to think about it," I explained.

"Okay," he agreed.

I felt a significant weight come off my chest at the fact that he didn't instantly respond with a "no." I wasn't sure what to expect, but "okay," was better than nothing.

We made our way back downstairs to the bar's central area, ready to call it a night. He still had a look of defeat on his face that I interpreted as annoyance at the fact I didn't want to talk about it again for a week.

Seth came out from near the kitchen and smiled at us both. We stood at the door and said goodnight, and this time Brandon didn't reach out to touch me. He understood.

TEN

Brandon

THE BREWERIES DOOR shut behind me, leaving me speechless and trying to process the many details of the story Kate had laid out for me.

It was challenging to sit looking into her eyes and listen to her tell a story about a man that violently abused her. All I wanted to do was take her in my arms and try and convince her that she was safe with me, but I withheld, knowing contact was the last thing she wanted.

I had an inkling there was something she held in that hindered her ability to be herself entirely. The story that just unraveled before me hadn't even come close to what I expected to be the reasoning behind her quirks.

As much as she didn't want me to, I couldn't avoid feeling terrible about what happened to her. Her facial expressions and comfort with the details behind her tragedy showed me she had accepted what happened to her. She made it clear she had no desire for me or anyone else to pity her, and I wanted to honor that request but believed I could be there for her and help find a way to help her finally move past her trauma.

I felt like I could be the one to fix her.

Rebuilding her would be a challenge because knowing it made her uncomfortable, I didn't want to attempt to give the impression that I was reaching her direction, and I didn't want to push things by asking her to go out with me anymore.

She had given me a week to think about it, but I didn't need it. If it meant she had a family member tagging along for the foreseeable future, I'd find a way to be okay with that. The hard part would be keeping my hands off her.

When I got home from the bar, I turned on Arrested Development, attempting to watch something comical before going to bed. I needed to clear the brutal images Kate had so vividly painted for me from my mind.

After an hour of lying in bed and staring at the blank ceiling, I got up and popped two Benadryl to help me fall asleep. Twenty minutes later, the pink pills kicked in and knocked me out.

Halfway through the week, I started missing being able to talk to Kate. I wanted to wrap myself in conversation with her while she sat across the bar from me, legs crossed at the ankles, her adorable facial expressions, and her hands flying all over the place as she blabbered on.

I hopped into the bar on Thursday night, hoping to get to spend some time talking with Seth. For the first time in a while, the bell chimed, and no eyes quickly looked my way. The taproom seemed desolate compared to its usual patron level, but I saw Seth, Luke, and Kate's mom all chatting behind the bar.

"You know she's not back, right?" Seth asked, leaning on the bar as I pulled up a stool.

"Yeah, of course," I said with a chuckle, "I came to hang out and talk to you if that's all right?"

"It is, but I'm sure you're sick of this place, and good God, so am I. So you wanna get out of here?" he asked, winking at me.

"Yes, please. What do you have in mind?" I asked.

"That Irish pub down the road does trivia on Thursday nights. We could head there?" he replied.

"Yeah, that sounds like fun, let's do it," I responded.

We entered the warm pub, the smell of sausage and mashed potatoes hitting me as soon as we breached the threshold. The taps housed many of the same selections that all the local places seemed to have, and I purposely selected one of the Dillon's beers.

I joined Seth at a padded booth in the back of the dining area with a piece of paper that had our team name written across the top, "Lip Rippers."

"You've just been so pathetic coming in and always ordering beer just to talk to my sister," Seth explained as he patted me on the back. "But, I'm glad you did."

Yeah, yeah," I responded as I smiled back, happy to have somewhat of a stamp of approval.

We quickly learned we were terrible at trivia, absolutely horrible. Out of fifty questions, we only got eleven right and finished at the very bottom of the roster. Accepting our defeat after a great night with a few too many beers, we stumbled out of the pub right before closing time.

"I don't know about you, big guy, but I'm a little hammered," Seth said as we headed down the sidewalk.

"Yeah, I probably shouldn't drive, and you definitely shouldn't. What's your address?" I asked, hoping to call him an Uber before calling myself one.

I looked up from my phone to see Seth sitting on the curb with his forehead resting in the palm of his hand and his eyes closed.

I chuckled at his hunched, drunken state.

"Okay, buddy, I got you," I said, pulling him up by the armpits and put my arm around him while we both worked to hold each other upright.

I gave the driver my address and shoved Seth into the passenger seat with the window open if he needed to vomit. The driver dropped us both off at my house, and I tucked Seth in on the couch before crashing into my bed, shoes still on.

I could hear Seth snoring on the couch as I laid in bed drunk, contemplating my ability to make adult decisions. It had been a long time since I had gotten so drunk, so I decided to place the blame on Seth.

My phone gently buzzed in my back pocket as I laid there, trying not to throw up. I rolled onto my side and fished it out, the screen revealing an unknown number that I didn't have saved in my contacts.

It was Taylor.

She had misspelled some of her words, and a few of them didn't make any sense. So I figured she, too, was probably in the same drunken state as me.

"Branddon. I've nissed you. I we should try us agein," I read.

Hearing from her out of the blue like that came as a complete shock. After laying there with my phone on my chest contemplating what, and if I should say something, I passed out.

I awoke to the sound of the toilet flushing. When I stood up, I swayed, unsteady on my feet and still feeling a little drunk. Seth laid back down on the couch, groaning from his hangover. After a quick call, I successfully called in sick to work, which technically wasn't a lie since I did feel like I could probably throw up at any moment.

Remembering bits and pieces of the night, I looked down at my phone to see if I had gotten a text from Taylor. Maybe it had just been a dream, and she hadn't reached out. But when I looked, the message was on my screen exactly as I remembered it.

At a loss for words, I decided to wait and see if she said something else. Talking to Taylor was something I hadn't thought I would ever have to deal with again.

"Ugh," I roared from my room.

"Ughhhh," Seth responded even louder as we both chuckled.

Desperate for coffee and water, I forced myself out of bed and made a pot. While the coffee brewed, I swallowed two ibuprofen and took two to Seth, accompanied by a glass of water. He rolled over on the couch and looked at me, pouting like a sick child.

"Thank you, sweetie," he said with a weak smile.

With the coffee freshly brewed, I got a cup and joined him on the couch, forcing him to sit up. His head slumped over at the neck, and he painfully chuckled while simultaneously groaning.

"Why did you let me do that?" he asked.

"You're a grown man. You made your own choices. You were the one saying another, and another, and another. And for some reason, I listened to you," I told him.

We flipped on the TV to take some time to rehydrate and sober up before going back to our cars.

"So what are you gonna do about Kate," Seth asked.

I looked over and noticed he had donned a pair of sunglasses that were now resting on his nose. Smirking at him, I couldn't help but laugh.

"The TV is too bright," he complained, putting the back of his hand to his forehead.

"Wow, you really went for it last night, I guess," I said.

He sat there and silently shook his head with his bottom lip puckered out.

"I'm gonna tell her that I'm here for her in whatever way she wants me to be, whatever she's comfortable with," I explained.

"I told you she was delicate, but good, I was hoping you would say that," he said, laying his head on the armrest, going back to sleep.

The TV droned on and on, but I had my phone in my hands, rereading Taylor's text repeatedly. She must have been drunk and likely woke up and reread it, instantly regretting her words.

As I sat there looking at her text, I decided to go glimpse at her Instagram page. Since I hadn't looked at it in a while, I was curious about what was new in her life. After a quick search, I found her profile and clicked on it, but the account showed up as PRIVATE, unlike how it used to be.

Since I had deleted her from my life, including all things digital, I had no idea what she had been up to the last couple of years. I then found myself curious, wondering what her life had become and what led her to message me. I locked my phone a few minutes later, and another text from her number popped up on my screen.

"I'm sorry, that came out of nowhere. I was out with the girls and got a little carried away." she wrote.

I knew sober her would regret it.

"But I meant what I said," she quickly added before I could respond.

Overdramatizing a breath in then out, I contemplated whether to respond. There were plenty of things rolling around in my head I could say to Taylor, both friendly and hurtful, but her communication had hit me out of nowhere, leaving me at a complete loss for words.

After I had thought it through, I finally came up with my response.

"Hey Taylor, you don't have to apologize, really, it's all good. But where is this coming from out of the blue? It's been years, and last I heard, you were getting married," I responded.

"We never got married. He failed out of pilot training like three months before he was going to graduate and cheated on be with some blond chick at a bar one night, so I called it off," she admitted.

Unsure of what to say back, I didn't respond and allowed her to continue typing as I watched the bubbles on the screen tap back and forth. I wanted to hear more about the things running through her head and out through her fingers.

The texts kept coming through, offering apologies in different ways about different things. She told me how stupid she had been for letting me go and the deep regret she felt. Hearing how much she claimed to have missed me shocked me.

She explained how she loved her new job and sincerely hoped that I was doing well. I inquired about what she was doing, and she sent a lengthy text back, telling me both the good and bad about it. Our messages shot back-and-forth for the next half hour, catching up on everything we'd missed.

Seth snored loudly, snapping me back to the reality of Kate. At that moment, I realized I had been sucked into talking to Taylor and hadn't even thought about Kate's feelings.

Taylor had been the first girl and still the only girl I had ever truly loved. Saying yes or no to being with her wasn't going to be an easy decision for me. I needed some time to think about it and decide how I felt about the idea of being back with Taylor. I wrestled both women in my head, trying to decide which would be best for me.

"I still want us," she said, redirecting the conversation away from talking about the Montana weather.

Staring at my phone, I kept my fingers still while I pondered my response. Seth snored from the other side of the couch as I locked my phone and closed my eyes, thinking what being with her would mean.

She added more, and I opened my phone again to read, "Take some time, and think about it. I'm moving to South Dakota this summer, I'd like you to come too and move in with me," she said.

The conversation quickly intensified, going from zero to sixty in less than an hour. However, something seemed wrong with the sudden escalation, leaving me to contemplate it even more.

"I'll think about it, okay?" I asked.

"Okay," she responded.

With my phone locked, lying in my lap, I went back to watching TV. Seth woke up a couple of minutes later, quickly suggesting we go get out cars from the bar, so I gladly hailed us an Uber.

"You're good people man," Seth said, patting me on the back when we returned to our vehicles.

"Thanks, I had a good night," I responded.

"Me too sugar," he said, blowing a kiss at me as he walked away.

Still unsure if I would go through with it after all the confusion in my inbox, I called Seth back. He stumbled back to me, smiling and squinting through his hangover.

"Can I get your parents' address?" I asked.

"Whatever for?" he said with a half-smile.

"I want to bring Kate some flowers over when she gets back," I explained.

"Eh, I'm not really supposed to, because of… you know, but okay, I'll text it to you," he replied.

As I took the hungover walk of shame back to my truck, I thought about all the ways being back with Taylor would be amazing. Her smile flashed across my vision, reminding me how it would light up my day no matter my mood.

When we were together, our relationship was great, and I believed we could be great again. Taylor had an infectious personality that could always make me laugh, and our conversations could lock me in for hours, always finding something new to discuss. On top of her character, I also missed spending time wrapped up naked with her runner's build figure.

The more I thought about it, the more I realized the fantastic sex came from the fact that she was the only girl I had ever genuinely loved, making it different simply for that reason.

Then the negative came back, reminding me of the hurt that Taylor had caused me. It had taken me so long to recover from it, and I was finally finding myself at a point where the emotions had subsided.

Bringing up the elephant in the room, I asked Taylor about her parents, admitting that I always felt like she treated me like I wasn't good enough for them. She acknowledged their opinion had once held weight, but she had changed her mindset, no longer caring. Her text explained that I had been an amazing guy that she threw away, worrying too much about what her parents would think. Then the guy they fell in love with and checked all their highly placed boxes ended up being a complete dirtbag.

"I know now, and I wish I could take it back. It was stupid," she said.

As hard as it was to acknowledge, I finally concluded that I just didn't want to have Taylor back in my life. As much as I thought she had always been the girl for me, I now found myself wanting Kate or just something new more.

"I'm sorry, I don't think we're gonna work out," I responded.

Accepting my answer, she continued to apologize, taking the blame for everything that transpired between us.

"I'll always love you," she texted.

Maybe we wouldn't end up together, but I, too, would always love Taylor.

We exchanged a couple more texts, leading to the conversation eventually fizzling out, and we stopped talking. Then, not wanting Kate to ever find out about this, I deleted the text thread and returned to my life.

I went in and joined Seth that night while he worked the bar. Sitting across from him, I declined his offer for a beer and just asked for water, still recovering from the night before.

"Same," he responded, rolling his eyes and raising his water glass as we toasted.

Our discussion soon shifted to talking about his sister. But, unfortunately, the fun party guy act quickly faded away, making way for the defensive big brother show.

"If you're going to do this, just be all in, not just playing games with her," he explained with a stern look.

"I'm not gonna play games with her," I promised sincerely.

Once he felt as though he had threatened me enough, we shifted back to talking about standard guy stuff. After a couple of waters, I went home, excited about my plans to see Kate the next day.

After a quick beard trim and shower, I put on something casually nice. Kate was expected to be home around noon, and I wanted to be there already to surprise her.

I stopped at the store on the way over, wanting to pick up some flowers for Kate. I grabbed a bouquet of multi-colored tulips, remembering she had said they were her favorite.

I heard the loud beep of the machine as I scanned the bouquet at the self-checkout register, and saw "MULTI-COLORED TULIPS" flash on the screen in bold, black letters.

"Why does that sound so familiar?" I thought to myself.

Quickly, my mind flashed back to the part of her story when Ethan had brought her a bouquet of those same flowers the night he knocked her out with a bottle of red wine in their kitchen. Trying to avoid buying something that would likely be a trigger, I returned them and snatched up a dozen roses instead.

Tiptoeing around things that might set her off was going to be the hard part about jumping into a relationship with Kate. She had told me her story, but now I had to try to remember all of the triggers she had mentioned.

Seth kept my phone buzzing, keeping me updated on their ETA and sending me silly GIFs that kept him "LOLing." Wanting to make sure I wasn't late, I showed up about thirty minutes early, just in case.

I pulled up to the neighborhood and realized Seth hadn't warned me about the sky-high wrought-iron gated community. After scrolling through the resident's list twice, I was sure there weren't any Dillon's listed on the screen, so I texted Seth, inquiring about how I was supposed to get into the fortress of a neighborhood. With no response, the gates opened up, allowing me to drive in.

For some reason, my nerves intensified as I walked up to the house and gently pushed the video doorbell. As I stood there and waited, I looked around and noticed three other cameras positioned on corners, strategically facing different directions. Then, a massive home opened up before my eyes as the ten-foot-tall wooden French doors swung open.

"Come on in, Brandon, and welcome," Mrs. Dillon said, offering me her typical warm and welcoming smile.

Mrs. Dillon led me through the entryway and down four stairs into their large living room. The area housed tall, vaulted ceilings made from exposed rustic wood, and my eyes instantly moved to the floor-to-ceiling whitewashed fireplace with a giant TV hanging above its dark wood mantle. Adjacent to the living room was a large kitchen, housing enough space to cook up a meal for a small army.

It looked like a house out of a magazine.

Three large jar candles were lit on the counter, filling the house with the warm smell of apple pie and cinnamon. The Dillon's home was warm, bright, and inviting. Beneath a large and fluffy grey rug, three sizeable tan leather couches sat centered on the TV in the living room. I spotted Seth sprawled out on the larger of the couches, watching hockey.

"You live here too?" I asked him.

"Yeah, it's a temporary situation. I've only been doing it for uh... thirty-two years," he said, smirking.

"He's not here to see you, Seth," Mrs. Dillon teased, swatting his feet off the couch armrest.

She turned away from Seth and politely invited me to join her in the kitchen. I joined her at the custom-made farmhouse table that could fit twenty-plus people.

We sat there and chatted while we waited on the duo to arrive. Mrs. Dillon took the time to ask questions about me and my past, with a genuine look of curiosity on her face.

"I really do care about your daughter, and I promise I will do the right thing, Mrs. Dillon," I explained.

"Please, don't call me Mrs. Dillon. Call me Claire," she asked.

"Yes, ma'am, Claire," I said, honoring her wishes.

"Okay then, that's all we need to speak about that topic then. Tell me more about you," she said with a kind smile.

As we talked, she asked me a few questions about where I grew up. She was genuinely excited to hear about my life before Montana and enjoyed the chance to get to know more about me. We talked back and forth for about half an hour, easily chatting as the topics flowed.

While we were caught up in our conversation, an odd sound rang through the house, causing Claire to look down and check her phone.

"They're home," she said with a smile, causing me to realize that sound must have come from a motion-triggered camera.

A few minutes later, Kate walked into the kitchen, a smile spreading across her face when she saw me sitting there with her mom, flowers by my side.

"Hi," I said, pushing the bouquet outwards in her direction.

Still smiling widely, she accepted them from me, closing her eyes and smelling their buds.

"Hi," she returned.

Mr. Dillon came in behind her, and she asked if he needed help getting stuff from the car. He looked over at me and offered a stern but welcoming nod, uttering no words.

"Seth," he turned, yelling towards the main part of the house.

Seth poked his head up from the couch and headed towards the kitchen.

Mr. Dillon kissed Kate on the forehead, "Your lazy brother can do it. Go see your friend," he said.

He softly smiled at me, then his daughter, before heading back into the garage with Seth. Kate quickly hugged her mom, then came back over to me.

"Let me just set my stuff down, put these in some water, and I'll meet you out on the back porch?" she asked.

"Sounds good," I responded.

Although I had seen a back porch on the other side of the living room windows, I had no idea how to get out there. Finally, Claire realized I was lost and motioned me back towards the living room and showed me to the door, leading me out to a covered patio.

ELEVEN

THE GLASS BACKDOOR opened outwards, leading to a wide-open wooden deck and large backyard below. Remembering Kate telling me how she and her mom had been working on sprucing it up, I looked around, admiring their handiwork.

To my left, a professionally installed built-in grill and outdoor kitchen sat in a u-shape at the edge of the deck and matched the color and style of the house perfectly. I saw a nice outdoor couch and circular fire pit Kate had bragged about building from concrete pavers to my right.

Doing a quick walk around the fire pit, I examined their meticulous craftsmanship, realizing the circle was almost perfectly round. The yard below had bulb lights dangling in the trees strung up all around, suspended by various wood poles buried in the ground.

While I waited on Kate, I got cozy on the cushioned outdoor couch. The backyard was magnificent, but I found myself wondering who the people that didn't allow guests were entertaining.

Kate finally emerged out of the back of the house and lit the fire pit, adding plenty of logs to keep it going, even though it was a warm December afternoon. She then made her way over to join me on the couch, sitting on the short end of the L-shape while I sat on the long side.

"Kate," I started, and she cut me off.

"Thank you," she said, remaining in place but leaning forward towards me.

She wanted to speak first, so I shut up.

"I really appreciate the flowers, and I appreciate you giving me the space this week. But I don't want you to feel like you have to do this. We can just be friends too. I know you and Seth already get along, so if that's what you want with me too, I get it. You won't hurt my feelings," she explained.

"Now, is it my turn?" I asked with a smile.

She motioned her hand towards me, inviting me to speak.

"Kate, I think you're a great girl, and I've enjoyed getting to know you and your family," I said, watching her break our eye contact, thinking I was about to tell her I didn't want to do this with her. "So, I want to keep seeing you. We can do things at your pace. Deal?"

She looked at me for a second before softly agreeing with a smile, "Deal."

The two of us sat there on the porch for almost three hours. Kate showed me around the yard, highlighting all the improvements they had done, and smiled as she detailed how her family enjoyed being outside together almost every summer night they were all home.

Kate shared with me the details of her trip to Missoula. Being one of my favorite Montana cities, we swapped stories about some of the hot spots we both loved. They had a great time and brought back some different food and beer options for the brewery.

After hearing all about her week, I shared mine with her, even though the most exciting night of the week had been the one night I spent getting hammered and playing trivia. Surprisingly, she found it hilarious, repeatedly saying how much she wished she had been with us.

"Kate, I hope you don't think I'm an alcoholic or have those sorts of issues. Honestly, I don't normally get drunk, but if I do, it's usually a pretty fun time," I reassured her.

"My parents own a bar. So I know you're not an alcoholic. I also know half the time you were only drinking another so you could sit there and talk to me longer," she said, flashing me a cheesy grin.

"You're not wrong. But overall, my week was boring, minus getting drunk and being complete losers at trivia with your brother. But I do want you to know that I wanted to text or call you the whole time but did what you said. My answer was always, let's do this. So, let's do this," I said reassuringly.

"Well, I didn't want you to feel pressured either way, but that's exactly what I was hoping you would say. I want you to know too. Just because I can't currently bring myself to hug or kiss you doesn't mean I don't want to," she paused, "because I do want to," she assured with a repetitive head bob.

"I understand. Kate, I'm not going to rush you. If you ever feel like I am, just say something or slap me," I said with a snicker.

"Deal," she added.

As it got later in the afternoon, her mom brought us out some snacks, and her dad even brought some samples of some new brews the brewery would soon have rotating. Mr. Dillon and I spoke for a minute, and just like his wife, he instructed me to call him Ryan.

The sun began to hide behind the horizon at about four in the afternoon. Although it seemed like a warmer week, the evening Montana winter air started to roll in quickly, leaving a bitter chill. Wearing only a light puffer jacket, Kate tried to hide her shiver.

"Well, this has been great, but I'll let you go get unpacked," I said, feeling cold myself.

"Yeah, okay, it has been good, thank you," she responded.

As she walked me to the door, she stopped.

"Hey, do you want to come over for dinner tomorrow night?" she asked quickly.

"Yeah, I'd love to," I said, gladly accepting her invitation.

That night I laid in bed with Tim curled up next to me and texted back and forth with Kate. After she asked what my house looked like, I tidied up quickly and sent some pictures of my small pad.

"I love it. It's quaint and homey," she texted.

"Thank you. It kind of looks like a shed compared to your parent's house," I said.

"Oh whatever, I hope to see it one day," she said as I smiled, hoping she would.

We sent messages constantly for a couple of hours until we both admitted we were beat and ready for bed.

The next day, I found myself sending Kate a good morning text and then talking to her throughout the day about anything and everything. My phone spent the day glued to my hand, needing a charge by mid-afternoon. Talking to her was easy and interesting. She repeatedly told me more small details about her past that she had previously kept close.

I learned she had left nursing school after the first time they wanted her to stitch someone up, causing her to pass out. Then, at her pace, she began slowly filling in some of the gaps from when she left Montana to when she returned.

It felt stupid, but I found myself waiting for her responses, smiling slightly every time I saw her name pop up on my screen.

I arrived at the well-guarded neighborhood and found myself stationed at the gate, unable to get in. Thankfully a red Mustang pulled up behind me and pushed their button, allowing the gate to open.

After parking my truck in the driveway, I grabbed the bottle of wine I had brought and made my way to the front door. Ryan stood in the entryway, holding it open when I arrived at the front. He glanced over his shoulder before shutting the door, joining me outside of the house.

"How did you get into the neighborhood?" he asked sternly.

"I was at the gate waiting, I was about to text Kate, but another car let me in," I answered.

"What car?" he demanded.

"It was a newer model red Mustang," I responded, widening my eyes, confused at his interrogation.

"Thanks," he returned and wrapped his jacket around himself tighter before heading down the driveway.

"Is everything okay?" I asked.

He stopped and came back towards me.

"People aren't supposed to let random cars into the neighborhood. We've told all the residents that, and they all agreed. Go ahead inside. I'm going to go talk with Mr. Trotman," he answered.

I made my way inside the house, knocking gently as I pushed the door open. Kate's smile from the kitchen was the first thing I saw as I crested the entryway. She and her mother were both working on something in the kitchen, leaving the whole house filled with the smell of bacon and potatoes.

I joined them in the kitchen, where Kate invited me to pull up a barstool while they finished up. Kate's long hair weaved in a braid that hung down her back and bounced around as she moved. A long sleeve black jersey dress that stopped at her knees loosely hugged her figure. On the front of the dress, seven wooden-looking buttons ran from her cleavage to just above her belly button. As usual, there didn't appear to be any makeup on her face, leaving her scar visible. As she diced tomatoes, I averted my gaze, so I didn't stare at her eye while also trying not to think about the horrible events that led to its appearance.

They worked in the kitchen with eighties hit songs loudly playing on a Bluetooth speaker. It seemed like they had a system going and knew where each other would be as they moved around the room.

Claire poured me a glass of the wine I had brought and scooted it to me across the counter. We spoke some when Kate wasn't tied up in with cooking, but I left her be, enjoying watching her cook and hum the songs she didn't know the words to while she looked beautiful as always.

Finally, Ryan came back into the house after we heard the noise set off by his motion.

He came over to the kitchen and put a hand on my shoulder, "will you join me out at the grill?" he asked.

I replied, "Yeah, sure," knowing it wasn't really a question.

His custom outdoor kitchen was illuminated by fancy Edison lightbulbs that hung loosely from the pergola above. He lit the grill, and I just stood there waiting for him to speak up.

"No one is supposed to let a random vehicle into the neighborhood. Mr. Trotman just got reminded of that, but I want you to know that you need to stop when you come through, letting the gate close behind you. Got it?" he said.

"Yes, sir," I responded, feeling like I was being scolded.

"Sorry, I'm not upset with you. We've just been over this with these people before. They don't know the full story, but they're aware there's someone we don't want getting access to our neighborhood. So I just want them to respect those wishes. It's not that hard. That's why we moved into a gated community. Got it?" he asked again.

"Yes, sir," I repeated.

"Good," he said, going back to his grill.

"So, Kate tells me you know all about HVAC systems. Guess I know a handyman now, huh?" he stated.

"Yes, sir, just give me a call if you ever need me to look at something, here or at the bar. I'll gladly come out," I offered.

"You can drop the sir kid," he corrected me.

"Gotcha," I responded with a chuckle.

He preheated the grill and seasoned some steaks for dinner while we talked. The conversation led to him asking me about my parents, which naturally resulted in him offering his condolences about my father. He seemed sad I didn't have a male influence growing up but happy to hear a loving mother raised me. It was apparent he was silently making sure I didn't check the same boxes that Ethan had.

He detailed the story to me about meeting Claire and the decision to open the brewery. He laughed as he reminisced about Kate learning how to pour a beer from the tap, a skill he had taught her. Then, just as he offered me a beer from the mini-fridge, Kate emerged out of the back door from the house.

"Everything okay out here?" she asked, shooting her father a sideways glance.

"Yes, Kate, we're fine. Go back inside; it's too damn cold out here," he answered.

I smiled at Kate while I stood there in a short-sleeve shirt and tried not to complain or shiver. Although I had grown accustomed to the cold, I still had some Florida blood trickling through my veins.

Ryan grabbed his spatula and pointed it at me, "I swear to God if I ever see that other boy again, I'll kill him. Don't ever give me a reason to add you to that list. Got it?" he threatened.

"Yes sir," I answered, adding the sir after being threatened.

It quickly became clear Ryan was a big fan of making sure you understood and acknowledged him by ending his questions with "got it?"

"Good answer," he said, going back to tending to the steaks.

After he asked, I told him about my tour in Afghanistan. He was interested in hearing about my time overseas, so I tried to tell him as much as possible, even though it was a relatively uneventful deployment. I was sure to subtly include the fact that I hadn't seen anything dangerous enough to mentally scar me and left in one piece so he could check that box off as well.

When Ryan had cooked the steaks just right, I carried them inside on a platter as directed. When I entered the doorway, Kate looked over at me, mouthing "sorry" at me. I shifted the meat to one hand and gave her a thumbs up. He only threatened my life once, so overall the conversation had gone well.

The Dillon women had finished up a fantastic spread while I was outside tending to the grill with Ryan. On the granite bar, four baked potatoes sat ready to be topped with all the fixings. Next to them, I saw a dish of parmesan Brussel sprouts and a loaded salad filled with all sorts of colors. Ryan came back into the house and complimented the women on their handiwork.

"Let's eat," he stated, rubbing his hands together.

"Thank you again for having me. This all looks amazing," I said as the four of us sat down at the table together.

"You're more than welcome," Claire said as Ryan nodded in agreement.

It was apparent how much Kate loved being around her parents. They had taken her in when she needed them most, and since Seth also lived at home, it was clear they had no issues with their kids sticking around.

A different chime sound sang loudly through the house, and mid-conversation, all three of the Dillon's at the table instantly silenced themselves, opening their phones. Unsure of what this new chime was, I set my fork down and just sat there in silence.

"That FedEx guy really needs to start coming earlier," Ryan finally said, the three of them putting their phones back down.

"It's the door chime," Kate explained, "sends everyone into full panic mode every time," she added before flashing me a gentle eye roll.

Everyone had finished their dinner except Claire, who was still picking at her baked potato while we made small talk around the room. Kate's parents were fun to talk to, and thankfully, they seemed to have a generally favorable opinion about the guy that had been hanging around so much lately.

Ryan talked about the new growlers they had found while he and Kate were in Missoula when my ears stopped working, and I instantly stopped caring about what he was saying. Kate had placed her hand on my leg underneath the table and was lightly resting it right above my knee. Out of the corner of my eye, I could see Kate looking at me. I turned and looked in her direction and saw she was wearing a soft smile and didn't appear to be panicking inside as her hand rested on my thigh.

Unfolding my hands that sat joined in my lap, I placed my hand on hers, feeling our fingers touch for the first time. Instantly at the feeling of my touch, she quickly retracted her hand, pulling it back into her lap.

"Shit," I thought to myself. "I pushed it already."

Placing my hands back in the center of my lap, I again focused on the conversation with the Dillon's, trying not to react noticeably. A few minutes later, Kate put her hand back on my leg, giving it a gentle squeeze.

This time I took what was given to me, being careful not to push it.

The rest of the evening was spent wrapped up in conversation, chatting with Kate and her parents at the dining table and trying to get to know each other better. The hand on my leg became lighter and relaxed as she slowly scooted her body a hair closer to me.

Finally, Claire gave Ryan a "let's leave them alone look," and they both suddenly decided they were tired. They piled all the dishes high in the single bowl sink, deciding they could wait to be done tomorrow.

"Goodnight, Brandon," Claire said as they made their way up the short flight of stairs to the landing their room was on.

The door to their room made a slight creak as they shut it, but I never heard a click to indicate they shut it all the way.

"Now what?" I asked.

"Would you like to join me in the living room?" she responded.

"Of course," I replied, following her out of the kitchen.

We situated ourselves on opposite ends of the oversized leather sofas, the fluffy couch nearly sucking me in when I sat down.

"They're comfy, huh?" she asked.

"Yeah, they are. Wow," I responded, bounding slightly to test the couch out more.

Kate sat on her end and hugged one of the large couch pillows. I sat on my end, slightly facing her with my left leg tucked under my right knee. She reached down to a basket that was beside the couch, fishing out the largest iPad I had ever seen. Her fingers gently moved across the screen for a moment before she turned it around and scooted halfway across the couch towards me.

"Can I come sit by you?" I asked.

She silently nodded and smiled at me. I scooted over, not going all the way, but leaving a couple of inches for her to come to me.

Thrusting the iPad into my lap, Kate started explaining the various things on the screen. The excitement overtook her as her finger ran across the screen, pointing to each small flourish and logo she had hand drawn in her digital design program.

"So, how did you do these?" I asked, genuinely curious about how she added such detail.

She took the iPad back, grabbing a tablet-friendly pencil out of the same basket. She sat back down, opened an app, and broke down some of the ins and outs of how she drew each item by hand. Enthralled to be sharing her skill with someone, her leg crept closer to mine and butted up next to it.

After she had shown me a couple of the basics, I tried my hand at the tablet. Not being a creative person and having the handwriting of a sixth-grader, I gave it a go. Although most of my attention was fixated on drawing something, I could feel Kate's eyes on my face. She redirected her attention and looked down at the tablet, giggling at my inability to even draw a straight line.

"Here," she said as she grabbed my hand and tried to help guide it.

As she touched my hand, I felt her touching my whole body all at once, and I couldn't see the tablet but saw myself laying her down on the fluffy couch and kissing her entire body.

"See, like that," Kate said, bringing my focus back to the drawing.

"Yeah," I cleared my throat, "that looks good," I said, not sure if that was referencing the quick fantasy or the drawing.

She continued the drawing, which ended as a simple sailboat filled with bright colors. Focusing on the art and not thinking about her body, I witnessed her talented hands draw as she moved the pencil smoothly over the screen, never skipping a beat.

The more time I spent with Kate, the more I liked her and felt the growing desire to put my hands all over her. It wasn't that I wanted to seduce her at that moment. I just wanted to touch her and have her touch me back, to feel a moment of intimacy with her.

Blocking out the thoughts, I diligently paid attention when she added animating features to the boat, bringing it to life on the tablet screen as it bobbled up and down on a wave.

"That's really cool Kate, I'm impressed," I complimented.

"Thank you," she smiled back as she made eye contact.

The tablet rested in her lap, and she realized our legs were touching. Her smile dropped, and for only a moment, she tensed up but then quickly relaxed, realizing it wasn't all that terrible.

We talked a bit longer, holding that position, enjoying looking at each other so closely.

"Every year, we decorate the brewery for Christmas as a family with some other people. Do you want to join us?" she asked.

"I'd love to," I said.

Kate walked me to the door, and we said our goodnights with no touching involved, just words floating in the empty space between us. That night had been a step in the right direction, leaving me confident things would only get better from there.

TWELVE

DURING MY WORK week, I found myself spending a ton of time on my phone. At the office, on the job site, in the bathroom, I spent every free minute I had texting back and forth with Kate most of the day.

It became clear she wanted so much more out of life. She touched on her hopes and dreams, only halfway painting the picture of what she saw for herself, leaving everything sounding somewhat diluted as I read what she typed out to me.

She knew what she wanted; she just let fear hold her back.

When I brought up solutions for reaching her travel and personal dreams, she started to rattle off excuses. She had to help at the bar, or school occupied too much of her time, but I knew the real reason was Ethan. I hoped that weight would be gone one day, and she would feel the freedom to live her life without fear.

I wanted to be the one to make sure that happened. I wanted to be the one to see her be able to live a normal life.

I wasn't sure how, but we never seemed to run out of topics to discuss. Kate would bring up something about the weather, and we would somehow keep talking, the conversation going on until it had morphed into discussing our favorite lunchmeat. I continuously asked her questions, trying to use every text message as a chance to learn more and more about her.

Sending her a good morning text became how I started my day, and saying goodnight to her brought it to a close. Kate's name popping across my phone screen both morning and night became a big part of my daily routine.

When Thursday finally rolled around, I donned the Busch Light ugly sweater I had bought the year before and headed into the brewery. As I approached the door, I stopped outside. I listened for a moment and heard festive Christmas music playing loudly from inside the building.

I pulled the door open, and the bell chimed, its sound finally making sense and aligning with the current season. Kate turned and looked at me and gently smiled as she twisted her hand. I looked at her with a confused face, and she pointed to the door, making the twisting motion again. Finally, I got the hint and locked the door's deadbolt behind me.

Making my way into the taproom, the pungent smell of cinnamon and spiced cider instantly hit my nose. The decorating brigade had already begun their work, erecting a massive tree in the back corner that stood at least fifteen feet tall.

Kate had decided on one of those classic red and white Santa hats with the ball on the end that tightly hugged her head. She walked over to me with an extra hat in hand, smiling as she wiggled it onto my head.

Her braid dangled down from underneath her hat, hanging down in front of her this time. She had on some nice dark-washed jeans and her high-top waterproof Vans and a turtleneck with chains lights printed on it.

One of the cooks I hadn't met before made his way to me with a steaming glass of hot cider I hoped would be spiked with something strong.

"Thanks man," I said, taking a sip of the strongly spiked drink.

"You're welcome," he replied as he moved his hand upwards until it was pointing at the ceiling.

Looking up, I found Kate and me almost directly under a fresh sprig of mistletoe hung from the loft.

I mouthed, "it's okay," to her as we smiled at one another.

"Cheers," Seth said as he walked over to us, as the cook realized we were ignoring the mistletoe. "Come with me, man," he said, motioning for me to follow him up the stairs to the loft.

The two of us ended up spending close to half an hour stringing lights along the wrought iron railing that lined the second floor. As the music blared, I found myself humming along, getting into the Christmas spirit for the first time in years.

From the balcony, I could see Kate decorating the tree with Ryan. She danced around the tree with an ornament in her hand, on the lookout for one last bald spot on the already covered tree. Her braid flipped around to her back often, moving with her as she danced and sang to the music.

When we were out of lights for the balcony, we went back downstairs and joined the rest of the decorating team. With the tree complete, Ryan had his arm around his daughter as they stood back, checking their work. Kate excused us from the decorating party, bringing me with her to the bar.

"We've been doing this every year for as long as I can remember," she said, looking around at the numerous decorations adorning the walls. "Do you have any holiday traditions?" she asked.

"Well, my mom and I always decorated the tree together while drinking hot chocolate the day after Thanksgiving. It's hard to get in the Christmas spirit in Florida when it's sometimes eighty degrees," I explained, laughing at her shocked expression. "And then on Christmas Eve, we always made chocolate chip cookies for Santa and loaded baked potato soup while we watched Christmas Vacation together," I said with a smile, remembering the good times I had on the holidays with my mom.

"I'm sure you still make Santa cookies, but do you still make the soup and watch that movie every year?" Kate questioned.

"No, not since I left home," I lied slightly, remembering the year I shared that tradition with Taylor.

"And then you just had Christmas day with your mom, or did other family come?" she asked.

"Nope, just me and mom. My dad's parents kind of cut us off after my dad passed, and then they died a couple of years ago. It always felt like my mom's parents were old, and they never really liked to leave their house up in Maine, and my mom doesn't believe in traveling in the winter. So we went there a couple of times, but they both died when I was in my teens, and my mom's sister is a fifty-year-old party girl," I explained.

"I get that," she said, "we're not super close with extended family either."

We continued talking about Christmas, Kate detailing how much she enjoyed the holiday season. She lit up when she spoke about her favorite holiday movies and telling me how much she wanted all the Christmas candies that hit the shelves during that time of the year. The Dillon traditions included an Asian menu for Christmas Eve, serving up dumplings, fried rice, short ribs, and more. Then for Christmas Day, they did the traditional holiday meal of ham and the classic sides.

The night was full of laughing, singing, drinking, and welcoming Christmas into the brewery. As the night ended, Kate walked me to the door to say goodnight.

"How would you like to go on a date, away from people, just the two of us?" she asked. I went to answer her, and she added to her question. "Well, kind of a date, and mostly just the two of us."

"Sure?" I responded, unsure of what she meant.

"My dad said we can use the bar's conference room and have dinner alone. I know it's not perfect, but how does that sound?" she asked.

"Of course, I'd love to," I responded, pleased she was making an effort to introduce some normalcy into our lives.

Her face became elated at my acceptance. "Okay, does Saturday night work for you?"

I quickly agreed. We said our goodbyes, and I left, hearing the bell and the lock of the door click behind me.

Saturday night, I dressed for our date in my usual casual getup. There wasn't much fancy about me, and that was something about me that was consistent. The one suit I owned, hung in the back of my closet, probably didn't even fit me anymore and would only be worn for a special occasion, which meant it had never been worn.

Since I couldn't pick Kate up in the normal going on a date fashion, I opted just to meet her at the brewery. We had talked alone at the bar before, but there were always others in the background. This time I wasn't just showing up and hoping she would be there or seeing her at work; it had been intentional.

The bell announced my arrival, and I looked to the bar and saw no one looking over at me. Only Luke was working, and I didn't see anyone from the Dillon family in the taproom. Seth emerged from the office just as I walked up to the bar. He had a fried cheese stick wedged between his teeth and hanging out of his mouth. He silently grabbed me by the arm, leading me towards the back of the bar.

"Don't you look nice?" he said as he talked with food in his mouth.

"Well, thank you," I replied with a chuckle.

We exited the taproom and entered the brewing side of the establishment. We walked between the giant stainless vats, fresh beer flowing inside them, and past the storeroom where they kept their brewing ingredients.

On the other side of the brewing room, I saw a long room that housed a wooden conference table. The room was enclosed from floor to ceiling with four glass walls, and a single door controlled its entry. There were decals stuck to the walls that showcased bits and pieces of the brewing process. I walked alone into the room and found a seat in front of one of the two beers placed across from one another. Seth left me in the room, gently shutting the door and leaving with just the tip of his hat.

I sat there alone for a few minutes, reading the different images and captions stuck to the wall. The tasteful room was purposely set to surround you with the vats around it, immersing you into the brewing experience.

A few minutes later, Kate rounded the corner of the brewing room and came into sight from my position. As she walked into the room, I stood and smiled at her, taking her beauty in.

Her hair hung loosely down from a side part, with one side tucked behind her ear. Usually, her hair was twisted back or tied up, but she had taken the time to roll some gentle curls into it for our date. Per her usual style, she had on jeans double cuffed at the bottom, exposing her ankles, and tan leather slip-on Keds. Her shirt appeared to be a light black chiffon material with a slight V cut in the center of its scoop neck.

On her eyelids, I saw a hint of smoke coloring rubbed on, and her lashes had a touch of mascara, making her eyes pop. As she sat down at her seat, her head turned to the right, slightly exposing where her scar would be, now hidden from me with a minute amount of cover-up.

"You look beautiful," I exclaimed as she joined me at the table.

"Thank you. You look really nice too," she said, eyeballing the denim button-up and black jeans I picked out.

We instantly started talking, and I told her about my hunting failure from that morning. Before I left, I texted her, telling her I would be out of service for a while but left out why.

"Sorry, guns," I quickly said, realizing she probably didn't want to hear about hunting or anything else that involved guns.

"Just because I don't personally want to shoot a gun doesn't mean I'm scared of them. You can talk about them. It's okay with me," she explained.

I let out a heavy sigh, feeling relieved that I could cross off something on my mental "don't bring it up" list.

Continuing my story, I told her about my cold venture into the woods that morning and how it had been a wash. She sat there as I talked, listing to me intently. Kate interlaced her fingers, and both elbows rested lightly on the surface of the table as she leaned forward ever so slightly. Her eyes were soft, and she appeared intrigued as I talked about my morning.

Her hands released from one another as she started in on her morning. She had spent all morning with her mom, looking for something new to wear for our date, but never found the right thing.

"I guess we both struck out this morning then," I said, causing us to laugh together lightly.

A few minutes later, Seth came back into the room with a large hot margarita pizza and two small salads. Kate smiled at me as she said, "your favorite, right?"

"If you guys need anything, just send me a text," Seth said, backing out of the room with a bow.

"Thanks for doing this," I said.

"My dad is in the taproom somewhere, and Seth is here, so they were quick to agree it was okay," she said.

"So, just curious, do you always want them around, or has it become a family rule. Will I one day be able to take you on a real date, just the two of us," I asked hopefully.

"I think so," she answered. "And both, Seth probably worries the most, but I also think he knows you're not a psychopath. But I guess it's sort of become a Dillon family rule. At first, it was just me wanting them around cause I was scared to be alone, but now I think they're just used to it and don't know how to stop. So now I'm their problem to babysit," she admitted.

"I've seen your family, and they love you. I don't think they see you as a problem or burden," I said reassuringly.

"I mean," she paused, "I am, but oh well, I guess."

"If you didn't already know, I want to take you out alone one day, but I'll wait. I hope eventually you can feel safe around me," I said.

"I am comfortable around you. I would go out with you alone right now, but honestly, I think they're still a tad wary about it. Not because they don't trust you or think you're a bad guy, they just don't know you well enough yet, but if you stick around, I'm sure they will," she explained.

"Well, I plan on sticking around," I admitted. "Shall we eat?" I asked, gesturing to the food.

We ate and drank, spending the evening in the glass box enjoying one another's company. Ryan brought us fresh pints of some new beers he had bought supplies for on their trip to Missoula to get my review.

Kate made me unconsciously smile when she talked. I often realized how caught up I would get in watching her eyes when she spoke, seeing her hands moving with her mouth through my peripherals, and sometimes failing to listen to the words she was saying.

I got to hear all about how she had recently gotten into playing the stock market through an app on her phone. She told me all about learning about day trading and bragged about the small amounts of money she was making that were slowly adding up. She used to enjoy the occasional trip to the casino, but now she spent her time gambling from the comforts of digital Wall Street.

The pizza was good, the conversation was good, and the beer was good. It felt as though we were on an actual date even though I saw Kate's brother and father casually stroll by the room every so often.

When the night was over, Kate and I started to head out to the brewery's front. As we made our way back through the brewing side of the house, Kate grabbed my hand, lacing her fingers into mine. My mouth cracked a small smile, and I looked down at her and saw her staring straight ahead and smiling too, not acknowledging me. She was trying, and I wanted to be the one to slowly help her fix her issues and get back to the normal life she deserved.

Ryan and Seth both smiled our way as we walked through the taproom hand in hand. The front of the house had gotten busy while we were tucked away in the backroom, hiding from the madness. When we got to the door, she released her hand from mine.

"Tonight was great," I said, "I already can't wait to see you again."

"Well, you have my number. I'm sure we will talk sometime soon," she said with a teasing grin.

THIRTEEN

A COUPLE OF weeks passed, and holding my hand was about as far as it had gone, but we were getting there. When I came over to her house, we often sat and talked on the couch, and as the time went on, she was no longer hesitant about getting close to me, often wrapping her leg behind mine at the ankle.

We carved out plenty of weekend trips to go skiing together with Seth. On the drive to the mountain, she would reach across the console and hold my hand, breaking her dedicated ten and two grip.

On the lift's ascent, I took a chance and put my arm around her, resting it on the back of the chair. I felt her slightly lean in closer into my side and smiled both inside and out.

During the week, Kate started working less at the brewery, freeing her up to take on more side jobs doing graphic design and send me snapshots of what she was working on for a local restaurant. Her keen eye for design had landed her a couple of jobs with nearby businesses that were keeping her rather busy.

With Kate tied up with work, I tried to stay busy myself. Winter started to set in as we neared the Christmas holiday, encouraging me to make sure I buttoned up a few last-minute chores around the house before going outside became unbearable.

We tried to make time for each other during the week, even if it just meant I came over for dinner. Usually, after we ate, I would stay, and we would sit in the living room together, watching a movie or just chatting while her parents purposely sat in a different room.

The weekends were when we got some more time alone. Most Saturdays, Kate spent time catching up on her hours at the brewery and couldn't always squeeze in a ton of one-on-one sessions with me. Sometimes I would join her, and I started learning a few things to help out, and Kate even taught me the skill it takes to master the perfect draft fill.

One weeknight, Seth and Kate made the executive decision to close the brewery early when the final customer left just after seven. This time of the year, the visitors had slowly decreased as people started to stay indoors, attempting to avoid the brutal Montana weather and roads.

Once everything was shut down and cleaned up, Seth hopped up on the bar.

"Ladies and gentlemen, it's trivia night," he yelled loudly, causing my stomach to turn at the memory of the hangover from last time.

Kate smiled and clapped her hands rapidly with excitement.

Even with Seth tagging along, it was always nice to be around her and do everyday date-like things. Going to trivia with my girlfriend felt normal and was something I was super excited about doing together.

Seth pulled me aside before we headed to the pub, "Hey…. so if I get too drunk tonight, which we both know I probably will, can you make sure we make it home?" he asked me with a hopeful smile.

"Yeah, of course," I said, returning a slight smile, realizing this proved he trusted me with his sister.

Inside the pub, Kate insisted she sat in a place where she could see the door. She still looked at people when they came in, but all around, she appeared to feel comfortable with her surroundings throughout the night. We laughed and joked, and compared to the last time; we improved our standings with the newest addition to our team.

When the pub was ready to close, we paid the tab and headed back to the brewery where we had parked our cars. As we walked down the sidewalk illuminated by the dim moonlight, I noticed some streetlights were out, making the path particularly dark.

At about a hundred yards from Kates's vehicle, three people appeared to be walking towards us on the patchily lit sidewalk. During Montana's winter months, people were often bundled up and hid beneath hats, gloves, and even baklavas if they would be walking outside for an extended period.

Unsure of who the people were, Kate slipped her head into the hood of her jacket, trying to mask her identity. My hands were in my hoodie pocket, and I felt her loop her arm inside of mine, bringing herself in closer to me.

The people got closer and finally made it into view under one of the working streetlights. Kate picked her head up, and after she realized she didn't recognize the people advancing towards us, her hand loosened its tight grip on my arm but didn't pull away.

Kate climbed into the driver's seat, and I walked around to the passenger side and checked on her half-shot brother as he stepped up and into the vehicle.

After blowing me a couple of kisses, he spoke, "Hey, I like you man, you're my favorite, stick around, okay?"

"Okay, Seth," I replied with a smile.

Kate laughed and rolled her eyes from her side of the car after helping me finagle his seatbelt into its buckle.

"Sorry about him, but thank you. I'll see you again soon," she said.

"I'm going to follow you home just in case," I replied.

"Why? Seth's here," she asked.

"I told him that if he got drunk tonight, I would make sure you made it home safe," I said, looking at Seth passed out in the passenger seat. "So, I get to make sure you make it home safe, Miss Dillon."

"Well, okay then. Thanks," she replied with a smile, looking over at her brother.

In addition to spending time together when we could, we were also constantly texting, learning tons about one another via our tiny phone screens. Talking about our exes was something we had silently agreed not to do, but occasionally Ethan would get brought up as a reference to something from her past. When she mentioned him, she was also able to say positive things about the guy, and sometimes it was difficult for me to remember that he had once been a great husband that treated her well.

It was hard, but I never got upset when she brought him up. It wasn't that I was jealous of him; I had just grown to deeply hate him for the emotional and physical scars he left Kate bearing.

With her being so open and honest with me, I concluded I should do probably the same. Taylor had been a big part of my life, and I thought it was only right if I shared our story with Kate. After I told her all about Taylor, Kate understood why I had taken so long to get back into the world of dating after Taylor broke me.

"Would you like to go see a movie this week with me? Seth or your parents, too," I asked Kate via text, trying to change the subject.

"No, I want to come over to your house and watch one. I'll bring Seth, not my dad J," she responded.

She later detailed that she wasn't a big fan of dark movie theaters for apparent reasons, but she was curious about seeing where I lived.

After I texted her back, agreeing to her idea, I looked over the top of my phone and realized that the house I had vowed to keep clean needed some serious attention if I was going to have company.

The doorbell sang loudly when the duo arrived for movie night. Seth was holding two large pizzas, and Kate had a pack of seltzers and a growler of beer in her hands. After she set her things down, I gave them the very short and sweet tour of my one-story, two-bedroom bachelor pad.

Seth quickly made himself comfortable on the couch he had passed out on during his first sleepover. Kate reached in her purse and widely opened her eyes wide towards me as she pulled out a movie.

"This is one of my favorites," I said when she pulled out an Elf DVD.

"I know," she said, grinning, "you told me."

We started the movie and enjoyed our pizza and beer. Kate sat next to me on the other couch, her left leg tucked under my right calve. She reached over and grabbed my hand and placed both of our hands in her lap.

About halfway through the movie, Kate rolled her eyes as Seth started to snore, with Tim curled up in a ball at his feet.

"He falls asleep during every movie," she whispered, laying her head down on my shoulder.

Feeling bold, I leaned my head down towards hers and kissed her on the top of her head. She didn't flinch or pull away but surprisingly pulled my arm in closer to her in response.

Before the siblings departed after the movie, Kate remained in the doorway to say goodnight. She moved towards me, wrapping her arms around me in a hug for the first time. I took her in my embrace and kissed the top of her head before sending her out the door.

I went over to the Dillon's for the Christmas Eve festivities, and per their request, I brought Tim along. Their house looked as though it had been decorated by a professional to be featured on a Christmas card. Wreaths in every window, perfectly straight white lights, and none of the obnoxious yard inflatables my mother seemed to love.

Once I came into the warm house that smelled of fresh baking pies, Kate pulled me aside in the formal dining room, directing me to close my eyes. When I finally got permission, I opened them and saw two wrapped gifts and a card.

She handed me the first package, which felt somewhat heavy and cylindrical in my hands. Once I had discarded the copious amounts of wrapping paper, I found myself holding a small stainless-steel drum-like object with airtight clamps holding down its lid. I again looked at Kate and furrowed my brow at her.

"Well, go on, open it!" she insisted, looking at the object with a smile.

The seals popped open one by one, and I removed the lid. I looked inside and saw a warm white chunky substance steaming from the container.

Returning my eyes to Kate, now even more curious, I raised my eyebrows and asked, "Sorry, but uh, what it is?"

She chuckled as she lowered her head. "I wanted you to have your old family tradition. It's loaded baked potato soup like you said your mom always made," she explained.

I smiled and shook my head, "Thank you, Kate, you made this just for me?" I asked in awe of her thoughtfulness.

"Well, Sam's Club made it. But I heated it up and put it in the container, and I even added some extra bacon and cheese," she beamed.

"It's perfect, thank you," I responded genuinely.

The following package she gave me felt cold to the touch in my hands with a bit of weight. I shook the object gently, leading me to no revelations about its content. After I ripped off the paper, I realized it was a package of ready-to-bake chocolate chip cookie dough.

"So you can make cookies for Santa," she said, visibly excited with her thoughtful gifts.

I again thanked her, amazed at how sweet her gestures had been. Last it was time to open the card that still sat on the table.

I removed it from the envelope and read the inside, "We're watching Christmas Vacation tonight."

I smiled in her direction and remained silent as she pulled me towards her into a hug, and I caught a whiff of her coconut shampoo.

The family allowed me to help in the kitchen, and oddly enough, I found myself cooking with SPAM for the first time on Christmas Eve. The holiday music played loudly on multiple speakers, and a lovely gathering of empty wine bottles began forming on the island's countertop.

The music paused as the chime that had previously rattled the Dillon family began ringing. All four household members took to their phones, checking to see who had set off the motion sensor at the front door. A moment later, the doorbell chimed. Waiting for their screens to load, showing them who was at the door, the Dillon's remained frozen in place.

A few seconds later, Ryan locked his phone and returned it to his pocket as he made his way to the door. While he went to answer the door, the music resumed, and the other three family members returned to what they were doing without saying a word.

The door shut, and I glanced over to see Luke walk in with two six-packs of hard cider in hand.

"Heyyyyy," he said, raising the bottles over his head.

"Heyyyyy," the three Dillon's in the kitchen echoed.

"What's up man, how's hunting season going?" Luke asked as he patted me on the back and sat down, joining me at the bar.

"Well, I think I'm done for the season and sadly didn't get anything this year. I was sort of busy and didn't get out there enough," I replied, eyeing Kate smiling, and dancing with her mom.

"Yeah, I didn't get anything either," he added.

The dinner ended up being more amazing than I expected. It was also the first time I'd had fried rice and dumplings on Christmas Eve, but I liked their tradition. Kate left the table, a moment later returning with my potato soup thermos and six spoons.

She passed out one spoon to each person at the table, finally handing me the last spoon and container. Kate stood at the head as though she was offering up a toast.

"Since Brandon's family isn't here, we are going to include his traditions with ours. So, everyone will take a bite of the soup and pass it around. Cheers?" she cheerfully asked as she raised a spoonful of the store-bought soup.

"Cheers," everyone echoed in unison as they also raised their spoons.

After dinner, I helped clean up while Kate popped my cookies in the oven. Once Kate had cooked them to the right consistency, she handed them out, forcing all the stuffed people relaxing on the couch to shove something else in their mouths.

Luke left after cookies, heading out to his next Christmas Eve invite, leaving the rest of us to get comfortable on the couch. The wine buzz had kicked in, and everyone was ready to settle down and enjoy a movie in the dark living room with the fire making the space warm and inviting.

Kate popped in Christmas Vacation, leaving me shocked that only her parents had seen it before. I held my tongue, and even though it was difficult, I didn't quote the whole movie like usual. She cuddled up next to me and held my hand in front of her mom for the first time. I saw Claire eyeball our interlocked hands and move her eyes to mine with a slight smile and nod to indicate her approval.

Par for the course, Seth laid on the couch and gave into his buzz as he started snoring before the movie was even close to being over, while Tim too took up residence on the couch, curled up on his feet.

Claire brought us over some popcorn and a mixed drink. Feeling full already, I set the popcorn aside but made room for the drink. I sipped it once, then took another, trying to figure out what was in the glass. The cold cider was one apparent ingredient, but they had hidden something else in it.

"This is good. What is it?" I whispered to Kate, shaking my glass and pulling her away from the movie momentarily.

"Hard cider, spiced rum, and a cinnamon stick. It was one of Luke's family traditions we adopted when my parents hired him and brought him into the family a couple of years ago," she replied.

"Good call," I responded, exchanging smiles and drinking some more of the new drink.

As the movie ended, Ryan woke Seth up by rapidly tapping his forehead and telling him to go to bed. He did as he was told, and Kate's parents told me goodnight, also going to their room, completely shutting the door this time.

"Now it's time for my favorite Christmas movie," Kate jumped up and exclaimed as I sunk farther into the couch, yawning.

Even though I would disagree that it's a Christmas movie, she put in Die Hard and joined me back on the couch, cuddling her body close to mine.

FOURTEEN

THE NEXT MORNING, I woke when the sun made its way through the back of the house's foggy glass doors. I looked around, quickly realizing I had fallen asleep sunken into the couch in the Dillon's living room, and noticed someone had covered me up with a fleece Montana State University blanket.

"Shit," I whispered as my hands reached up and covered my eyes.

I jumped to my feet and hurriedly started to gather my things. I looked all over the room for Tim when my eyes caught sight of Ryan sitting at the kitchen table with his gaze glued to his open laptop, enjoying his morning coffee. His hand raised slowly, and he motioned towards me and invited me to join him without removing his eyes from the screen.

"Mornin'," he said, shutting his laptop and giving his attention to me. "Late night?"

"Morning, sir," I responded, feeling somewhat guilty I had spent the night. "I guess I fell asleep on the couch. I'm sorry, I didn't mean to sleep over; it won't happen again."

"Listen," he said, pausing to take a sip of coffee and clearing his throat. "We worry about Kate, but at the end of the day, she's thirty years old. I hope she finds someone else to look after her like Seth, her mother, and I do. And between us, I'd really like this house to be kid-free one day."

"I understand. I'll never do anything to hurt her; I can promise you that," I said firmly.

"I don't think you would either, but I also trusted Ethan with my baby girl, and he treated her right for five-plus years before things went off the rails. So, you have to understand my worry," he explained.

"I understand your worry," I replied, "I'm not trying to rush anything, but know I care about her, and I only want what's best for her."

"Good. Well, then, don't drink and drive. So, if that means you have too much while you're here, you're more than welcome to sleep on the couch, and only the couch," he said, pointing to me at the last part of his speech.

"Thank you, I understand," I replied, sipping my coffee as I softly chuckled.

"Oh, and Merry Christmas," he added, "I put Tim out."

I looked out the glass door next to the living room and saw Tim enjoying jumping around in the deep snow, his belly almost grazing it.

"Thank you, Merry Christmas to you too," I responded.

We awkwardly sat there for a couple of minutes, drinking our coffee, not saying anything to one another. Then, finally, Tim interrupted the quiet when he returned to the door. I let him in, making sure I dusted the accumulated snow off his legs before he tracked it through the house.

I ran my fingers through my greasy hair and felt it spread all over the place and realized I desperately needed to brush my grimy teeth and take a shower.

There wasn't much to get, but I gathered all my stuff, including Tim.

"Thank you again. I'm gonna head home now," I explained.

"You're coming back for Christmas, right?" he asked.

Kate had never specifically invited me to Christmas. Maybe it had been implied, or she planned to, but she had never formally asked.

"Um, I guess so?" I replied questioningly.

"Well, you're welcome to join us. Hope we see you in a little," he said.

The holiday ended up being a complete success. There were a couple of gifts that the family exchanged, but the area under the tree was barren for the most part. I regretted not getting Kate something small to open on Christmas after the thoughtful things she had given me the night before.

I watched Kate smile while sitting in the living room in her Christmas pajamas, shooting her brother with a Nerf gun like they probably had when they were kids. The already long list of things I liked about her kept growing every time I saw her cheerful smile spread across her face.

Christmas dinner had all the usual items. The full table housed a baked ham and a full spread of traditional homemade sides that led to me overstuffing myself. Claire kept the wine bottles coming, and I tried not to overindulge two nights in a row.

We spent the evening eating, drinking, and even survived playing a game of Monopoly together. The Dillon family was a blast to be around, and it became a Christmas forever lodged in my memory.

Kate and I rang in the New Year together at the brewery with her family. Of course, I wanted more, but standing behind her and wrapping her in my arms felt like enough for me that night. I knew the following year would be even better with her being such an integral part of my life.

Our chaperone dates continued.

We tried to switch it up, making sure we didn't do the same things every time we went out, even though our small town had limited options. Sometimes we would go back to the meeting space at the brewery, while other times, we just hung out at the bar while she worked.

We did more movie nights, both at her house and mine. Seth came with her, and as expected, always fell asleep before the movie credits rolled.

Kate and I also went on a couple of double dates with her parents. Sometimes they would sit at the booth with us, and other times they would sit a couple of tables away, giving us some privacy. Slowly but surely, it felt like we were starting to have a more normal relationship.

The cold weather finally broke towards the end of February, and spending the day outside became bearable. Desperate to get out of the house and enjoy the nice weather, Kate, Seth, and I made a trip to the local state park for a short hike through the woods.

We followed the precut path that weaved through the dense forest alongside a snowy stream and eventually found ourselves at the base of a forty-foot-tall waterfall. Ice had formed on the outside of the fall, allowing the water beneath to rush into the shallow pool below.

Seth ventured over to the fall, wanting to reach underneath and feel how thick the layer of ice was, while Kate and I sat down on a wooden bench that provided a view of the fall. She rested her head on my shoulder and wrapped her arm around mine, trying to warm herself up. Although I hadn't said it out loud yet, I recently admitted that I had fallen in love with her.

"Kate," I said quietly, turning my head to look at her.

"Yeah?" she mumbled from her position tucked in next to me.

When I didn't say anything back, she looked up at me, her eyes meeting mine. My left hand lifted and gently landed on her chin. I looked at her for a moment before lightly pulling her face close to mine.

My other hand stayed in my lap with her wrapped around my arm. Her eyebrows slightly raised in the middle, and she allowed her lips to open a sliver as her eyes gave me the look of, "it's okay."

With her face only inches from mine, I slowly eased the rest of the way. Finally, our lips met, and I felt Kates's grip slightly increase on my arm. After a moment, the rigid feeling faded, and she kissed me back.

Even though I wanted to push my tongue in her mouth, I held back, leaving my lips on hers loosely as I rubbed my hand on her cheek. When I pulled away, I sat back in my seat and smiled as I looked at her.

She quickly locked onto my eyes, and I saw a slight grin appear on her face before she redirected her eyes, moving them around in front of us, avoiding eye contact after our kiss. Finally, she relaxed and returned her head to its resting place on my shoulder.

"Was that okay?" I asked

"It was perfect," she replied, cuddling closer to me.

After a couple of weeks, our kissing slowly progressed, and it got to where every time we were alone, we found ourselves making out like high school kids. Her lips matched with mine felt right, but I silently kept craving more of her.

When my lips pressed against hers, my hands wanted to be all over her, not missing one inch of her body. The urge to take her shirt off and feel her bare skin on mine and finally be able to rub my hands across the feather tattoo on her lower back always slipped into my mind. I wanted it all, but I was patient and desperately hoped we would eventually get there.

One warm Saturday, I went over to the Dillon's house for an early evening cookout. As usual, Ryan invited me out to the grill to join him as he cooked the meat.

"Ryan," I said, stealing his attention away from the burgers in front of him, "I have a question for you, and feel free to tell me, no, but I hope you don't."

"Go on," he said, crossing his arms and fixating his glare at me with an intrigued look on his face.

"If she's okay with it, I'd like your permission to take Kate out on a real date," I paused, "alone."

He just looked at me for a moment, providing me with no hint as to what his answer might be. He flipped the steak and closed the lid of the grill, turning his body square to face mine.

"She's a grown woman and can make her own choices. We kind of just kept this overwatch thing because we thought that it was what she wanted. Maybe it isn't anymore, though. So, if she's okay with it, I'm okay with it," he finally answered.

"Thank you," I replied.

We ate our dinner together. Then I started a fire, and Kate and I sat outside by the blaze while we cuddled up and talked while enjoying the evening being together. I loved sitting next to her and watching her smile and ramble as the flames illuminated her face.

When I got home that night, I sent her a text.

"I'd like to take you out on Saturday to that new steakhouse that just opened if you wanna go," I stated, knowing her dad and Seth were working that night.

"I can't, my dad and Seth are working, but you can come over if you want," she said as expected.

"I talked to your dad, and he said if it was okay with you, we could start going out just the two of us," I replied.

She didn't respond for a couple of minutes, and I stayed seated on my couch, anxiously awaiting her response.

"Okay, let's do it," she finally responded.

"I'm going to call this our first date then," I responded.

"Well then, just so you know, I don't kiss on the first date," she added playfully.

For the first time in a while, I felt overly worried about what I would wear. The place was supposedly nice, so I opted to wear what people often referred to as Montana Casual; a pair of dark brown Kuhl pants and a black polo. For the occasion, I even trimmed up my beard and brushed my hair nicely, surprisingly not donning a baseball cap.

As discussed, I drove over to her house to pick Kate up at five on the dot, only to see Ryan standing alone in the driveway and waiting for me when I pulled up. He had moved things around on his schedule, passing off his shift at the bar just in case his baby girl needed him.

He often waved and gave the subtle appearance of being happy to see me, but the face I saw showed the classic dad scowl he likely used on Kate's high school boyfriends.

"I'm trusting you," he said, pointing a finger hard at me when I met him in the driveway.

"You know I'll take care of her," I assured him, patting the Smith and Wesson Bodyguard I had concealed in my waistband.

"I know you will," he said, placing a hand on my back, guiding me towards the house.

Kate stood near the bar in the kitchen talking to her mom. Upon hearing the door open, they stopped their conversation as both the women directed their attention towards me.

She looked stunning.

Kate pushed her lightly curled hair back, sending it to hang in loose waves down her back. I saw her wearing her classic look of cuffed jeans that hugged her thin frame, brown slip-on Keds, and a navy-blue shirt with a wide neck that showcased her collarbones.

A touch of eyeshadow and some eyeliner was easy to spot, causing her eyes to pop more than usual. As beautiful as she was with the makeup on, I appreciated that she always looked just as good without it.

"You look amazing," I complimented her as she blushed, shyly tucking her hair behind her ear.

"So do you," she echoed.

After a lengthy and private goodbye to her parents, Kate came over to me on the couch and nodded her head towards the door, saying, "let's go," out of the corner of her mouth. We sprinted out the front of the house, and I opened her door and helped her climb into my truck. For the first time, we were truly alone, and Kate didn't seem bothered by it at all.

The hostess sat us at a table in the back I specifically called ahead to reserve. Ever since being shown a plethora of different pictures of Ethan, Kate had started to let me be the one to sit facing the door and be her lookout.

The restaurant's romantic ambiance was somewhat dim, and I loved watching the shadows that danced around the booth as Kate's hands flipped around while we chatted.

We spent the night laughing together as we ate perfectly cooked steaks and split a bottle of aged red wine. The time alone was perfect without wondering if anyone else was nearby, hearing or watching us. She was all mine and comfortable in the moment.

Every time I saw the door open, my eyes briefly left Kate's, allowing me to do a quick scan. Not once did she not trust my watch or turn around to look herself. Kate seemed naturally comfortable and at ease being alone with me. The mood that moved across the table gave me the impression she was relieved she could just be a normal person on a regular date for the night.

She finally trusted me.

The newly opened restaurant ended up being a success, and someplace I would consider taking her again. Not even glancing to read the total, I paid our tab, and we made our way back to my truck, hand in hand.

For our first date alone, dinner was all Ryan was willing to let me have, so I started to take her home as soon as we finished. I was grateful for the time alone and didn't want to push my luck by asking for anything more.

"Hey, pull over," Kate said, halfway back to her house.

"But I said we would go home after diner," I explained.

"We can have a few more minutes alone," she replied.

I pulled off and veered into a gravel cutout in the road that overlooked one of the falls that gave the city its namesake. The infrastructure around the fall left the dammed section of the Missouri partially illuminated at night, leaving the water barely visible over the guardrail.

As I put the truck in park, Kate flipped up the center console of my bench seat, allowing her to slide over next to me. She placed her hands on both of my cheeks and just looked at me, smiling widely.

"Tonight was great. Thank you for taking this on and for asking my dad. I just wanted to tell you that before we were in my driveway with him peeping out the window," she said, quietly chuckling.

"Of course, I'm glad we finally got to do it," I replied.

She pulled my face to hers and kissed me while running her hand from my cheek down to the back of my neck. Then her hand grabbed mine and moved it down to the left side of her chest, and squeezed it slightly.

I took a moment, enjoying being able to touch somewhere new on her body. My hand stayed on her, moving from her breast up to her shoulder and back down. The moment took over, causing the fingers I had near her waist to start inching their way down in between her legs. She quickly realized my intent and grabbed my wrist, and moved it back up to her waist.

While kissing her, I smiled and said, "Sorry."

She didn't respond verbally but smiled for a moment beneath my lips and continued kissing me. I reverted to caressing her breast for a minute until she slowly pulled away from me and rested her head on the headrest behind her as she remained smiling in my direction.

"I love you Kate," I blurted out.

After a very short pause, Kate's smile grew slightly wider, and she responded, "I love you too Brandon."

I smiled back as a feeling of calm washed over me, relieved she didn't think it was too soon or too much. Telling her those three words had been weighing heavily on me, but suddenly, the moment just felt right.

Kate leaned back over towards me and put her lips back on mine. It wasn't a sexual kiss, but it was just one riddled with a passion that I couldn't explain.

Her lips released as she rested her forehead on mine, and I could feel her smiling as she placed her hands on my face. I grabbed her hand and felt my tires slip on the loose gravel as we pulled out and finished our drive back to her house. Kate sat on the bench seat next to me for the trip's duration, her hand on my thigh and her head on my shoulder.

I helped Kate out of the truck, and we walked together to the front door. While standing closely in the entryway for a moment, and I could see her smile in the glow of the porch light as we repeatedly talked about how much we enjoyed the night. Pushing the hair behind her ear, I kissed her goodnight, feeling overly satisfied with how our date had gone. As soon as Kate went to turn the front door handle, Ryan twisted the knob too, opening it for her.

"Everything go okay?" he asked, standing in the doorway with a refined look, his eyes glaring a hole into me.

"That it did, better than okay. Thank you again," I said, staring at Kate with a smile while I talked.

Based on his look, I gathered my overly enthusiastic answer must have come off as suspicious to Ryan.

"Well, goodnight," he said, opening up the door for Kate to come inside.

"Goodnight," I replied, turning around and heading to my truck alone.

I quickly started taking full advantage of my new freedom just to go over and pick Kate up for Saturday afternoon ice cream dates or for anything else we wanted to do, just the two of us. It was a relief to no longer only see her when it worked with someone else's schedule.

The weather started improving quickly as spring finally settled in. On the weekends, we often found ourselves going on walks and hikes in the woods, enjoying the break from the bitter cold. Being alone outside and sharing my love for the mountains with Kate and Tim became the highlight of my week.

I took her to the river a couple of times, trying to teach her how to fly fish. She gave it a go the first two trips but eventually decided it wasn't the hobby for her. Her favorite part about tagging along on my weekend explorations became setting up her chair and enjoying the warm sun beating down on her skin while I waded into the cold summer water.

With Kate being alone with me at my house more often, I had taken extra steps to make her and her family more comfortable. We both had our phones set so her parents could always see our locations, just to ease their minds and for extra security. I also took the time to get a wireless camera system installed around the house at Ryan's request. So, when the UPS man came to the door, I heard the same jingle that would ring throughout the Dillon home.

My mom planned a trip to come up and visit in the late spring. After she had fallen in love with that time of the year in Montana, she tried to make it up at least once a year when winter finally faded, but before the summer set in. She booked her annual trip to see me, but I knew it was primarily to meet the girl who occupied most of our conversations.

Her flight landed on time at the small airport, and I saw her eagerly running through the only terminal to see me in the same way she did when I got home from Afghanistan. She wrapped her arms around me, hugging me for a lengthy amount of time as her cheek rested in the middle of my chest.

As we drove, I droned on and on about all the new things I had been doing in Montana until she cut me off mid-sentence.

"I love you, son, and I love seeing you and hearing about your life. But, when do I get to meet the lovely Kate?" she asked.

"Tonight, mom, geez," I replied, hiding my excitement about getting to introduce the two.

The Dillon's had made up some burgers and invited us over for dinner to get the chance to meet my mom. Our parents meeting each other so early in our relationship may have been hasty, but since she visited so rarely, I didn't know when the next chance would be.

She cheered, all giddy like when I detailed out our plans for the evening. Being a classic southern woman, she demanded to freshen up and look her best before going to their house.

Briefly, I shared some details about Kate's past with my mom that I hadn't told her before. She didn't get the full story as I did, but she knew enough to understand the basics of the situation. With my mother's love for physical affection, I had to pre-warn her not to bombard Kate with hugs. I also asked her to pretend like she didn't know and not appear to treat her any differently.

After a quick stop at Albertsons to grab a bottle of wine, we headed over to have dinner with the Dillon's.

My mom strolled into the entryway of their home, instantly stunned at the decor and size and complimenting them multiple times. Being someone that didn't make a ton of money, she had always dreamed of owning a house of such magnitude.

Kate and my mom hit it off right away. Thankfully, as she sat on the couch and talked to her, she left out her usual routine of divulging all my embarrassing childhood stories. Instead, she repeatedly detailed how happy she was that I had met Kate after being so alone for so long, reminding her I'd been somewhat of a loner before.

My mom was overly kind, continuously telling her how sweet and pretty she was. A couple of times, I saw her unknowingly reach towards Kate then retract her hand when she remembered her feelings about being touched by someone unfamiliar.

Kate kept saying, "you're so welcome," smiling as she entertained my mother's speech of gratitude.

At one point, Kate even reached over and placed her hand on my mom's leg as they laughed about something together. Her forward act of affection shocked me, but I took it as a sign that she was becoming more comfortable with new people and was happy around my mom.

Claire and Ryan also loved getting to meet my mom. Since they had taken such a liking to me, I think they had finally accepted I was sticking around for the foreseeable future. The three of them sat at the table and discussed their shared love of red wine while my mom asked tons of questions about the brewing process.

We finally called it a night, and my mom said her goodbyes to the Dillon family, thanking them for their hospitality. She repeatedly thanked them specifically for taking me in during the holidays, saying she was grateful I wasn't a "sad single guy alone at home anymore."

In the truck, all my mom could do was talk about how perfect the night had been and how much she already loved the Dillon family. She very quickly got over her head, leaving me to tune her out when she started talking about marriage and grandbabies.

The rest of her visit went great. I had taken the week off work, allowing us to do all of the classic tourist stuff she loved about Montana. We drove out to West Glacier National Park and explored some of the smaller state parks. On a few of the local stops, Kate joined us, causing my mom to fall more in love with her as the week went on.

Eventually, it was time for her to return to the Sunshine State. As we parted ways at the airport, she gave me some motherly wisdom about love.

"Brandon," she said, grabbing my hands.

"Yes, mother," I replied sarcastically.

She swatted me on the arm for my sarcasm.

"That girl is too sweet. I'm so glad you met her. It's awful what happened to her, but I know that you will always do right by her and take care of her. Don't let her go. I think she's worth it," she said.

"I know mom. I'm not letting her go," I replied reassuringly.

She waved goodbye, ascending the escalator to her terminal. There were tears in her eyes as she left her only child behind. But honestly, I figured she was probably just dreaming of the idea of grandkids again.

FIFTEEN

ENJOYING THE LAST bit of summer, we expanded our adventures and began visiting other towns around Montana, soaking in our chances to get some new experiences together. While visiting a local brewery, I picked up a map that detailed every Montana brewery across the state, and Kate and I decided to work towards filling it in.

I took her out rafting and exploring the rivers, and we climbed in and out of the mountains hiking with Kate's navigation skills guiding us. On occasion, she continued joining me at the river, working on her tan and keeping me company while I tried, and often failed, to pull in rainbow trout.

I would force Kate out of bed early on Saturday mornings, dragging her to the local farmer's market. After a couple of visits, Kate became a big fan of homemade soap, and both of our bathrooms had a small basket of them piling up.

As summer came to a close in early August, the evenings rapidly started to cool off again, causing the jackets to emerge from the back of the closet. Kate and I transitioned to doing more outdoors during the day while spending our evenings with the heat turned on indoors, watching movies, or playing games together. There was unspoken comfort and security in being tucked away in my house, monitored by a security system.

My permissions grew as time went on. What started as Kate allowing me to grab her breast had become permission to rub my hands all over her body. I took full use of it while trying not to cross any invisible boundaries and make her feel uncomfortable. I had worked so hard and waited so long, and I didn't want to ruin anything.

Once, it had gotten to us both throwing our shirts to the floor while we laid on the couch, passionately wrapped up kissing one other. I hoped that it would continue and result in her pants coming off as well, but a few minutes later, she backed up and appeared uncomfortable with her exposed skin.

Her sudden discomfort wasn't solely from her past trauma with Ethan but from her pregnancy that left visible stretchmarks zig-zagged across the lower half of her abdomen. When her shirt was off, she constantly used her hands and arms to try and cover her skin.

Not once had I thought of her stretch marks as ugly or even remotely a turn-off to me. Instead, I thought the scars served as one of the few memories she had of the son she never got the chance to watch grow up. So every chance I had, I tried to reassure Kate that everything about her was beyond perfect to me and that I loved her the way she was, stretch marks and all.

One movie night, I decided that we had waited long enough, it was time, and we couldn't wait any longer. Kate needed to watch Super Troopers.

When she arrived, I had two individual liters of cola, a bottle of syrup, and some poutine on the coffee table, ready for our movie night. A confused look spread across her face as she hung up her coat and saw the arrangement spread out on the coffee table.

"Don't worry. You'll understand soon," I explained.

About ten minutes into the movie, Kate silently grabbed the PlayStation controller and paused the movie. I watched her stand up and turn towards me before she sat down on my lap, facing me, with her legs straddling my hips.

With both hands, she grabbed my face and looked directly at me with a gaze that was still and quiet. The distinct look of gentle happiness that I had grown accustomed to seeing appeared to be missing.

"What's wrong? Is everything okay?" I asked.

"Everything's great," she said, a soft smile showing on her face.

"You don't look very happy," I responded.

"I love you," she said.

"I love you too?" I returned, getting more confused.

"I want you. I want to do this," she answered, rubbing her hand over the top of my head, pushing my hair back.

By "this," I assumed she meant sex.

Usually, I would have been overjoyed at the invitation, but at that moment, I felt nerves running through my body in the same way she likely did. Knowing my bedroom talents in the past had been well up to par, I wasn't worried she wouldn't enjoy it, but I worried that taking it to the next level would be detrimental to our relationship we worked so hard to craft.

It freaked me out that it scared me.

"Kate, it's okay. I love you," I said, trying to reassure her that we could wait.

"No, I don't want to wait anymore. I love you, and I want this. It's okay. I trust you, and I think I'm ready," she said, her eyes regaining their customary encouraging twinkle.

"Okay, but only if you're sure. Tell me if you don't want to, or if you want to stop, though," I said.

"I've thought about it a lot lately. I'm so sure, and I promise I will," she responded, her lips moving to mine.

We started kissing in a manner that was already familiar. Her soft lips moved naturally with mine, and her tongue smoothly found its way in and out of my mouth. I was comfortable with that part of the act, and I could tell by the loose feeling of her body she was too.

Finding my hands onto her hips that straddled my lap, I moved them up and down her torso, feeling the bones of her ribs rubbing the bottom of my palms. I brushed up the back of her shirt as I ran my finger along her spine, the excitement of grabbing more than her breast growing.

I wanted her bad.

For so long, I wanted her naked next to me, feeling her warm skin rubbing against mine as I felt up and down her entire body. My hands were both anxious and excited about being able to explore parts of her that I hadn't yet charted.

Her hands grew more comfortable on my body as we continued kissing. She moved in a random pattern from my face, down my shoulder blades, through my hair, and to the back of my neck while trying to find a comfortable place to rest.

Kate let go of me and pushed herself back. She crossed her wrists down at her waist and raised them, allowing her shirt to slip off over her head quickly. As she leaned back down to resume kissing me, I put my hand out to her chest, stopping her advance.

The soft glow from the kitchen light illuminated her from the side, allowing me to see almost all of her. Her hair hung down in front of her shoulder, and I brushed it to her back, trying to get the complete picture of her body unobscured. I took a moment to appreciate her small but well-rounded breasts, lightly rubbing my index finger along the black lace that crested her bra cups and working up the straps to her collar bone then back down again. As I came back down, she breathed harder than usual and opened her lips slightly.

My finger continued downwards, and I found myself thankful she had decided to wear a front clasped bra. Both of my hands joined at the hook and worked together to unlatch it gently.

Releasing from the middle, the bra sprung loose, exposing half of each breast. I placed the palms of my hands on top of Kate's shoulders and rubbed them down her chest. When I had both hands covering her, I paused for a minute and leaned forward as I gently kissed her cleavage.

At that point, Kate's arousal was visible. Her eyes were closed, and her head slightly tipped back as my hands worked my way over her body. My excitement was also noticeable, and Kate hadn't adjusted from where the bulge in my lap pushed on her inner thigh.

My hands continued outwards, her cross-back bra easily sliding off her shoulders and down her arms and finally landing on my legs. Kate made her way back down to me and began slowly resumed kissing my neck. I turned my head in enjoyment and let her have plenty of room to move her lips along my skin. I opened my mouth and breathed softly, signaling my pleasure.

As she brought her lips back to mine, she placed her hands on my shoulders and pulled me from my leaned-back position on the couch. Her lips parted from mine, and she put her hands at the base of my shirt. I saw her beautiful smile flash my way as she slid it over my head, and my top joined hers on the floor. I brought my lips to Kate's and placed one arm around her lower back while the other slid under her opposite thigh. With a good grasp on her body, I gently stood up and kept her with me in my arms, lips locked on mine.

Both of us topless, I carried her to my room, gently laying her on the bed. I kissed her body from a half-planked position, moving from her abdomen up to her lips and back down again. She gently ran her nails down my back and entangled one leg in mine. I scooted her up, allowing both of us to be entirely on the bed. Turning her with me, I laid down on my side next to her and took my lips from hers. For a moment, I held myself up and gazed at her while she opened her eyes and looked back at me with a comforting smile.

With my hand that wasn't squished beneath her, I brushed the stray hairs from her face as she closed her eyes and smiled. I grabbed her lower back, pulling her in towards me, and continued kissing her.

Laying on our sides, Kate scooted back closer to me and weaved her top leg over my bottom one. Her pelvis was touching mine, and she was ever so slightly rubbing against me, pushing into me a little more every time.

I felt Kate's fingers flirting with my waistband. She slid her pointer finger into the rim of my pants, and it glided sideways from my hip to just below my belly button. Once she had traced that area twice, her entire hand slid down into my pants and underwear.

Surprised by her slipping into my pants, I slightly flinched and moved upwards just an inch as she grabbed onto me. She returned her lips to mine, gently biting on my bottom lip. Ready for my turn, I put my hand on her exposed shoulder and lightly pushed it down onto the bed, causing her hand to slip out of my pants.

My hand moved all over her, rubbing every inch of her skin as her head moved backward, slightly digging into the bed as she enjoyed my touch. She made soft little moaning sounds as her breathing intensified. My hand found my way to her hip and then laid flat over her belly button.

I used two fingers to run back and forth at the edge of her jogger pants as I gazed up to Kate and saw her open her eyes and gently nod at me.

Taking my permission, I slid my hand from her stomach down into her pants. I moved around in her underwear, enjoying touching somewhere new on her body and causing her hips to move slightly upwards as she enjoyed the attention.

After a few minutes of Kate enjoying my hand in her pants, she moved hers to my face, pulling me to her lips. When we started kissing, Kate moved, causing my hand to slip out of her pants. She worked her hands downwards and put them in the edge of my waistband as she pulled and tried to get my shorts and underwear to slide off. I eagerly reached down to help her take off my pants, and once when I threw my clothes to the floor, I moved my hands to her waistline.

My hands grabbed the edges of her joggers, and her lips stopped moving, and she pushed back slightly and looked at me. There was no smile on her face as she stared up at me.

"I love you," she said faintly.

"I love you too, Kate," I whispered back.

Her hands moved down to mine on her waistline, with our gaze still locked on one another, and I wondered what would happen next. A few seconds later, she kissed me once and smiled as she pushed my hands downward, helping me slide her pants off.

We laid there for a minute together, fully exposed. My left elbow was tucked under me, allowing me to see Kate fully as she laid completely bare on her back. I looked at her body, admiring it up and down, and felt my love for her swelling up inside.

"Are you sure?" I asked, placing my hand on her stomach.

"I'm sure," she responded.

I quickly ripped open a condom and slid it on after fumbling with it for a minute. Then, with her permission, I climbed on top of her as she spread her legs for me. Finally, feeling like she had agreed enough times, I eased myself inside of her.

"Is this okay?" I questioned.

"It's perfect. Stop asking," she said with a smile and pulled me down to her, placing her lips on mine.

Kate's lips moved over to my neck as I continued loving her. The hands that had previously been stuck to my ribs wandered and moved their way from my back to my butt.

After a few minutes, I paused and pulled out of her for a short break. The pause was partly due to being overly excited at the moment, leaving me slightly winded. But, also because it felt so good, and I wanted her so bad, my body was trying to tell me it was time. But I craved more Kate, and I wasn't ready for it to be over.

Her hand moved from my side to my face, running across my beard gently. She pushed my hair that was starting to curl in front of my forehead back to the top of my head. A calm smile spread across her face that kept her teeth hidden as she just looked upwards at me.

Once my short break was over, I moved to center myself on top of her again, but Kate had other plans. She wrapped her fingers around my shoulder and placed her lips on mine as she rolled me onto my back.

She got on her knees over top of me, holding herself up by her palms. I wrapped my arm around her and pulled her down onto me, causing her body to stiffen involuntarily. In response, my grip around her released, and I took my hands off her body and laid them next to me. She propped herself up and looked at me with an awkward look on her face.

"Sorry, I'm sorry, I didn't mean to," she said, gently shaking her head.

"No, I shouldn't have pulled you like that. I'm sorry," I replied.

"It's okay, I promise," she responded, leaning downwards as her lips gently met mine again.

She stopped kissing me and positioned herself on top of me with a seductive smile that spread to her eyes. She situated herself, finding the right place, and I slid back inside of her. With her hands placed on my chest, she moved in a rhythmic motion as I watched her from below. Her eyes were closed, and her mouth was slightly open as small moans escaped it. I reached my hand up and grabbed her breasts, and began caressing them as she rode on top.

My hand made its way to her face as Kate laid herself down on me. She opened her eyes, looking into mine gently while continuing to move up and down. Moments later, her eyes closed as she buried her head on the pillow near my head. Her cadenced grinding sped up, and her breathing escalated. She mover her head and dug it into my chest, and my hand felt her back slightly arch as I felt her tighten around me. After a momentary pause, she sped back up, and her moaning grew louder. Her hand wrapped around the bottom of the back of my neck, and her face lifted and came in full view for me.

With her eyes closed and mouth slightly open, she held her breath for a second and then let out four loud gasps as she climaxed around me. I found myself incredibly turned on and grabbed tightly onto her hips. After a couple of deep thrusts inside of her, I found myself joining in on her orgasm.

Both fully satisfied, Kate pulled off me and laid beside me. My eyes were still closed from our moment of pure pleasure when she placed her lips on my cheek and gently kissed it. Her hand moved to me, and she played with the few hairs that popped out of my chest.

We laid there for almost an hour, both fully exposed and ignoring the outside world around us. During that time, I took my hands and rubbed them all over Kate's body while we chatted, trying to learn everything I could about it and her body.

As I explored her nakedness, I saw new scars I learned the origin of and tried to put my fingers on every freckle and mole she had. She allowed me to flip her over, and I kissed her back and finally got the chance to touch her tattoo all over.

"I got it in high school with my best friend. I got kind of sick of it for a while, but she had type one diabetes, and I lost her pretty suddenly a couple of years ago, so now I'm glad I have a piece of her with me," she told me as I ran my finger across the birds that were flying out of the feather.

While we laid there quietly, I couldn't help but wonder if she was just as happy at that moment as I was. The smile she wore and the gentle look in her eyes as she leaned in to kiss me hinted that she was. I could have laid there all night, holding her in my arms.

Sex had never been that amazing.

SIXTEEN

WE DIDN'T HAVE sex again for a couple of weeks, but it was just as incredible as the first time when we did. I loved Kate for her, and although the sex was nice, it wasn't necessary to me.

She became entirely comfortable with me touching her and all of the other physical acts we tried. As our relationship progressed and the sex happened more, the instances of her appearing tense when we found ourselves naked and alone quickly dwindled.

Kate was beautiful, and I wanted to make sure she never forgot that. So I tried to make her comfortable in her body with everything I did, trying to assure her she didn't need to feel ashamed by things like her stretch marks. I loved her, and they were a part of her.

I slowly started to introduce Kate to some of my friends. Most of the people that invited us over were military people or people from the base, so we didn't have to worry about her high school friends showing up and bringing up her past.

Every time we were out, she seemed just as cheery and bubbly as she did when working behind the bar. It was refreshing to see Kate start to finally let loose and have fun around people she barely knew. She deserved to be free and not have to feel held back by Ethan or the dark events of her past.

I felt good being the one that was fixing her from the inside.

After her first couple of friendly outings, Kate started branching out more and socializing with my friend's spouses, and girlfriends without me glued to her hip. After seeing it at a couple of cookouts, Kate had taken a liking to playing corn hole, and every time we were out, and boards were available, she challenged someone to a match.

No matter what we did, our dates always seemed to find a way to be fun as long as Kate was there with me. We just enjoyed being around each other, and there never seemed to be a dull moment between us. Kate was highly adventurous, and her inability to just sit on the couch and watch TV led to her always coming up with something new for us to try.

As the cold winter silently slipped into town, the business at the brewery slowed down quite a bit, and Kate found herself working there considerably less. However, her graphic design side-hustle had taken off, and she often had a full plate of commissions for artsy menus from restaurants across the entire state.

Kate always had someone with her whenever she was away from her parents' house, and I wasn't around. If she was at the brewery, Seth or Ryan was always there, at least in the building with her. I had also agreed to the spoken rule that she was also never to be left alone at my house.

I had fallen madly in love with Kate, and she had become my other half. I was willing to do whatever it took to help her, and her family never forget that she was safe and comfortable with me.

One night, after being at my house alone for a couple of hours, I looked at my watch and realized it was after eleven. I jumped up and started to get dressed in a hurry so I could take Kate home.

"Come back to bed," she said.

"It's almost midnight. Shouldn't we get you home?" I asked.

"I decided to start sleeping over here. I'm a grown woman," she responded. "If that's okay with you, of course?"

"Seriously? Of course it's okay," I said joyously, hopping back into bed and pulling her naked body close to mine.

Wrapping myself in Kate and keeping her warm in my chilly house while she curled up next to me and slowly fell asleep became my favorite nights of the week. Having her in my bed at night and waking up with her beside me just felt like the way life was meant to be.

When she would sleep over, we woke up before the sun, and Kate would whip up a fresh pot of coffee while I got ready for work. On my way in, I would drop her off at her house, leaving her in her parents' hands for the day.

When we weren't together, we would text back and forth like two high school kids. With all the new and exciting things to learn about Kate, I looked forward to seeing what the next thing I unearthed would be.

Just as the first snowstorm moved into the area, our first Thanksgiving together came and went. We celebrated just the two of us at home and made a classic holiday meal that ended up half-burnt, causing us to laugh and have a frozen pizza instead.

Again, I partook in the annual decorating of the bar with the Dillon Family. The blaring holiday music and boxes upon boxes of decorations that came out of the wickets helped the Christmas spirit set in for the second year in a row. That year, the best part was pulling Kate's body in close to me and kissing her under the mistletoe.

With all the time we spent together, Kate had accumulated almost one of every toiletry at my house. It didn't take long before my shower and bathroom countertop was overrun entirely with women's products, and I couldn't have been happier. After agreeing she was right, we went out and bought some fancy towels, allowing Kate not to feel like she was drying off with a shop rag anymore.

She also started to leave clothes over at my house that had quickly gathered on top of my dresser. I took the time to clear some room for her, hoping she would feel more at home and get her clothes out of the corners of my room.

Covering her eyes, I walked her into my room and only uncovered them when I had two empty drawers and half of the closet ready for her to move some stuff in. She turned around, and a grin spread across her face slowly as she thanked me.

For my birthday, Kate had gotten me a framed canvas of us on top of the ski resort mountain, the first photo we took together. Even though I thought it would be a mounted elk, it was quickly hung in the living room and was the first official thing ever to adorn my flat white walls.

As Christmas grew closer, I looked forward to spending the holidays with the family that adopted me. It had been a long year that proved somewhat tricky at times, but I was happy with where it ended up. In the beginning, there were plenty of instances where I got sick of always being around her family or asking for permission like Kate was a child. Even when I thought I was done feeling micromanaged, I couldn't imagine what things would be like without Kate.

That previous summer, Seth met a girl while out one night at a karaoke bar he had been seeing for a couple of months and brought her to Christmas that year. Courtney worked as a trauma nurse at the downtown hospital and was a single mom to an oddly tall eight-year-old boy.

After they met, Seth ended up spending the night, and early the following day, he had a curious little boy old asking what he was doing while Courtney was attempting to sneak him out the back door. They kept seeing each other, and their quirky personalities seemed to be a good fit for one another. Courtney was genuinely friendly and appeared more than capable of putting up with Seth's and all of his various shenanigans.

Seth and I had become pretty good friends. If Kate was out of town or busy and I found myself bored, Seth and I would often spend time together, doing something just the two of us. We would go to trivia nights or just hang out at the bar, sharing some beers and having guy time.

After inviting him, Seth had even started tagging along on guys' night. All the guys in our group liked Seth and generously welcomed him into the fold. Seth's one rule was that if he was coming out with the crew, there was no way they were going to his family's bar.

Kate and I enjoyed going on double dates with Seth and Courtney. They liked many of the same places that we did, and it was nice to go out with someone new. I loved sitting at the table and watching Kate's bubbly personality shine as she talked to Courtney, and I could see she was happy to have found a girlfriend to laugh and joke with.

As we made our way out to the car after a group dinner one night, Kate debated if she was going home with Seth or me. In the end, she chose to go with her brother, defending her decision by saying she needed to get some clean clothes.

While lying in bed alone, I decided I was ready to ask Kate to take the next step in our relationship. I wanted nothing more than her to move in with me and have my house become ours. I didn't want to come home any other nights to a bed without her.

Popping into the bar one afternoon when I knew Ryan was in and Kate was home working on a project with her mom, I went back to the office to try to talk to him. I said hi to Luke at the bar when I passed by with my fists nervously clenched and stood at the cracked door for a moment before finally knocking.

Ryan yelled, "come in," from his desk, and I pushed the door all the way open and casually strolled in, trying to abandon my nerves.

When I broke the threshold, I found Seth also in the room, sitting at the adjacent desk with his feet kicked up, tapping away on his phone. Seth looked up and shot me a curious look. Unsure what I was doing there, he quickly said, "Hey," then directed his attention back to his phone screen.

"What can we help you with, sir?" Seth asked sarcastically in a deep, manufactured voice.

I quietly chuckled before turning my attention to the other side of the room and looking at Ryan.

"Mr. Dillon, could I talk to you for a second?" I asked.

"If you call me Ryan, you can," he responded, still not looking up from his screen.

"Ryan, can I talk to you for a second?" I rephrased.

"Sure, what's up?" he asked, finally giving me his full attention.

"Could I talk to just you, like in private?" I asked.

Silently, he stood and headed towards the taproom while motioning for me to follow him. I looked over at Seth, who winked at me and gave me two thumbs up as I followed his dad out of the office.

"Beer?" he asked over his shoulder as we walked to the bar.

"Sure," I responded, pulling up a barstool.

"Go take a break," Ryan told Luke.

"Aye aye," Luke responded with a half salute to Ryan and a nod towards me as he walked away. Ryan made his way to the tap, and knowing my favorite of their brews, poured me a pint of Lip Ripper. My nerves were slightly growing as I prepared to ask the man who kept his daughter so close and protected for so long if she could now leave his zone of protection to come live with me.

He set my beer down on the counter, not removing the hand he had tightly wrapped around it. When I realized he hadn't let the glass go, I looked at him and saw his gaze directed straight at me.

"No," he said, shaking his head.

His hand remained locked on my beer, his eyes fixated on mine as I searched for my response. My face twisted into a look of confusion.

"I haven't even asked my question yet," I thought.

I looked at him for a moment before finally speaking up, "No?"

"Not yet," he quickly responded, "I'm not saying no forever, but I am saying no for right now. I appreciate you coming to ask me, though, I really do, but I want you to wait a little longer," he said, finally releasing his death grip on my beer and stepping back.

"A little longer for what?" I asked.

"Before you ask my daughter to marry you," he responded, furrowing his brows in confusion.

I took a sip of my beer and chuckled.

"Well, I'm glad to know it isn't a no answer forever. And I would come and ask you that first, but no, that's not what I came here to ask," I replied.

"Ah, well, that's good to know. I did feel just a little bad about saying no. Alright then, what's on your mind, kid?" he responded.

"I love Kate, and I love having her around. So, I came here to ask you if it would be okay for me to ask her to move in with me," I responded. "Full time."

He didn't respond as quickly as I had hoped but looked at me while he sipped his beer for a moment, contemplating his response to my question. While he thought, the bell chimed, causing us both to turn our heads in the direction of the singing door.

"Hang on," he said, moving over to the computer to help the new customer.

His demeanor quickly changed from the stern father's look he had with me to a cheerful customer service manner as he served the new patron.

"Saved by the bell," I thought as I sat there, drinking my beer in large gulps while worrying about what his response would be.

After he had expertly poured the new customer a beer and started his tab, he came back over to my end of the bar and put the heels of his hands on the bar, placing his weight partially on them. He looked at me for a moment, glaring a hole into me. My eyes darted around a little, uncomfortable with just staring back at him.

"You looked when the bell went off," he stated.

"I did," I responded confidently.

"And you still have all those alarms and cameras?" he questioned.

"I do," I answered.

He looked down at the ground and thought for another moment as he shifted his position and leaned against the wall as he crossed his arms.

"Alright," he finally answered, "you have my blessing."

"Tha.." I started to say when he leaned forward and put both hands on the edge of the bar again, placing himself roughly six inches from my face.

"But I swear to God, you better not let anything happen to my baby girl. Because if you do, I'll have two men on my shit list, you got it?" he whispered to me threateningly.

My voice slightly cracked when I responded, "Got it."

At my response, Ryan backed away from the bar and moved into a less intimidating position against the wall.

"Thanks," I added.

"You're welcome," he said, raising his empty glass towards me, "Refill?" he offered.

Although I still had a third of my beer left and was unsure I wanted another, I felt obligated to have a second.

"Sure, why not," I answered.

I decided to go the simple direct route and flat out ask her to move in, no cute gesture or game, just simple and easy. I went down to the local hardware store and got a key made especially for her.

That night, Kate came over for dinner, and we ordered some pizza.

We sat in the kitchen and talked about Christmas the following week. I regretted not paying for my mom to come to spend the holiday with us, but I had thought about it too late, and she hated the Montana winter cold anyway.

After dinner, we enjoyed some time watching TV together. While we were sitting on the couch watching an episode of our new show Dexter, I reached over and grabbed the tiny box I had placed her key inside.

After I thought about it for a minute, I put the case back on the end table, deciding to just casually bring it up the idea of moving in together later to see what she felt before I asked.

When we finished with TV for the night, Kate kissed me on the cheek, telling me she would sleep over. We brushed our teeth and got ready for bed in our usual fashion, but when we climbed under the sheets, Kate rolled over to me and started kissing on my neck. Before I knew it, I was on my side facing her, enjoying her lips on mine as my hands ran all over her body.

Kate nuzzled her body in close to me as she drew random patterns on my chest with her index finger.

"Move in with me," I blurted out as my finger traced her hip.

She stopped her tracing and sat up on her inside arm. I turned further onto my side to look at her, hoping to get a better read on her thinking. The moonlight shone in from the window, reflecting off her face, showing me a broad smile on her face. Her eyes looked into mine as she placed the hand closest to me up to my face.

"Yes," she said.

I rolled my eyes in relief and let out a loud sigh, grabbing her and pulling her body on top of me. She started laughing as I flashed a goofy smile at her and kissed her repeatedly, beyond happy she had accepted. I stopped and gazed at her smile. Brushing the hair from her eyes, I moved my hand to the back of her neck and pulled her face in towards me as I began kissing her.

After a moment, I stopped my lips, guiding her to my side with my arm wrapped around her. She snuggled up beside my body and closed her eyes. A few minutes later, Kate started to breathe harder as though she had fallen asleep while I laid there awake, looking up at the ceiling. At that moment, it felt impossible that I could have been any happier. Kate was my dream girl, and her moving in was the first step in finally making her mine.

SEVENTEEN

WITH CHRISTMAS BEING just days away, Kate and I decided to wait until after the holidays to get her larger furniture moved from her parent's house to ours. When she told Claire and Ryan I asked her to move in with me, her mom pulled her into a hug, expressing her excitement.

Ryan said, "I'm happy for you," then looked over her shoulder in my direction, giving me a stern nod.

"Hey, I got one kid out of the house for you. You're welcome," I said internally with a subtle chuckle.

While we unpacked her never-ending pile of boxes, we found things that we didn't need duplicates of and items I never realized had been missing from my life.

"What the heck is this?" I asked as I waved an odd object from the kitchen box in the air.

"It's a thingy. It separates the egg white from the yolk," she said with a smile, causing me to laugh and toss in the drawer alongside the other gadgets we would never use.

She went around subtly adding her feminine touch to the place, and for the first time, I had a top sheet on my bed and not just a well-loved comforter.

We spent Christmas the same as it was the year before. Kate took the time to make my traditional potato soup from my mom's recipe instead of buying it premade from Sam's. She did a great job, and to also keep her traditions alive, we had the soup for lunch and planned to have our fried rice and potsticker dinner with her parents.

When we arrived at the Dillon house that night, there was a fresh dusting of snow that had just begun to fall. Kate grabbed my hand and pulled me back before I opened the front door. I followed her finger, which pointed upwards, and saw a sprig of mistletoe that was once fresh but had since died from the cold and had an icicle hanging off it. I pulled Kate towards me and kissed her, holding her close.

We entered the warm, sweet-smelling home with Tim leading the way and found everyone already half-drunk in the kitchen, cheering with excitement to see us. Seth had his arm draped around Courtney, and they were both holding a heavily poured glass of wine. Her son Levi was sunk into the plush leather couch, sucked into playing his handheld video game with a look on his face that clearly said, "I don't want to be here."

Claire and Ryan were singing in harmony to the music as they worked on the family dinner in ugly Christmas sweaters while Luke sat at the bar with them, chatting away about who knows what.

Luke left before dinner to have a Christmas Eve meal with his parents before going out to party with friends, and the rest of us sat down to eat the classic Asian-inspired feast that the Dillon's loved. Levi wasn't interested in the food and spent most of the time just pushing things around on his plate.

I began to picture Kate and me there, sitting in the same room with our kids, finally filling more of the seats the massive table could hold. It hadn't been something we had discussed, but I could see myself having all of that with her when I had never seen it with anyone else.

Snapping back to reality, I helped clear the table.

Once we cleaned up the meal, Claire motioned me over to the fridge and showed me the fresh chocolate chip cookie dough she had been chilling in a large metal bowl. Calling out to Seth, I invited him to join Kate and me in the kitchen and bring Levi to help with cookies, hoping it would brighten the kid's sour mood.

He took my advice and was finally able to get Levi unglued from his video game. They joined us in the kitchen, and Kate threw a small chunk of cookie dough at the kid that missed his hand and landed on the counter, causing him to chuckle subtly. Finally, we coaxed a laugh out of him as he ate the ball before joining in on the holiday tradition.

Eventually, everyone except Claire and Ryan joined in on the cookie rolling, and we prepped five sheets of homemade dough for the oven. Levi had gotten into the spirit and finally had fun dancing to Christmas tunes in the living room with his mom.

Kate snuggled up next to me on the couch for the annual playing of Christmas Vacation with an extra spiked hard cider in hand. It meant a lot to me that her family had taken my traditions and added them to theirs.

When the movie was over, Seth was not surprisingly asleep. Courtney covered him up with a blanket before thanking the Dillon's and scooping up Levi to head home. With Seth finally alone on the couch, Tim jumped up and made himself comfortable at his feet.

I stood up, ready to leave, when Kate asked, "Die Hard?"

"How about we go back to our house and watch it this year?" I suggested, sticking my hand out to help her off the couch.

We made our way home with a bag of fresh-baked cookies and watched Die Hard on our couch together, falling asleep together before it was over.

That year under the tree, laid some new fishing gear Kate had gotten me. I was so wrapped up in spending my summer with Kate I hadn't spent as much time in the creeks as I would have liked, leading me to realize how much I had also neglected hunting that year. Since she often complained I didn't knock the mud or snow off my shoes well enough, I got her a set of laser-cut floor mats for her truck so she wouldn't have to complain about my mess anymore.

Kate and I rang in the New Year at the brewery again, and I felt beyond happy that I was able to place my lips on hers when the clock struck midnight.

Throughout January, Seth, Ryan, and I worked to get all of Kate's bigger stuff over to my house and out of storage where it had been since she moved back from Ohio. With somewhere to finally put it all, we picked through her unit, trying to find the things we needed.

Kate being there made our house feel like a home.

She started by hanging some generic farmhouse decorations on the walls and suggesting we light a ceremonial fire to burn the ratted mat I had outside our back door. It wasn't a fancy house by any means, but it was ours, with her touches finally making it feel like a home.

For the rest of the winter, we spent a lot of time together in the house. On the weekdays, I was busy with work, fielding calls, and closing work orders from all the people who never stopped complaining about the temperatures in their office. On the colder weekends, Kate and I found things to do around the house, trying to keep ourselves busy while stuck indoors. She dove deep into home improvement projects and constantly tried to find something to do. She often encouraged me to get on YouTube and learn some techniques to spruce the place up.

Over the season, we painted the flat white living room a soft grey, updated the lighting and mirror in the bathroom, and ripped out the dingy carpets, replacing them with walnut knock-off laminate flooring. Kate didn't say anything about the wine stains still lightly seeped into the padding in the living room as we pulled the carpet from the nail boards beneath.

My dilapidated home was quickly being updated into something that looked like less of a bachelor pad every day. The house had desperately needed the update, and her ideas ended up making a big difference in its appearance.

The more we did around the house, the more I thought maybe one day we would sell it in the hopes of getting something bigger together. The place was good for just the two of us, but it lacked much room for anything or anyone else. Forever with Kate was something that had begun to manifest in my mind, leaving me finding myself hoping that our future would bring about a need for a house with more rooms.

One brutally cold February weekend, I got a call from Ryan while on the job. Since he usually just texted me, it was surprising to see him calling me out of the blue. Worried something was wrong with Kate, I quickly answered.

"Hey Ryan, what's up?" I asked.

"Hey Brandon, if you can, I need your expertise. I just got to the brewery, and it's gotta be fifty degrees in here," he said.

"Okay, I'll take lunch in about thirty and head over," I responded.

I took my lunch early, grabbing my bag of personal tools and heading over to the brewery. Ryan went to the back with me, directing me to the location of the furnace. As we rounded the back corner of the brew room, I heard a high-pitched squeal coming from the closet.

"I can tell you right now. It's probably your belt," I diagnosed.

"Can you fix it?" he asked.

"Of course I can," I responded.

I jotted down a list of things for him to grab, sending him to the store so I could start getting to the belt to make the repairs. I got to work, took pieces off, and made other checks to ensure the fix would be simple.

When he returned with all the needed parts, we worked together to replace the belt while I taught him some basic fixes. Over the past year and some change, Ryan and I had become close, so I didn't mind spending alone time with him.

The overall concept of growing up with no male influence had just become normal to me, and I hadn't thought of it any other way. It was just my mom and me, and we got by, forging a special bond. She tried to do all the things my dad would have done and was always trying to make the extra effort to help me feel like someone wasn't missing from my upbringing. With Ryan around, he quickly became like a father figure to me. He showed me a few simple fixes on cars and taught me about the brewing process. In turn, I took the chance to teach him some things about fishing and basic HVAC skills.

When I was out of the house for work or any other reason, Kate was still going to the bar or her parents' house so that she wouldn't be alone.

"You still want to go home all of the time or to the brewery. Do you not feel safe here alone?" I asked.

"It's not that," she responded, looking down at the ground. "It's not that I don't feel safe at home. I just haven't been alone in years. It still feels weird to me. I'm sorry," she answered.

"Kate, it's fine, I understand that, and you don't have to apologize. I just want to make sure you feel safe in our home, even if I'm not there. I don't want you to feel like you moved in with me, and it's not the same fortress your parents had you protected with. But not wanting to be alone, I get that," I replied.

"I'll get there, I promise," she replied, wiping away her sad look and replacing it with a happy one.

"You're more than welcome. I'd do anything for you," I said, taking her into my arms and holding her close.

Finally, the cool weather dissipated slightly, making way for some warmer weekends. We took the mild days as our chance to get outdoors and tried some short hikes nearby or walked around some local small towns, enjoying the short breaks from the painful cold.

I loved that Kate and I could always find things to do together that we both enjoyed. Sometimes living in such a cold climate was challenging and forced you to stay indoors, but knowing I could be snowed in with Kate and still have fun made it worthwhile.

The sex between us had remained amazing, and Kate had become completely comfortable with me handling her body. She no longer had any shyness and was an open book when it came to telling me what she did and didn't like.

It seemed like we forgot the Ethan problem with all the fun of moving in together and getting to know one another. The constant worry of him being somewhere in the world was no longer in the forefront of our minds, enabling us to live a more relaxed life. There were many times I no longer checked places before we went in, and half the time when the doorbell chimed, I just assumed it was a delivery person and didn't even bother to look at the camera. We had become complacent and hadn't even realized it.

While sitting at the bar one night chatting with Seth while Kate worked, I glanced across the crowded taproom and saw her talking to a male customer. The white button-up shirt he wore hung tight to his body that appeared to be we built, contrasting against the summer tan he still kept. While she talked to him, he stared at her and smiled, flashing his shiny white teeth in her direction.

I couldn't help but notice the extra-large smile she had on her face while she stood there, listening to him talk. She seemed comfortable around him and didn't appear to be standoffish the way she had been when she first met me. She said something to him that was inaudible to me, and he busted out in a loud laugh that Kate then joined.

The two of them must have stood there and talked for close to fifteen minutes when I looked down, realizing my glass had run dry.

"Hey, I'm gonna go home. Will you bring her home tonight?" I asked Seth, motioning my hand towards Kate.

"Yeah, you good?" he asked.

"Yeah, I'm good," I lied. "Just tired."

I wasn't good, though. As I walked out to the truck, I felt irritated that Kate was blatantly flirting with someone right in front of me. Being the jealous guy had never been a role I played, but there I was, finding myself upset at the way she had become lost in conversation with a stranger. When I was almost at my truck, I heard hurried footsteps coming up from behind me.

"Brandon, wait," I heard her voice calling.

I turned around and saw Kate about ten feet from me.

"I thought I was going to ride home with you? Why did you leave?" she asked.

I rubbed my head from my forehead to my temple before jutting my hand out towards her.

"Oh, I don't know, maybe because you spent the last twenty minutes flirting with some stranger right in front of me. It took you months to even let me touch you, and now you're getting all close-up and chatting it up with some new guy? What the hell, Kate?" I demanded.

I looked away for a second and let out a loud sigh as I shook my head gently, my volume growing when I continued talking.

"How do you think that makes me feel Kate, you're my girlfriend, and I was the one that fixed you, and look at you now! Do you just always come to the bar and flirt with the guys that are buying drinks?" I asked, both my hands moving like Kate's did when she talked.

She just looked at me for a second, silently gathering her defense internally. I watched the anger boil up in her face as she stared at me. Over her shoulder, I could see Seth coming towards her after hearing me raise my voice. She raised her hand behind her, motioning for him to back off.

"Not that I should be even remotely defending myself, but I can't believe you just said those things to me. Fixed me? What the hell? I didn't need you to fix me, so number one, screw you, and you know that guy, Kurt, yeah, we went to high school together, and he just lost his wife three years ago to breast cancer. She and I had lost touch, but we were best friends when we were in school, and now he's a single dad to two kids and moving to Arizona next month because he can't make it here on his own anymore. So we were just enjoying sharing funny stories about Christa," she explained.

"Kate…" I started to say as I slumped my shoulders down in defeat when she stuck her hand up at me, shutting me up.

"No, and the fact that you would ever say things like that to me is beyond disappointing. I seriously can't believe you right now," she continued, shaking her head at me.

My head hung downwards in disappointment, and my mouth remained shut as Kate stood there on the sidewalk, scolding me. She was right, and I knew it. Seth walked up just as Kate was finishing her lecture, her hands calmly returning to her side.

"Everything okay here?" Seth asked with wide eyes looking between us.

Kate just stared at me with a blank expression before responding to her brother.

"Everything's fine," she answered, "Let's go back."

"Kate, I'm sorry," I blurted out as she turned to walk away.

She quickly turned back around to me.

"Don't wait up for me. If I don't go home with some random guy from the bar like you seem to think I would, I'll be sleeping at my parents' house tonight," she replied loudly, storming off.

"Kate, please," I pleaded as she kept on walking.

"Fix me? Wow," I heard her say under her breath.

Seth turned around and shrugged his shoulders at me before following his sister back to the bar.

I drove home feeling like an idiot. My behavior had been unacceptable, and I instantly regretted the things I said to her. I trusted Kate completely, and I never thought she would do anything to hurt me or cheat on me. I just worried about her too much.

When I got home, I sent her a text and apologized.

No response.

And then I sent three more, detailing my stupidity and begging her to forgive me and come home.

I got no response to any of them.

I decided I would just call her and apologize over the phone, but it went straight to her voicemail. A few minutes later, my phone pinged, and I scrambled to grab it.

"Hey man, sorry, but I'd just give her some time to cool off. She gets pretty wigged out when people yell at her," Seth texted.

I shouldn't have said any of it, but I definitely shouldn't have lost my cool and raised my voice at her. Instead, I accepted her wishes and put my phone away for the night.

I finally climbed into bed alone and just laid there on my back while I looked at the ceiling. It had been a while since my house had felt so empty and alone. When I lived on my own, the room never had the growing heavy air of loneliness like someone was missing.

For two whole days, I didn't hear from Kate. I thought about going over to her parent's house but didn't, deciding she would let me know when she was ready to talk.

It was a hard two days, and I missed her like crazy. When she wasn't around, my eyes were opened to how utterly important she had become to me. She was my person and everything to me, and not just sending her a text to tell her I loved her or asking her about her day was killing me.

Day three was enough for me. I wanted to clear the air and get her back. I shot her a text and didn't try to apologize or make excuses. I just asked her if we could talk. She didn't text me back right away, but thankfully, she agreed to meet me when she did. After four nights of sleeping without her or talking to her, we met up at the brewery.

The bell echoed off of every wall when I walked into the empty taproom. Kate looked over my way, missing the smile and bright eyes she usually gave me. After a quick scan, I realized she was the only one around, and no one would be there to witness her yelling at me.

With Kate's favorite latte in hand as an apology token, I made my way over to the table where she was sitting. She had her hands folded on the table while her leg bounced impatiently underneath. She glared at me, remaining dedicated to her silence. She was still upset, and I knew I wanted to do whatever it took to make things right with her. So I started the conversation, talking at a fast pace to spit all my words out.

"I'm so sorry, Kate. That was so stupid of me, and I can't believe I did it. I was a complete jerk, and I overreacted to absolutely nothing. I think the world of you, and I know you would never do anything to hurt me. I should have just asked, and again, I'm so sorry. I promise you it won't happen again," I said.

She glared at me across the table for a moment, locking her eyes on me and remaining quiet.

After taking a sip of her latte, she finally spoke, "Thank you for your apology. What you said was insulting and disrespectful. It made me feel like you don't trust me, and that's a problem with me. I don't have a lot of friends, but it's nice when I get to see the few I do have."

"I know, and I'm sorry. I love you, Kate. I promise I trust you completely," I said, sounding like I was begging.

"But fix me? Is that what this is? Do you just want to fix me? I'm like a project to you?" she asked.

"God, no, not at all. I never saw you as something to fix, but someone I wanted to help put back together after everything you went through. I didn't mean for it to come off like that," I defended.

Wanting to touch her, I reached towards her hands, hoping to hold them as I recited my apology, but she pulled away and placed them in her lap.

She looked over at me, "I hate bringing him up, but I've been in a relationship with someone that was always jealous. Over time I realized I lost all my friends because of how he treated me when I chose to hang out with them and not him. I'm not saying you will, but I'm not going through that again," she stated.

"I know, Kate, and I swear I will never be like that. I'm sorry for how I acted, and I promise it will never happen again," I responded, hoping she would hear the sincerity in my words.

"Okay, I accept your apology," she said.

With a sigh of relief, I got up and walked to her side of the table.

"Can I hug you now?" I asked, holding out my arms out for her.

She looked at me for a moment, then finally showed a soft smile in my direction.

"I suppose," she answered, standing up and stepping into my embrace.

I pulled her in close and rested my chin on her head. As I held her in my arms, I breathed in the fragrance of her coconut shampoo, something I hadn't even realized I had missed about her until that moment.

"I missed you," I whispered to her.

"I missed you too," she replied.

I pushed her out and held her by the shoulders at arm's length.

"I promise not to be a jealous jerk ever again, but you have to promise me something too," I said.

"What's that?" she asked, raising an eyebrow.

"The next time we get into a fight about something, no matter how stupid it is, I want you to promise me that you won't just leave and run off to your parents' house. We have a life together now, and we have to work out our problems together," I answered.

She thought for a moment, "deal," she answered as I pulled her back into my arms.

The following week, we ended up attending a going-away party for her friend Kurt and his kids. There were a couple of other people from high school at the house that Kate made sure to point out to me. They stared at her and whispered to one another a couple of times but never spoke to her. She walked around the party proudly and acted as though she didn't know half the room knew her story.

After a few minutes of joking, Kurt pulled me away from the crowd, saying he had something on his air conditioner he wanted me to look at, even though it was still a couple of months till his renters would need it.

"Hey man, is she doing okay?" he asked me when we were alone.

"Yeah, why?" I responded, unsure of how much he knew about Kate and her life.

"I know about the whole Ethan thing. Sadly he and I were best friends in school, and Christa and I heard about the situation and felt terrible Ethan ended up that way. I can imagine it's a sensitive topic, so I never wanted to ask Kate, and I don't know Seth that well, so I figured I'd just ask you," he said.

"Yeah, she's doing well. A lot better than she was when I first met her a year and a half ago," I responded as we walked back towards the house.

"Good, glad to hear that. You've got yourself a winner there. She's a great girl," he stated.

I looked across the yard and saw Kate talking and laughing on the enclosed back porch with Kurt's oldest daughter. She stood there in the same way she always did, looking beautiful and happy, and it was impossible to believe she had ever been hurt by someone she loved.

"She is. I'm very lucky," I said.

EIGHTEEN

FINALLY, summertime arrived in Great Falls, and we were taking every chance we could to enjoy the beautiful weather.

Late in the summer, I was inside having my morning cup of coffee and watching Kate play with Tim in the yard. Seeing her, entirely in love with my dog, I realized how much of a small family we had become in the almost two years we had been together.

Everything was going so well for us.

Since she had been with me, Kate had also started to become more comfortable around new people. I loved watching her blossom as she got back into the swing of having an everyday life that wasn't riddled with fear. She shook stranger's hands and was able to be herself even when she found herself in a large crowd.

Thinking about how happy our little family made me, a plan began brewing in the back of my mind that I would need a diamond ring to accomplish. Although it was still months from execution, I wanted to be prepared when the right time sprung upon us.

To make some extra money, I started taking pointless online college classes. The GI Bill I earned while on Active Duty paid for my courses while also providing me with a small stipend on the side that I was able to tuck away in the hopes of buying Kate a ring and getting her to agree on an elaborate international honeymoon.

In addition to earning extra money from my GI Bill, I started picking up some on-call work with a local HVAC company.

Occasionally, I would get pinged after hours or on the weekend with a request to go out and do some minor repairs. A couple of employees were on the phone tree, so if I was busy or didn't feel like it, I could pass on the job, handing the extra money off to the next person.

It was nice earning extra income since Kate had become fully committed to fixing the house up. Unfortunately, her projects weren't cheap, so I found myself dipping into my secret ring fund for her DIY ventures.

Continuing with the tradition of family labor, Kate found herself getting pretty busy at the bar helping out as the adults from the local small towns headed to Great Falls for one last trip to the city before the cool winter air returned. Ryan kept expecting the rush to die down, but the people just kept coming in for their handcrafted drafts. The bell rang off the hook as Kate kept on smiling, whisking herself behind the bar and doing her job effortlessly.

The one thing I didn't like about Kate working late nights at the brewery was falling asleep without her next to me. Ryan, Seth, and I had agreed that they would always make sure she got home safe if it would be a late night and I wasn't waiting up for her.

When she came home, I would feel her climb into bed with me, her cold arm laying across my chest as she curled up beside me to get warm under the covers. I would wake up in the morning, kiss her on the cheek, and then tiptoe around while I got ready, trying to stay quiet enough to let her catch up on her sleep.

I woke up to go to the bathroom and felt the bed next to me oddly still cold and empty. I patted around in the dark, feeling for her body, but felt no one there. I reached over and flipped on the light to see her side of the bed vacant. I grabbed my phone to check the time and saw it was after one in the morning, and the screen filled with notifications.

One Missed Call: Kate

Three Missed Calls: Seth

Six Missed Calls: Ryan

Two Text Messages: Kate

One Text Message: Claire

Two Text Messages: Ryan

I threw off the blanket in a hurry and grabbed whatever clothes my hands could get to first. I put the phone on speaker and instantly called Kate back while hurriedly dressing.

No answer.

I tried calling Ryan, then Seth, ignoring the text messages as I frantically tried to get ahold of someone in the Dillon family. On the third call, Seth finally answered his phone.

"Seth, what's going on?" I asked as I grabbed my keys and prepared to walk out of the door.

"Everything's okay, she's fine, but you should probably get down here," he said, not adding any more detail.

"On my way," I replied.

I grabbed my stuff and ran out of the house as fast as I could. Seth didn't tell me anything, and even though he reassured me she was okay, something had happened that alarmed the entire Dillon family.

The pedal hit the floor of my truck as I sped the seven miles to the brewery, running a red after a thorough check for cars. When I finally pulled onto the breweries street, I saw the flashing red and blue lights bouncing off the dark downtown walls from the three police cars parked directly in front of the building.

After slamming my truck door, I ran to the entrance of the bar, my heart racing. A young cop stood outside and saw me running towards the door. He put one hand out towards me and placed his other hand on the grip of his gun. I quickly stopped and raised both palms in his direction.

"Sir, can I help you?" he asked loudly.

"I need to get inside," I responded, still holding both hands up.

"Sir, this scene has been secured. I can't let you in," he replied.

My heart pounded harder at the word "scene." Was he saying this was a crime scene? Was something wrong with Kate?

"Scene?" I asked, "I need to get in there now." I shouted.

"Sir again, I cannot let you in. I need you to step back right now!" he said, escalating his voice more.

I didn't respond and just stayed in place, unsure of what to do. The officer removed his pistol from the holster and held it in his hand loosely by his side. His gaze remained locked on me as I stood there, trying to figure out how to get inside. My hands that were calmly in the air transformed into fists. It took everything I had not to throw this guy into the wall and go inside, but I knew better. Kate was in there, and I just wanted to be with her and know she was safe.

I loosened my grip, showing my palms again, and told the officer. "Okay, okay," I said with a more apparent sense of calm in my tone.

Keeping my hands up, I backtracked and walked back to my truck before fishing my phone out of my pocket. I quickly called Seth, and he didn't answer, and just as I went to call Ryan, Seth's return call was incoming.

"Hey," I said quickly.

"Hey are you coming?" he asked me.

"Yeah, I'm out front, but the cop wouldn't let me in," I detailed.

"Alright, I'll go out there," he said.

"Thanks, man," I responded and made my way back to the door.

"I'm sorry, sir. I didn't know," the officer said to me when I returned to the front of the brewery, and Seth let me in.

I brushed past him, paying him no attention as I made my way into the Dillon's brewery.

The bell chimed when we walked back in, and a huge relief washed over me when I saw Kate sitting in the back at a table with her parents. She looked to be all in one piece, as did the bar. There was no sign of any blood, bodies, or struggle. Since my mind had been playing every bad scenario repeatedly, I felt relieved seeing for myself that she was okay. She still had on the same green shorts and black shirt she wore when she left the house that morning, and her hair hung down tightly over her right shoulder, still perfectly braided.

As I hurried over to her, Kate jumped down from her high-top chair and met me halfway across the room. I outstretched my arms in her direction and firmly took her into my embrace.

I held her close while she nuzzled her head into my chest. I rubbed her from the top of her head down to her shoulders repeatedly, trying to hold back my tears.

I never wanted to let her go.

After kissing the top of her head multiple times, I grabbed her face by the cheeks and looked at her. Tears welled up in her eyes as she looked up at me.

"Talk to me, Kate. What happened? Are you okay?" I asked.

She stammered for a minute as she tried to find the right words to say to me. I could tell she was upset, and I prayed to God it wasn't Ethan.

After she took a couple of deep breaths, she withheld her tears and spoke, "Ethan was here," she gasped as her bottom lip quivered.

I pulled Kate back into me and held her close, "I'm so sorry," I whispered into her ear, directing my eyes towards Ryan, who nodded.

We just stood there alone in the middle of the taproom while I held Kate close to me. She pushed herself back from me and wiped her eyes clean before grabbing my hand and pulling me, guiding me over to the table where the officer was sitting with her parents. Kate sat down as I stood behind her with my hands on her shoulders.

The officer started speaking again, "Okay, thank you for your time, ma'am, that's all we need for tonight. We'll let you know if we hear anything else. Good to see you, Ryan," he said as he reached out, shaking Ryan's hand.

Kate asked me for a minute alone with her parents. From the bar, I watched them exchange a few words and even a laugh, ending with the three of them in a group hug.

"Are you ready to go?" she asked.

"Yeah, you're coming home with me?" I asked.

"That's where I live, isn't it?" Kate responded.

"Of course," I answered, relieved she wanted to come home and not go back to her parents.

"Good, take me home, and I'll tell you everything. But, my parents want Seth to come with us," she said.

I paused for a moment. I understood the desire to keep their daughter safe, but it made me feel inadequate when they did stuff like that. But I didn't know the whole situation, so I agreed to Seth coming along.

We went home and got ready for bed silently. Kate still hadn't told me much, causing my curiosity to continue to grow.

After Seth was all tucked in on the couch, with Tim curled at his feet, Kate and I went into our room. She sat down on the edge of the bed and put her hands in her lap, and her feet kicked slightly as they dangled.

"I'm sorry, I just wasn't ready to tell you until we were away and alone. There was so much going on, and you joined in right at the end. I wanted you to hear it from start to finish," she said.

I sat down on the floor in front of her, ready to hear the story.

NINETEEN

Kate

TWO WEEKS BEFORE Ethan showed up at the bar, I was home alone while Brandon was off at work. Sucked into the couch, I sat there, doodling away on menu ideas for some rich person's new sushi bar in Kalispell.

On the armrest of the couch, my phone buzzed.

I picked it up and flipped it over, looking to see what telemarketer I would get to hang up on. The hair on my arms stood up when I saw Ethan's grandmother's name scrolling across my screen.

A speedy debate raged in my head as I tried to decide if I should answer the call or not. For all I knew, it was Ethan calling me after he had stolen her phone or done something horrible to her. But remembering I had asked her to contact me about anything Ethan-related, I decided to answer it.

"Hello?" I asked shakily.

"Kate, it's Shannon Hall," she said in her decades of chain-smoking voice, washing a feeling of relief over me.

After a minute of small talk bantering, she spit out her news, finally getting to the point of her call.

"Ethan came by," she said.

My body instantly froze in place, silently trying to comprehend what she had said. After internalizing her words, my eyes shot to the front door and saw the deadbolt still secured.

Shannon detailed that he had just rolled into town and stopped in unannounced to see her. Being a nice Montana fall day, she had only the screen door closed, leaving the house door wide open to air out. She was on the couch watching TV when he casually strolled into her living room wearing a smile.

He immediately grabbed her phone from the coffee table and moved it out of her reach, hindering her ability to call anyone, and told her he just wanted to talk. He didn't offer any details about where he had been or what he had been doing the past couple of years. She asked, but he avoided the question, or his answers remained vague, but she noted he referred to himself as Mike once.

Overall, she described his appearance positively. His clothes appeared new and clean, and he had buzzed his hair down to the same length all around. He wore a smile the whole time and seemed to have a positive attitude and she never once felt threatened by his presence. He weaved together of the story of being back on all the medications and told her he had been stone-cold sober for almost six months.

They just sat there and talked for close to half an hour while she facilitated most of the conversation, trying to pull information out of him.

The most important thing she inquired about was his reasoning for coming back to town. Again he seemed to repeatedly dodge her question, saying "it's nothing," or "oh, don't worry about it." His lack of interest in providing answers worried her that something would eventually set him off if she kept prodding.

Finally, she peeled back the onion some, and he vaguely stated why he had come back. Shannon told me he claimed someone had something he came back for and repeatedly told her he was looking to collect what he was owed. He promised her he wouldn't start any trouble and promised he would take his stuff and go.

When his dad died, he hadn't left him anything of value, and even though the house was in Ethan's name, he couldn't collect it while he roamed the country as a wanted man. So it sat on its trashed empty lot as it further dilapidated from years of neglect. Now and then, I would drive by it, hoping I wouldn't see a random car parked out front, leaving me to believe he was holed up inside.

Shannon's concern grew that the things he described were in her possession, even though she couldn't think of anything specific she had that was labeled his or even worth anything. He explained he would try and get his stuff that night and be gone first thing in the morning, no trouble caused.

Giving me a heads up he was in town was nice and just what I had requested when I moved back. I politely thanked her for calling and asked her to pass me any updates she got, silently praying there wouldn't be any.

When I hung up, my first instinct was to call Brandon and repeat everything she had told me. I knew that he would want to know, but I also knew it would cause him and my whole family to enact some secret panic plan they probably had stashed in the back of their minds.

I decided not to call him or to tell him or anyone at all. I'd only just gotten my life back. There was no way I wanted to go back to the secluded and scared existence I had once lived.

That night I had a shift at the bar I was supposed to work that I weaseled out of by faking a migraine. Brandon came home and took care of me, trying his best to help me feel better with foot rubs and a warm bath. I felt safe there with him, tightly locked in our house for just that one night, hoping Ethan would be leaving the next day.

The following day Seth sent me a text, giving me a hard time about calling in sick. He said the place was packed and that mom had even made an appearance to help. There was no hint that Ethan had come by, and I hoped he retrieved stuff and left, never even thinking about stopping by the brewery.

The week that followed, I was a little more cautious but tried to be subtle to avoid acting so different that it alerted Brandon or my family. I purposely worked fewer shifts at the bar, blaming it on graphics orders I needed to do anyway, and I suggested we spend the weekend painting the shed out back to stay close to home.

Often, I laid in bed at night and pictured the ways that Ethan would try to get to me. There was the grocery store, the brewery, and even when I took Tim for a walk. The fear of him finding me started to keep me up at night. That was the moment I decided it had to end, and I wasn't going to let him play games with me anymore.

I jumped right back into my regular routine, letting the fear go. I started working at the bar again, going grocery shopping alone, and went out for a run around the neighborhood, knowing the cold would roll in soon. It felt good to let life happen and not constantly worry and fear something I had no control over.

Three weeks later, while still trying to live my life, he showed up.

The bell sang loudly through the taproom, and I paid it no mind while I continued helped a man decide on a beer. I completely missed that while I talked to the customer, Ethan had situated himself on a barstool at the opposite end of the bar. After I finished with the guy that reeked of onions, I looked down the bar top, trying to see who had come in.

And there he was, Mr. Ethan Hall in the flesh.

My eyes shifted towards the office where I knew my brother was sitting, more than likely just sending stupid memes back and forth with Courtney or Brandon. As my eyes stared at the door, praying for Seth to emerge, Ethan snapped his fingers, causing me to redirect my attention to him instantly. He shook his head, knowing that my first instinct would be to call for help. His hand lifted off of the bar, and he beckoned me over towards him with one finger.

My entire body screamed internally.

I had vowed to let the fear go, but there it was, staring me in the face and filling me with utter panic. I just kept talking to myself, "this isn't happening. He isn't actually in front of me."

Every word in my vocabulary was trapped deep inside of me, and my throat had run dry. The idea of calling to Seth was off the table as I stared at him silently, too scared to say anything.

I was locked in.

So I did as I was told and found myself walking over to his end of the bar. As I neared him, my vision thinned down to a narrow tunnel, only seeing Ethan directly in front of me. Hanging down at my side, my hands were ever so slightly shaking as I pushed them to my thighs to silence the apparent appearance of fear. The last thing I wanted was to arm him with the knowledge of how terrified his presence made me. But, although fear had set in, I wasn't worried he would try something or cause a scene in a room full of people.

When I got closer to him, he warmly smiled at me. It wasn't the sadistic smile I remembered when he slammed my head into the wall of our laundry room, but I saw a genuine smile, a smile I had seen on his face a million times, a smile that felt honest.

As I studied what I could see of him, I noticed he looked well. The look of a strung-out drunk had faded from his face, making way for hints of the kind gentleman I had once loved deeply. He looked clean and collected in his collared shirt and faded Washington Nationals hat.

My hands found the counter behind me, and I pulled myself as close to it as I could. My hip dug into the edge as I leaned into it, trying to be as far from him as possible.

"Hey there, Katie girl," he said coolly, instantly taking me back to my old life.

My teeth clenched together, rendering my jaw frozen. As I glared at him, I dug my toes into the bottom of my shoes, trying not to appear afraid. The words in my body were buried deep down as I stood and stared at him, speechless. I had every intention to scream, but when I tried, both my lips and jaw refused to open.

My voice was trapped.

My hands hung in front of me, ready to grab something to bash his head in if the opportunity arose. Knowing him, I assumed he was armed and didn't want to risk getting hurt by making the first move. I located two dirty pint glasses to my left in my peripherals that I knew I could chuck at him if need be.

Suddenly, he started with some small talk, and I stood there stiffly, forced to listen to what he had to say.

"So, Katie girl, how has your day been? Oh, and your parents, and Seth, how have they been? I do miss them," he said as if nothing was wrong.

I remained silent and just looked at him.

He didn't respond to my silence, and he emitted a slight chuckle when he asked if I remembered when we almost got caught having sex in the brewery's office when we had been left there alone in high school. A chill shot down my back at the thought of being naked with him.

Even though I didn't respond to any of his questions, he continued talking to himself while telling me about his adventures. He had been all over the place since he moved out of Ohio, working at various auto shops around the country. The way he spoke about seeing the sites and loving life out of Ohio made it sound like he had left because of his personal choice.

Obviously, the work he was doing was for under-the-table pay.

"They know me as Mike, so don't call me Ethan when you meet them," he said, waving his hands in the air and chuckling at his ruse.

My silence remained, but there was no chance I would ever be meeting his work buddies. Allegedly he was now clean and claimed to have been sober for an indefinite amount of time. With his improved appearance, I believed that part of his rambling to be genuine. He had been sober before, and it was only a matter of time till he relapsed.

Upon the realization his small talk was getting him nowhere, he switched his method to an apologetic stance. Even though he tried, his apology lacked the sincerity a sane person would have had.

"Katie girl, you know my meds were all messed up, and Dr. Branch attacked me. I would never want to hurt a woman. I only did those things because I love you, and I just can't do life without you. I've tried over the years, but I'm here now. You don't have to miss me anymore. I want us back. We've been through a lot, and I know we can get through this together," he said with a cavalier tone, almost sounding like he was trying to justify his criminal actions.

At that point, I realized he must have been off his meds if he legitimately thought that we could work our issues out.

I remained silent.

It didn't matter what words he strung together. I wasn't going to apologize for shooting him, divorcing him, or the plethora of other things I had done to break free of him. Our relationship was over just like it had been the day he smashed a bottle of red wine over my head. There was no coming back from that.

My body stayed where it was, pressing my hip firmly into the countertop, my lips sealed. There were plenty of things I wanted to say to him and had prepared myself to say to him for years, but the words were stuck inside as I stood there frozen in fear, unable to pull them out. Oddly, my silence didn't seem to bother him, and he continued having his one-way conversation.

"Kate, I love you, and I want you back," he said, causing a pit to form in my stomach.

With still no response from me, he kept on rambling.

"I know you'll remember how good we were together, so I'll let you stew about it. But, God, you're so pretty. I missed that face," he said with a smile, looking me up and down.

My eyes must have stared a hole into him by that point.

"Just think about it okay, "I'm gonna leave. But Kate, I still want you, and I also want my thirty grand for my half of the house profits," he replied, standing up and pushing in his chair.

I watched as he walked out of the bar, and the bell echoed louder than it ever had before as he exited the room.

Allowing my fear to take hold, my breath caught up to me, and I began gasping for air as my body involuntary fell to the floor. Tears flowed down my face as I scooted under the bar top and pulled my knees in close to my chest.

"Help, help her!" one of the customers that had joined the line yelled when he saw me hit the ground.

Seth ran to the bar and threw open the swinging door to get to me. He found me as I looked straight ahead and let the tears continue to roll down my cheeks. He used all his strength to pull my dead weight from below the counter and into his arms, finally helping me feel safe. On his knees by my side, Seth fumbled with his cell phone and called the cops.

"I need everyone to leave. Don't worry, your tabs will be on the house. Please drive safe and have a good night. We are sorry for the inconvenience," Seth shouted to all the taproom's patrons.

At that moment, I felt more scared of Ethan than I ever had been before. The way he sat there and talked to me like nothing had ever happened was eerie. Anger started to brew inside of me, and I vowed that I wouldn't let him lock me in again the next time I saw him.

After I knew the brewery was empty and my brother locked the door, I came out from behind the bar. Seth left me alone for a moment to start making phone calls but didn't leave my sight. While he was on the phone calling the cops and dad, I called Brandon.

No answer.

I had to shake the notion that Ethan had stopped by to see Brandon before coming to see me. I started to imagine how upset he would be with me when he found out that I hadn't told him about the phone call from Shannon. Once Seth had contacted the cops and dad, he returned to me and admitted his call to Brandon also went unanswered.

Knowing Brandon and the long day he had, there was a good chance he passed out on the couch, beer in hand. I kept telling myself it would be okay. He was safe at home and would get the missed calls at some point.

We picked a high top in the restaurant's back and sat down, allowing me the chance to give Seth a quick rundown of what happened while we waited for the cops.

Our parents surprisingly arrived right before the cops did. As soon as he had me in sight, my dad ran in my direction, grabbing me and pulling me in tightly to him. Both parents quickly attempted to console me, but at that point, I still had some fear in me, but mostly anger was what had begun to boil inside of me. I was angry that I had worked so hard to cut him out of my life and pissed he was back, ready to destroy it all.

When the cops arrived, my parents joined me, and we went over the details of what happened. Briefly, I described our history, then detailed the phone call and the bar encounter. I watched the officers as they took hurried notes, fingerprints, and nodded their heads. They could write down as much as they wanted, but Ethan had evaded the authorities for years, so I doubted the two small-town Montana cops in front of me were going to be the ones to bring him in finally.

The bell rang, and I looked towards the door, seeing Seth walking in with Brandon on his wing.

"Finally," I said out loud, running over to him and landing in his embrace.

I never wanted him to let me go.

I saw the fear in his eyes as he pulled me in close, and his arms wrapped around me, instantly making me feel safe. Tears flooded my eyes, not because of my fear of Ethan, but gratitude that all the horrible things that passed through my mind earlier when he didn't answer my call weren't true.

I briefly explained that Ethan had shown up at the bar, saving the rest of the story for when we were alone.

We finished up our discussion with the police, placing the whole story and reins in their hands. I talked to my dad alone and had Brandon wait by the bar.

After arguing with him for a minute, I told my dad he wasn't coming home with us and finally agreed to let Seth come instead. He made a joke trying to make me laugh, so I faked one, hoping it would get him off my case if I came across as okay. Brandon was my safety net now, and I didn't want to step on his toes or violate his pride by having my big brother have a sleepover.

Thankfully we were finally on our way home to go to bed and pretend like the events had never happened. I knew I was going to have to explain everything to Brandon. I also knew he wouldn't be happy I failed to tell him about the phone call. I worried that the whole incident would send us all into lockdown mode. We worked so hard to get to be where we were. The last thing I wanted to do was backtrack.

So, I got ready for bed, sat on the edge of the bed, and told him, hoping it wouldn't change our lives.

TWENTY

Brandon

KATE GAVE ME all the details.

Sitting on the edge of the bed, she laid it all out for me while her hands remained still, almost frozen in her lap.

Kate's safety was important to me, but I didn't want her to think that she had to hide things from me to continue living a normal life, which maybe wasn't something I had made clear before.

"I wish you had just told me about the call," I said when she had given me the whole story.

"I know, I should have. I just didn't want to go back to feeling like a hermit again. I was hoping he would just go back to wherever he came from, and maybe he did, but clearly, he didn't stay," she responded.

"I don't want you to feel like that, Kate. You can tell me things like this, okay?" I replied.

"You're right. I'm sorry," she said with a defeated look.

She didn't seem as rattled by Ethan's appearance as I had expected as she calmly told me the story with a straight face.

With enough talking about it for one night, we turned off the lights and shut the door, sealing off the sound of Seth snoring in the living room. We climbed into bed, and I pulled Kate into me, trying to feel as close to her as possible.

Tears welled up in my eyes as I felt her warm body pressed next to mine, taking in the familiar smell of her hair products and rubbing my finger across the small scar she had on her lower back. I quietly held her in the calmness of the dark and tried not to think about the worse ways the night could have gone.

"I don't want to go back to the way things used to be," she stated, hearing her choking up a little.

"Kate, they won't, but we should probably go back to being a little more cautious," I said, trying to reason with her.

"Okay," she agreed.

Seth was up before us, making coffee in the kitchen while I found myself unsure of what to do. I didn't want to go to work and leave Kate at the house alone, but I also didn't want to tell her I wasn't comfortable with her staying behind.

"Will you go to your parent's house while I'm at work?" I asked as Kate walked out of our room, looking like she hadn't gotten much sleep.

"Sure," she responded blankly with a subtle eye roll, hinting my request had upset her.

"Just for a couple of days. Please, to make me feel better?" I asked.

"I don't want to, but I'll do it for you," she said, half-smiling.

I dropped Kate and Seth off at their parents' and went to work, still spending the day worrying about her.

We went back to halfway acting the way we used to. We weren't complete shut in's, but we were operating on a renewed sense of awareness, ensuring we remained vigilant in our daily lives.

We were going to the brewery more often for dates, and if we wanted food from somewhere else, we just ordered it as take-out instead. I was again trying to make sure I was doing the simple things I had slacked on before maintaining our sense of security.

I again started looking at everyone's faces and scanning the area anytime we were out. Kate insisted on going grocery shopping still and heavily sighed when I argued that I wanted to come along with her. I wasn't trying to be overbearing, but I worried for her. I was trying my best to keep her safe while also supporting her in having her own life.

"Okay, enough," Kate said randomly, cutting me off mid-conversation one evening when we were sitting at a table in the family brewery.

"What?" I responded, confused.

"I'm over it. I'm so beyond over it. I want to be alone again, in my house. I'm not doing this scared thing anymore and running to mommy and daddy's house. I'm okay, and I don't need you constantly trying to fix me," she said, with her hands flying all over the place while she spoke.

She let out a frustrated grunt as she scooted her chair back and walked away from the table.

"Where are you going?" I asked.

"I'm going to tell my dad too," she replied, not slowing her stride or looking back at me.

I sat there at the table alone, clearly having no say or input to the matter. Her mind appeared made up, and she didn't want to go back to a life of being scared, becoming the girl that lived in fear again.

A few minutes later, Kate made her way back to the table. Ryan came out of the office and looked at me, shrugging his shoulders in my direction. I returned the shrug as we silently agreed to respect her wishes.

"Now then, can we get back to our pizza?" she asked, pointing roughly at the food while tossing her braid over her shoulder.

"Um, sure," I replied, realizing there would be no discussion.

Kate went back to working the bar and staying home by herself when I wasn't there. I remained silently vigilant when I was gone, ensuring I checked the cameras around the house every time they pinged. She repeatedly promised that she was being more careful.

I showed her where the guns were in the guest room and gave her the code to the safe just in case. She still wasn't interested in handling them, but I felt better knowing she knew where they were and how to get them if she needed to.

Things were feeling slightly off between us after Kate's demands of making her own choices. But it was her life, so I was trying to give her the space she wanted. So I stopped sending her texts all day to check in on her and instead just checked the cameras as we tried to live out our new normal.

A week after she rattled off her demands, it was evident she was still upset about it, and it was starting to affect our relationship. Rarely was she affectionate towards me, and she often just rolled over and went to bed without even a hug or kiss. She had become noticeably distant and quiet in everyday life. I found myself desperately wanting to clear the air and make things right, so I quietly set up a surprise date for us.

One evening, I went into the living room and saw Kate sitting on the couch doing some work on her iPad.

"Put this on," I said, throwing a sundress and sweater her way.

Her eyes moved from the dress to me and back to the dress before finally landing on me.

"Where are we going?" she asked skeptically.

"You'll see," I replied. "Just put the dress on and get ready."

"Alright," she responded.

We arrived at the steakhouse in town, and a slight smile spread across Kate's face she tried to hide. The restaurant was where we had gone on our first date, which was also the same night that I first told her I loved her. Per my request, the hostess nestled us in at an intimate table in the back, where we finally got the chance to sit and talk.

"Kate, I know things have been different lately between us, and I want to get back on track, get back where we were," I said, hoping she would agree.

"I know, it's been weird lately, but I was just over everyone treating me like a child, you included," she explained, flipping her hands slightly on the table.

"You're right, and I'm sorry," I replied.

"It's okay, but yeah, let's get back to being us. I'm an adult and want to be treated like one. So I don't need to be fixed constantly," she said.

"Deal," I answered, abandoning the idea it was my responsibility to help her recover from every issue in her life.

The rest of our dinner went great. Finally, Kate seemed to be back to her usual bubbly self, pushing away the attitude she had before and showing me the sunny side of her I had missed deeply.

As soon as we were back home, Kate pushed me up against the wall, her lips on mine. Kissing her back, I reached my hand around her body and squatted down, and put my other arm on her leg as I lifted her into my arms. Then, with our lips still locked, I carried her through the house, finally making it to our bedroom.

Her dress came off quickly, revealing only a bra and thong. My hands worked speedily and removed them both, tossing them to the floor.

After our makeup sex, I laid next to Kate and ran my finger down her spine as she fell asleep. At that moment, I realized I wanted nothing more than to spend every night for the rest of my life in this exact position with the same girl. I felt the feeling wash over me; there was no doubt in my mind, I wanted to marry that girl.

The next day, I took time from my lunch break and drove down to the brewery, knowing it was where Ryan would be.

I wasn't nervous about asking Ryan for Kate's hand in marriage because I felt as though I had proven myself to him on more than one occasion throughout our relationship. I had taken care of her and done everything he asked of me to ensure her safety, so I had profound confidence he would say yes.

The closed sign displayed on the glass door forced me to use the key Ryan had given me for emergencies. The door opened slowly, and the bell jingled, signaling my entry. Courtney and Seth were the only people in the room as they sat at a high top, sharing a pizza and some wings.

"Whatcha doing?" Seth asked, motioning me over to their table.

"Well, I'm here to see your dad. Is he in?" I asked.

"I think he's in the back. Whatcha need him for?" Seth responded.

"I just need to talk to him about something. It's no big deal," I replied shortly.

Seth's eyes widened as they looked at me, and a smile turned up in the corners of his mouth. Unexpectedly, he moved closer and wrapped both arms around me as mine remained stiffly stationary by my side.

"What are you doing?" I asked.

He pushed out of the hug, holding me by the shoulders at arm's length.

"I'm so happy for you guys," he answered joyfully, pulling me back into his embrace while I looked at the ceiling.

Hearing what he said, Courtney chimed in before I could reply,

"Oh my gosh, that's so exciting!" she said, joining her hands at her heart and smiling.

"What are you guys talking about?" I repeated.

"You're going to be my brother," Seth exclaimed.

"Okay, well, I'm here to ask your dad," I replied, realizing Seth knew what was going on. "You don't think he'll say no, do you?" I asked, starting to worry he would.

"Nah, I doubt it. He likes you," he answered, placing his hand on my shoulder.

"Okay, good," I said, feeling relieved, "But listen, you can't ruin the surprise, don't tell Kate I was even here. Got it?" I asked.

"Got it," Seth and Courtney said in unison.

Ryan was back in the brewing room, kneeling down running some tests on a new beer he was working on perfecting. In the almost two years I'd been with Kate, I learned about the whole fermentation process, realizing it seemed more scientific and specific than I could have ever imagined.

"What can I do for you?" Ryan asked, sensing my arrival.

"I was hoping we could have a little talk," I replied.

"About what?" he asked, dropping his tools.

"Can we go out there and sit down?" I replied, motioning back to the taproom.

"I guess so," he responded, making his way towards the door.

I found a place out front, and Ryan stayed behind the bar, cleaning two glasses. Turning around, I saw Seth and Courtney staring in our direction. Seth stuck a big thumbs up at me, and Courtney swatted at him, trying to get him to leave me alone.

"Beer?" he asked.

"Thanks, but no. I'm just on my lunch break. I have a couple of more jobs to do this afternoon still," I replied.

"Gotcha," he said, placing my cup down and filling his with a red ale, "so what's on your mind, kid?"

I took a deep breath in then let it out. The nerves I thought I didn't have were finally catching up to me.

"Well, Ryan, you know I love Kate. She's my whole world, and I would do anything for her. I came here today to ask your permission to ask Kate to marry me," I said, watching him for any ques of a response.

His face remained unchanged as he stared at me. I stared back at him, awkwardly waiting for him to speak.

"Sure," he finally said, more casually than I had expected.

"Well, okay. Thank you," I replied.

"You're part of the family now. We're happy to have you, so yeah, you have my blessing," he added.

"Thank you," I said, letting a deep breath out and placing my hands on the bar top as I stood, "Well, I hate to ask and run, but I have to get back to work. I want to do it here if that's okay. Just gotta think through all the details first," I explained.

"Sounds good to me," he replied.

After saying goodbye to Seth and accepting another hug, I went back to work, planning how to ask the girl of my dreams to marry me.

TWENTY-ONE

I PLANNED EVERYTHING out. All Kate had to do was show up and say yes.

I never saw myself being a guy that would get married. I adopted the mindset that my life would end up with my title being "long-term boyfriend." But the more my mind rolled over the idea, the more I was certain Kate was always meant to be my wife.

Kate's first marriage had ended so awfully, and I initially worried maybe she wouldn't be interested in ever doing it again no matter who was standing at the alter. However, when we flirted around the topic, she seemed okay with the idea, never really giving off the impression that she was totally against it.

The confidence helped ease my anxiety about asking the woman I was madly in love with to spend the rest of her life with me. My nerves were still off the charts, but I wasn't as scared as I had expected myself to be. I knew Kate was the only one I could see myself going to bed with every night and waking up next to every morning, and I believed she felt the same way.

My future with Kate started to look more vivid as I planned out my proposal. I could envision us building up her design business and it eventually being her only job. We would sell my bachelor pad and buy a bigger house. The path I saw had us moving out of town and getting something with an acre or two for us, and perhaps even a couple of kids to enjoy, all she had to do was say yes.

I was out replacing a thermostat on the north side of town at my second job, as far as Kate knew. She begged me not to take the call and just enjoy spending the evening relaxing at home on the couch with her.

I crafted my story and told her it would only be an hour fix that would bring home two or three hundred dollars. She sighed, knowing it was worth the money and went over to her parent's house to help her mom with some baking.

It had taken me weeks to find the right ring. I wanted something plain and simple but beautiful. Kate wasn't much of a jewelry girl, so I tried to find something that fit her simplistic style. The solitaire princess cut diamond that finally called out to me sat in four posts on a white gold band. After grabbing another ring out of her jewelry box, I had it sized just right, ensuring it would fit her dainty finger.

I convinced Ryan to close the bar for the night on a Tuesday, allowing us to have the whole place to ourselves.

My plan of action was typical and predictable, and I decided to ask her to spend the rest of her life with me in the brewery's back room, where we had our first kind of date. I kept the setup simple and only had a pizza and beer on the table, hiding that this dinner would be extra special.

Ryan called and told Kate that he needed some help with the quarterly finance books, prompting her to come in. At first, she was reluctant, dodging the chore and complaining she was tired. But, he remained persistent and told Kate it needed to be done that night, and finally, she agreed.

"She's out front!" Seth texted me with multiple smiles tacked onto the end.

Standing alone, I instantly saw her when she rounded the corner with her hand wrist-deep in a bag of Cheetos. Thinking her dad would be in the room alone working on the books, a look of confusion spread across her face when she saw only me.

She hadn't taken any time to get ready to come to help her dad and still had on the clothes she had been sitting on the couch in when I left to organize the ruse. She stood in front of me in dog-hair-covered yoga pants, a messy bun, and one of my t-shirts. My eyes looked her up and down, and I knew she couldn't have looked more stunning.

"What are you doing here?" she asked, smiling.

"I wanted to have dinner," I responded.

"Okay?" she said with a questioning tone.

"Sit, please?" I asked, motioning her to the chair across from me.

She walked into the room and joined me at the table, setting her bag of Cheetos to the side. Using her coated orange fingers, she grabbed the napkin in front of her with a forced smile.

"Yeah, my bad," she responded, cringing and cleaning her hands.

We started in on the pizza and sipped our beers quietly in the glass box. Although we chatted like we were on a regular date, I knew Kate could see right through me and knew there was more to the evening.

"Excuse me for a second," she said, getting up and heading out to the bathroom when we had finished our food.

I sat and nervously rapped my fingertips on the tabletop, and Kate soon returned and slipped back into her seat. In the bathroom, she twisted her hair into a loose French braid that hung over her shoulder.

"What?" she said, realizing I was staring at her.

"Kate, I love you. It's been a tough couple of years for us, but I know how happy we make each other and how much it's all been worth it," I paused, taking the time to stand up and walk over to her before I finished my speech.

She adjusted in her seat as a smile formed across her face. She turned to look me straight on as she fixed her posture and folded her hands delicately in her lap.

"You mean everything to me. From the moment I saw you, I knew that all I wanted to do was get to know you, and now I just want to spend the rest of my life learning more about you," I added.

I shoved my hand into my pocket and pulled out the ring I had dropped in loosely. I looked up and saw Kate's hands cupped over her mouth, and her eyes doubled in size.

I got down on one knee in front of Kate, holding the ring between two fingers for her to see. "Kate Amanda Dillon, will you do me the greatest honor in the world and be my wife?" I asked.

"Yes, yes, yes," she cried instantly.

Getting up from my knee, Kate stood and jumped into my arms.

"I love you," she said, planting a kiss on my lips.

"I love you too," I mumbled against her lips.

We finished our beers together in the room. I smiled as I watched Kate repeatedly stick her hand out and grin as she looked at the shiny diamond I picked out for her.

In the taproom, the other members of the Dillon family, Luke, and Courtney were waiting anxiously. Their eyes all moved to Kate's finger when we walked out, and they instantly started cheering when they saw the diamond ring. I reached down and grabbed her hand and raised it high with mine before turning her towards me and planting a kiss on her lips.

"Congrats, sweetheart," Ryan said, giving his daughter a side hug.

"Thanks, Dad," she responded.

Ryan came over to me and motioned for me to join him at the bar.

Kate's dad poured me a beer and said, "Thanks."

"Thanks for what?" I asked.

"She hasn't been this happy in a long time, if ever. I couldn't have asked for a better future son-in-law," he replied with a gentle look in his eyes.

"I'm glad to do it," I said.

The small party continued for about another hour. We had some beers, ate more pizza, and enjoyed being together. Our memorable night had gone just as perfectly as I had hoped it would.

Ready to take my fiancé home, we said our goodbyes to the family and started the three-block walk back to where I had hidden my truck. Kate's hand sat lightly in mine the whole ride home while I enjoyed the feeling of the diamond on her finger, symbolizing our future.

On our way into the house, we started kissing on the porch, caught up in the night's events. Kate playfully threw off my hat, and it landed in the yard as she began to run her fingers through my hair. Forcing myself to take my lips off of hers, I pushed back from Kate and entered the code on the digital keypad, unlocking the back door to the house.

When the door swung open, I felt an unusually cool air blow towards me as though the heat had kicked off. Thankfully, that was the easiest thing for me to fix.

Kate smiled at me as she took Tim out back while I checked the thermostat. I flipped on the hallway lights and quickly realized why the house had cooled off so much. In front of me, I could the main door to our home was wide open.

Reaching into my pocket, I quickly grabbed my phone and clicked the button on the side.

Nothing.

In the excitement of the night, I didn't even realize that my battery had died, rendering me incapable of checking the cameras. I slowly meandered through the house, glancing into the rooms just to make sure everything was clear. I stepped out of the hallway to go close the door and check the thermostat when I realized someone was sitting on my couch.

As soon as our eyes met, I knew the figure sitting in my living room was Ethan Hall.

TWENTY-TWO

ETHAN SAT IN front of me for the first time.

"Hey there, Brandon," Ethan said smugly, crossing his legs.

As he sat back further, I caught a glimpse of the 1911 pistol that rested in his lap. He moved one hand and placed on the gun while the other stretched across the back of the couch.

His appearance wasn't disheveled or strung out, and he didn't look like the mess like I had always envisioned. He had on loose-fitting tactical OD green pants with a baggy black crew neck t-shirt. His hair was buzzed short, and the stubble on his face looked only a couple of days old.

My eyes looked towards the open doorway. I could see damage to the splintered wooden frame from where the deadbolt failed when he kicked it in. But, as crazy as Ethan was, he wasn't stupid. He knew what he was doing and must have known that we always came in the back door.

"He's been watching us," I thought to myself as a chill shot down my spine.

"What are you doing here?" I asked.

"Well, plain and simple, I want my wife back," he responded as an eerie smile spread across his face.

"I think we both know that's not happening," I responded, purposely pulling the edge of my jacket up and exposing my waist so he could see I, too, had a weapon.

"Katie girl!" Ethan called out loudly from his position.

Being focused on Ethan, I didn't hear Kate coming in the back door and tip-toeing down the hallway. I looked towards her and saw her shoulder firmly pressed against the wall, stopped in her tracks. A confused look spread across her face, but I could see she knew who's voice she heard.

"Go to the guest room," I directed Kate, knowing it was where the gun safe was.

"No, no, no," Ethan quickly interjected, "I saw what's in there. You can stay out here with us," he added, tapping his hand on the couch as an invitation for her to sit down.

Kate listened, not trying to cause any issues. She shuffled directly behind me and placed one hand on my lower torso. I reached back and grabbed her hand and pulled it near the front of my hip.

"Will you put your gun down so we can talk about this?" I asked.

"Sure, but only if you do it first," he answered with a nonchalant shrug.

"Okay, same time," I responded, taking my gun out of my waistband and setting it on the floor a couple of paces in front of me, not releasing my hand.

Ethan followed suit, placing his gun down on the floor between his feet, and we both pulled our hands back together. I needed him disarmed because if he had decided to use his weapon, I wouldn't have even known about it until it went off.

"Katie girl, I've changed. I've got it all figured out now. I'm sorry for what I did to you, and I swear on my life it will never happen again. I don't know what got into me, but we can get through this," Ethan said, trying to look through me to Kate.

I could feel the anger welling up in me as he talked directly to her. Kate wasn't his property, and I wasn't letting her leave with him for any reason and would protect her with everything I had. If it were up to me, Ethan wouldn't be leaving our house alive.

When he stopped talking, she let my hand go and peered around me, bringing herself partially into Ethan's sight.

"Ethan, we can't go back to what we once were. This is over, it's been over, and I need you to accept that and let me live my life again," she stated, standing next to me, now in his full view.

Ethan took his eyes off hers, allowing him to glance down at her hand. His eyes stopped when he eyeballed the diamond I had slipped on her finger only a couple of hours prior.

"What..." he said, a sad look crossing his face. "What's that?" he stammered, his finger slightly shaking as he pointed at Kate's hand.

"She agreed to marry me, and now here you are ruining our celebration," I answered, taking Kate's hand back in mine.

"We're still married. I never signed any divorce papers. So, how do you plan on doing that while you're still with me?" he asked, clearly growing more upset as he spoke.

There was confusion and sadness on Ethan's face as he stared at Kate. I glanced over at his left hand and saw that he still had a gold band on his finger.

"I didn't need you there to get a judge to agree to it. You beat me, kept me hostage, and killed someone while you left me tied up in our basement. It was easy to argue the grounds for a divorce," Kate responded, stepping one pace ahead of me.

Trying to stop her from advancing any farther, I moved my hand forwards and placed it on her shoulder, gently pulling her back to my side. I tried to give Kate the space to fight her own battle but also wanted to ensure I kept her close to me. I couldn't begin to try to figure out what was running through his mind or what he planned on doing to her when he didn't get his way.

"I just want you back, Kate," Ethan said, a look of sorrow becoming even more apparent on his face.

"No, you don't get to have her back," I said, raising my voice and taking a step forward.

Ethan stood slowly in front of the couch. I pulled Kate in closer to me while he turned and walked two paces over to the wall directly to his right, examining the picture of us on a snowy mountain. He let out a slight chuckle and rubbed his thumb and pointer finger across his forehead, looking down at the ground.

"I just want my wife, that's what I came here for, and I'm not leaving until I have her," he responded, turning towards us again.

His demeanor had changed from sad to what appeared as confident as he moved his hands and head together while he spoke.

"I think I've made it pretty clear; she's not going anywhere. I helped her put her life back together after you destroyed it," I replied.

His hands started to form into tight fists down at his sides, and he pressed his lips together as he became more agitated. Ethan leaned his head back as he took a deep breath in and closed his eyes. He released the breath in his lungs, and the rest of his body relaxed in suit. He moved his hand down to the bottom of his shirt and pulled it upwards, raising the edge of it to just below his nipple.

"You think you didn't break me?" he loudly responded as anger shot through his eyes, "I had to fix this myself because of the lies you were telling about me. Thankfully, you didn't hit any organs when you shot me in our kitchen."

With his lower torso exposed, it was easy to see a scar the size of a half-dollar exposed on the edge of his side. The built-up tissue was jagged and raised, making it stick out from the surface of his skin and clearly not something fixed by a professional.

"Lies? What lies? What did you expect me to do?" Kate asked, her voice raised to match his.

"Lies about what happened, none of that happened, and you know it, you shot me and ran out. And expect you to do? Oh, I don't know, not shoot your husband in his kitchen, for starters," Ethan responded, taking one step closer to Kate.

With Ethan and Kate now getting closer to one another, I could see she no longer had the same crippling fear towards him she once displayed. She was bold, and where there had once been fear, I saw courage. She had a sharp sternness in her voice and strength in her eyes as she glared at him, hating him for the violence he had put her through.

With the tensions between the two quickly rising, I felt it was time to end the conversation and do whatever it took to get him out of our house and away from Kate.

"Here's the deal, you can leave now, and we won't call the police. Does that sound good to you?" I asked.

"No, no deal. Kate, do you want to come with me or stay here in this dump?" he asked, waving his hand around the room.

Kate held her breath as she compiled her response. I watched her shoulders relax and felt her grip on my hand loosen as she unleashed on her ex-husband.

"You psychopath, have you not heard a single thing that we've said? I am not and will not ever be with you again. You are a maniac that deserves to be locked up," she replied, an agitated vein now visible in the middle of her forehead.

Ethan silently stared at her blankly as the painful words that fell from Kate's mouth sank in.

"Wrong answer," he finally said.

Suddenly, Ethan started to move quickly towards our position. I reached down to grab my gun, and before I wrap my fingers around it, Ethan kicked it out of reach and sent it sliding under the couch.

"Go to the guest room!" I shouted at Kate just before Ethan landed a blow to the right side of my face, sending rippling pain to the other side of my head.

Instantly, I swung back with my non-dominant hand, hitting him directly in the nose with the side of my fist. He stumbled a couple of steps back with blood spurting from his nose and his eyes streaming with tears.

He wiped his face on his shirt's sleeve, and his bloody smiled quickly flashed at me before he charged in my direction. Trying to control him, I dipped my shoulder down and landed it hard in his gut, stopping his rush. When I made contact, I felt only a skeletal frame with skin wrapped around it from the many years of neglect to his body.

Ethan instantly backed away from me. His hands fell to his knees as he bent at the waist, desperately sucking for air.

Just as I went to throw a better-aimed punch at him, he raised his hand and said, "Okay, okay."

Even though he was raising a white flag, it was too late. There was no stopping what we had already started. My blow hit him in the side of the ribcage as he adjusted one of his hands to rub his new injury. Grabbing him by the shoulders, I threw him down to the ground and climbed on top of him, not cradling his fall and causing his head to slam down hard on the wooden floor.

His hands instantly shot up to his head, holding it as he groaned in pain and slightly squirmed on the ground. His groans quickly morphed, forming into a smile, then maniacal laughter as he began to chuckle. The hollow sockets that held his eyes looked back at me with blood running down his cheek.

Quickly coming off his head, Ethan's hands threw another punch at me. I thrust one back in return just as his fist landed under my left eye. My hand instinctively came up to it after missing his face, rubbing it for a moment.

Out of nowhere, Ethan thrust his hips up into the air, forcing both my hands to land near his ears. He interlaced his fingers and grabbed onto my forearm before ripping it out from underneath me and pulling me down flat onto him. He quickly rolled me over, taking me with him and pinning me to the floor.

He moved one of the legs I had behind him flat on the hardwood floor and placed his knee on top, using it to pin mine down.

"Ahhh," I yelled as he dug his knee harder into the meat of my inner thigh.

In our roll, we knocked over the living room end table, sending water all over the floor from a plastic water bottle and shattering a glass vase that was just out of my reach.

"Now, are we ready to stop?" Ethan asked, now holding my hands by the wrists above my head.

"Nah," I said, smiling as I wiggled one hand free and threw three more sloppy punches at Ethan. One successfully hit his face, landing directly under his right eye, and the other two were blocked when he released my other hand.

Before I could pull back to throw a fourth fist, Ethan grabbed my hair and used it to pull my head up before slamming it down on the floor, sending the room into a dizzying spin.

It took everything I had not to pass out, but as far as I knew, Kate was still in the house, and I had to make sure he didn't try to take her while I laid unconscious on the floor.

For a moment, I laid beneath him, defeated and watching my world fade in and out. Ethan hunched over me with one arm on the floor and the other wiping his face, trying to catch his breath from our quick altercation.

I used my elbow and knocked the arm he was bracing himself out from underneath him. He managed to catch himself with his other hand before he fell completely. As he rose, I landed another hard blow right in his ribcage, hearing a satisfying crack as my fist made contact.

Just as I went to hit him again, Ethan momentarily collapsed on me. My mind was spinning, but I assumed something had hit him from behind. It seemed like he felt the blow, but it wasn't enough to knock him out.

He shakily picked himself up on his palms and, once more, grabbed the sides of my head and slammed my head down on the floor, this time harder than the last. When it was apparent I was on the brink of passing out from the pain, he climbed off me, leaving me on the floor.

Through my blurred vision, I could see that Kate had come back into the room and held something she had used to strike the back of his head. Ethan stood there, the two of them frozen in place, staring at each other.

"Let's just go," he said, "if you love this guy, you'll come with me and let him find someone that's not as screwed up as you are," Ethan said.

"No," I groaned as I squirmed on the floor, my vision rapidly fading.

Kate tried to move to her right to make her way towards me, but Ethan quickly blocked her path.

"I'm not screwed up. Thanks to him, I'm not the screwed-up person you made me anymore," she responded.

"Whatever, Kate, let's go," he said, reaching out to grab her.

Dropping the object, she turned to run, and Ethan quickly took a few steps forward, grabbing her by the shoulder and promptly wrestling her down to the floor.

Forcing myself to snap out of the pain, I tried to stand as quickly as possible, knowing he had Kate pinned to the ground in a vulnerable position.

As I stood, my body swayed slightly, and I saw Ethan land two punches to the side of Kate's face. Ethan grabbed her by the chin with one hand and pulled her in by the nape of the neck as he planted a kiss on her lips. He released her and smiled, leaving his blood spread on her face.

On the ground, I saw the lower receiver of an AR-15 I had been building lying near the couch that Kate had used as a weapon. Unsure I'd be able to bend over and come back up without fainting, I charged towards Ethan and used my body weight to knock him off of her. I ran at him sideways and tackled him, my shoulder hitting him directly in the side. He flew off her and slammed into the living room wall, his shoulder penetrating the sheetrock.

I tried to help Kate up and out of the room before Ethan had a chance to stand up. She seemed shaken from his assault but relatively stable on her feet. She stood tall and kept trying to help me get vertical more than I was helping her.

"Go!!" I yelled, demanding that she leave the house before the fight got even worse.

Kate's feet moved quickly down the hallway as she listened to my instruction.

Ethan took my one knee stance as an opportunity and quickly had me back flat on the ground. We were both exhausted and fading fast, and Ethan was using the little strength he still had to hold me down. I tried to fight him, but I struggled to get out of his grip with very little success.

With me pinned beneath him, we both just laid there for a moment as we tried to slow our breathing.

"Okay, okay," I said finally, realizing he was holding all the cards and I had run out of gas, "let's stop, please."

Ethan silently remained on top of me, holding me down. His breathing had grown heavier, and he had his eyes closed as he used all of his weight to push me down on my wrists.

"Oh, now you wan…" came out of his mouth right before his eyes squeezed shut, and his body fell downwards and landed flat on mine.

All of his body weight fell onto me, leaving me weighted down on the hardwood floor.

His shoulder laid on my chin, and his arm had my head pinned to the floor. Ethan's blood trickled onto my face, and his sweat rolled off his head and stuck to my skin. Slowing my breathing down, I tried to feel if his chest was rising and falling.

I felt nothing but his body weight lying on me.

Finally, I gathered enough strength and moved my hands under his body, and pushed, finally rolling him off of me. His frame flopped onto the floor, landing on his back next to me with a solid lifeless thud.

I propped myself up and saw Kate down near my feet with her legs crossed and blood splattered across her shirt.

"Kate, are you okay?" I asked, feeling an adrenaline rush.

I got on all fours and slowly crawled over to her, dragging one of my knees.

"I'm, I'm okay, I think," she stammered, her entire body trembling.

Turning around, I looked at Ethan. He was laying there still, his eyes halfway open, revealing a lifeless and hollow stare at the ceiling.

"I, I, I didn't know what else to do, I was panicking and couldn't get the gun safe open, so I used that," she said, pointing to the AR lower. "And I left just like you told me to, but the second I stepped outside, I knew I would never forgive myself if something happened to you."

She paused, trying to catch her breath. I pulled her in close and held her while we sat on the floor next to her dead ex-husband.

"I'm so sorry," I said repeatedly.

"So I grabbed the golf club and hit him in the head as hard as I could," she stammered.

I could feel Kate lightly shaking in my arms as I held her. Her eyes were stuck downwards as she stared at her shaking hands.

"And I came back in here, and the golf club was just what stuck out to me," she added.

"It's okay, we're okay, it's over," I added, pulling her back into me, staring at Ethan's dead body.

After a few minutes, we both calmed down enough to be able to comprehend what had just happened. We talked through it, making sure we both had the same recollection of events.

Ethan broke in.

Said he wasn't leaving without Kate.

A fight broke out.

Kate smashed him over the head with my favorite driver.

He bled out in my living room.

After fumbling with my phone to make the needed calls, Kate's parents arrived right after four police cars and two ambulances flooded the road, their red and blue lights illuminating the entire street. Shock spread across both of their faces as they took their daughter into their arms and saw their former son-in-law lying motionless on our living room floor. Kate finally stopped shaking and appeared calm, happy that he was no longer a threat to her.

Taking turns hugging Kate, both of her parents also took me in their embrace, repeatedly thanking me for defending her.

After being declared dead on the scene, Ethan's body was bagged up in a thick black bag, the sound of the zipper echoing through the house as they sealed him inside. After they moved him, all that remained was a bright red puddle of blood from his head wound.

He was carried outside, and I saw multiple cameras flashing through the open front door. The news teams had gotten wind of the incident and darted at the chance to cover something of such magnitude in the small town.

The police came in and took some pictures, trying to get us to recreate the play-by-play of what happened. They started to ask some questions, and I swayed back and forth, struggling to keep my eyes open. When the officers realized I was in no shape to give a statement, Kate and I were ushered into an ambulance. Ryan stayed behind to help the police finish our house as Claire chased us to the hospital.

We were poked and prodded under the painful fluorescent hospital lights as we got examined by multiple doctors.

Thankfully Kate was relatively okay and had only suffered from some minor bruising to her face. The nurse allowed her to shower off and gave her some clean clothes, allowing her to wash Ethan's blood off her.

After a CT scan and a couple of x-rays, the doctors diagnosed me with a fractured orbital socket and a good concussion. They wanted to keep me overnight to check on things and make sure I was better in the morning.

Claire did the difficult task and called my mom, telling her the story of what had happened. She cried tears of joy at the news of our engagement but started sobbing and talked about buying a plane ticket out when she heard about the scuffle.

The doctors finally allowed me to shower with Kate's help and gave me a rear-opening gown to get comfy. With Ethan's blood and sweat washed off of me and down the drain, I laid down in the railed bed with

Kate by my side. I downed the small cup of pain meds I was offered and felt my vision growing hazy as they entered my bloodstream.

"Thank you," Kate said, pulling the covers up to her chin.

"For what?" I asked.

"Saving me," she added, looking up at me, tears filling her eyes.

My eyes turned and looked down towards hers.

"Kate, I'll always be there for you, don't ever doubt that. You're my family now. But, thank you, you saved me more than I saved you," I replied, tears starting to fill my eyes too.

She scooted up and kissed me for the first time since we came home from our engagement earlier that night, causing me to wince at the pain from my broken face.

"Sorry, sorry," she said, going back to lying by my side.

"It's okay. It was worth it. I love you," I said.

"I love you too," she replied, nuzzling in closer to me.

TWENTY-THREE

AFTER A FEW more tests and a novel's worth of prescriptions, the medical team finally released us, allowing us to go home to finish our recovery. Claire brought both of us some clothes, and we both gladly changed out of our hospital gowns before leaving. Our bloody clothes were thrown in biohazard bags and ended up in a furnace somewhere.

Once fully discharged, Claire was waiting out front to pick us up from the hospital and bring us back to their house, free of any dead bodies.

Seth and Ryan were working on getting everything cleaned up for us and hoped to be done in the next couple of days so we could go back home if we chose to. As if I didn't want to sell the house before, I now had a valid reason to talk Kate into moving.

"Hey, we should move to a house where you didn't kill your ex-husband" sounded like a good argument to me.

Seth pulled me in for a hug and kissed me on the cheek when we got to the Dillon's house. He then held Kate by the shoulders for a brief second as he looked her over completely before wrapping his arms around her.

I hadn't thought about it, but Ethan being gone would take a massive weight off the entire Dillon family. They no longer had to feel like their lives were forever plagued by what happened to Kate in her previous relationship.

It felt nice to bathe in the large walk shower in Claire and Ryan's master bath. I closed my eyes and enjoyed the feeling of the jets pounding my body on full blast, the water falling to the floor. I looked down at my feet and watched it run clear and free of blood as I enjoyed the warmth.

I slightly flinched when I felt Kate's hand on my shoulder as she joined me and wrapped her arms around my waist from behind. The feeling of her skin brushing against mine calmed any anxiety that was still trapped inside of me.

"We're okay," she said as she rested her cheek near the middle of my back.

"We'll always be okay," I said, turning her around and pulling her into a hug.

My boss gave me the rest of the week off, giving me the time I needed to recover. After a couple of days, my face began feeling better, but my whole body felt sore, bringing meaning to the phrase, "I feel like I got hit by a truck."

After staying with Kate's parents for two weeks, we finally decided it was time to go home and face the memories our house had recently acquired. We both were uneasy as we stepped into the living room, shocked that Ethan's dead body was nowhere to be seen.

Seth and Ryan did a great job getting the place fixed up. The wall that Ethan fell through was patched, the front door sat on a newly painted frame, and if I didn't already know, I would have never believed there had been a dead man bleeding out on the floor two weeks prior. I could almost feel the death in the room as I looked at the spot where his corpse had been and only saw fresh carpet.

I thanked them multiple times for doing what they did, knowing it must not have been easy to clean up the massive puddle of blood. They, of course, wouldn't hear my thanks, constantly repeating they were happy to do it and wanted nothing in return.

Wanting to feel at home again, Kate decided a shower, some pizza, and a movie were in order before we finally climbed into our bed. I agreed and went out to the car to bring the last of our stuff inside.

With all of our luggage in the house, I sat down on the couch, trying not to replay what happened as I glared at the blank TV. When I replayed it the night my mind, I could still feel the haze in my eyes and the throbbing beneath my skull.

"You okay?" Kate asked as she saw me in a trance staring at the floor.

"Yeah, yeah, I'm good," I replied with a smile.

Two weeks later, we were watching some early morning TV, and I shifted my gaze over at Kate for a minute and saw her curled up on the couch. She had one foot tucked up under her as she ate a bowl of cereal that sat propped on her knee. Her eyes were locked into the morning news, and she had a wet spot from spilled milk on my t-shirt. Everything about her was so perfect, just the way she was. I smiled her way gently and realized I didn't want to wait any longer to make her my wife.

"Wanna go get married today?" I asked.

Kate turned her attention away from the TV and looked at me, partially confused, a spoon still hanging from her mouth.

"What?" she asked, still chewing her last mouthful.

"Wanna go do the courthouse thing today?" I asked.

She stared at me with a blank face for a moment as she finished the food in her mouth.

"You're serious?" she asked, her eyes brightening up.

"I've never wanted anything more in my life," I said, leaning over and brushing the hair out of her face.

She looked back to the TV screen for a moment and thought about my proposition.

"Okay," she answered, looking back and showing me the giant smile that had grown on her face. "Yeah, okay!"

She set the bowl of cereal down on the coffee table and jumped on my lap, grabbing my face and kissing me repeatedly. She suddenly stopped as she released her hands from my face. Kate looked at me, then over my head as she blankly stared out the window behind the couch.

"I have to call my parents. I have to find something to wear, they have to make plans, we have so much to do," she said, excitedly jumping up and skipping to the kitchen.

"Babe, what about your mom?" she asked, peeking her head around the corner.

"Don't worry about it. It's all good," I replied.

While Kate made plans, I went online and booked a week-long trip to New Zealand, just the two of us. Our honeymoon would be the perfect escape to forget about everything that happened and start our new lives as a married couple from a place of peace.

When Kate felt ready, we hurried down to the courthouse and paid our fifty-three dollars for a piece of paper that permitted us to get married.

Kate wore a simple white sundress and had just a touch of makeup on as we signed our names on our marriage license. I found myself unable to take my gaze off the beautiful woman who couldn't stop smiling that was minutes away from being my wife.

I grabbed Kate's hand and pulled her around the courthouse with our permission slip in hand. We knocked on doors until we found a judge that was willing to do the ceremony on such short notice and paid thirty-two more dollars for her to deliver our nuptials.

We said our vows with Kate's parents, Seth, Luke, Courtney, and my mom on FaceTime, promising to always to love and care for one another.

We had been through so much together, and this was it. We were finally going to start our new life as a couple. There was no psychotic ex-husband in the picture or lingering fear holding us back from living our lives to the fullest anymore.

It was Kate and me forever.

Made in the USA
Columbia, SC
25 January 2022

54348098R00141